"You seldom find such telling evocation of striking witchcraft scenes, and the weaving of the whole tale is like viewing one five-hundred-year-old masterpiece just about to be cut finished from an artist's loom."
—Andre Norton

Set against the turbulent backdrop of the Italian Renaissance, *Damiano* is the first volume in a compelling tale of magic and faith by a remarkable new fantasy author.

Praise for R. A. MacAvoy's
Tea with the Black Dragon:

A deft blend of the oldest of magics in a dragon and the newest of sorceries in computers...I thoroughly enjoyed it."
—Anne McCaffrey

"A promising debut for a fantasist with an unusual perspective...A highly entertaining read."
—Chelsea Quinn Yarbro

"A very different fantasy...It's a wonderful book, with beautifully drawn characters and a tremendously varied and unexpected background. I wish I'd written it."
—Elizabeth A. Lynn

"A refreshing change from the more familiar epic or heroic fantasy. I recommend it highly."
—*San Francisco Chronicle*

DAMIANO

R. A. MacAvoy

BANTAM BOOKS
TORONTO · NEW YORK · LONDON · SYDNEY · AUCKLAND

DAMIANO

A Bantam Book / January 1984

ISBN 0-553-23575-3

Published simultaneously in the United States and Canada

Bantam Books are published by Bantam Books, Inc. Its trade-
mark, consisting of the words "Bantam Books" and the por-
trayal of a rooster, is Registered in U.S. Patent and Trademark
Office and in other countries. Marca Registrada. Bantam
Books, Inc., 666 Fifth Avenue, New York, New York 10103.

PRINTED IN THE UNITED STATES OF AMERICA

O   0 9 8 7 6 5 4

What thou lovest well remains, the rest is dross
What thou lovest well shall not be reft from thee
What thou lovest well is thy true heritage
    Ezra Pound, The Pisan Cantos, LXXXI

This novel is dedicated to Pierre Bensusan, the musician, whose face on an album cover inspired the character of Damiano and whose music could inspire Raphael himself.

DAMIANO

Chapter 1

A string buzzed against his fingernail; the finger itself slipped, and the beat was lost. Damiano muttered something that was a bit profane.

"The problem isn't in your hand at all. It's here," said Damiano's teacher, and he laid his ivory hand on the young man's right shoulder. Damiano turned his head in surprise, his coarse black ringlets trailing over the fair skin of that hand. He shifted within his winter robe, which was colored like a tarnished brass coin and heavy as coins. The color suited Damiano, whose complexion was rather more warm than fair.

"My shoulder is tight?" Damiano asked, knowing the answer already. He sighed and let his arm relax. His fingers slid limply across the yew-wood face of the *liuto* that lay propped on his right thigh. The sleeve of the robe, much longer than his arm and banded in scarlet, toppled over his wrist. He flipped the cloth up with a practiced, unconscious movement that also managed to toss his tangle of hair back from his face. Damiano's hand, arm, and shoulder were slim and loosely jointed, as was the rest of him.

"Again?" he continued. "I thought I had overcome that tightness months ago." His eyes and eyelashes were as soft and black as the woolen mourning cloth that half the women of the town wore, and his eyes grew even blacker in his discouragement. He sighed once more.

Raphael's grip on the youth tightened. He shook him gently, laughing, and drew Damiano against him. "You did. And you will overcome it again and again.

1

As many times as it crops up. As long as you play the
instrument. As long as you wear flesh."

Damiano glanced up. "As long as I . . . Well, in that
case may I fight my problem a good hundred years! Is
that why you never make mistakes, Seraph? No flesh?"
His toothy smile apologized for the witticism even as
he spoke it. Without waiting for an answer, he dropped
his eyes to the *liuto* and began to play, first the treble
line of the dance, then the bass line, then both together.

Raphael listened, his eyes quiet, blue as lapis. His
hand still lay on Damiano's shoulder, encouraging him.
Raphael's great glistening wings twitched slightly with
the beat of the music. They caught the cloudy daylight
and sent pearly glints against the tiles of the wall.

Damiano played again, this time with authority,
and smoothly passed the place where he had to change
the meter—two strokes, very fast, plucked by the middle finger. When he was done, he looked up, his face
flushed with success, his lower lip red because he'd
been biting down on it.

Raphael smiled. His wings gathered forward and
in, making a sort of private chamber within the drafty
Delstrego hall. "I liked that," the angel said. "—The
way you played it, too, first éach line, then both."

Damiano shrugged and flicked his sleeves from his
hands, his hair from his face. Though his expression
remained cool through this praise, he squirmed on the
bench like a child. "Oh, that was just to warm up to it.
I wouldn't perform it that way."

"Why not?"

"It's too simple. There's nothing to it, just playing
the one line, without even any trills or ornament."

The archangel Raphael took the little wooden instrument out of Damiano's hands. He edged away
along the bench, and his wings swept back in a businesslike manner. His face, as he retuned the strings,
was chiseled perfectly, almost harsh in its perfection,
unapproachable, forbidding. But the high B string rang
flat (the pin tended to slip), and his left eyebrow shot

up in theatrical shock, along with his left wing. Damiano smothered a laugh. Slowly Raphael began to play the melody "Ce fut en mai," which is a very simple tune, one he had helped Damiano to learn three years previously. He played it a number of times through, without trills, without ornamentation, without counterpoint of any kind. He did, however, play it differently. The first iteration was jolly; the second, sad. On the third trip through, the song bounced as though it were riding a horse, and the fourth time the same horse was being ridden into battle. The fifth became a dirge, and when it all seemed over for good (like an eventful life—that song—now over for good), he played it through again like the dance it was. Damiano listened, his amusement turning to awe.

"I'll keep my mouth shut from now on," muttered the youth.

"I would be sorry if you did that, my friend," said the angel. "I like to hear you talk." The smile he turned on Damiano was terrifying in its mildness, but Damiano was used to Raphael's smile. He grinned back.

"Please, Seraph, while you have the lute, play me again the French piece from last week. I can't grasp the cross-rhythms."

Raphael lifted his golden gull-wing brow again, but as no musician needs to be asked twice, he began to play.

Damiano watched and listened, thinking: I am privileged like no other man on earth. I can never deserve this, not though I transmute lead to gold and flesh to fire, not though I keep my chastity for life.

It then occurred to him that perhaps not every young man in the Piedmont would consider it a reward worth remaining a virgin for—hearing an angel of God play the lute of four courses. Even Damiano himself had his moments of dissatisfaction (with virginity, that is, not with Raphael).

And then angels were not a popular object of study, even among the order of alchemists, since they had no material power to offer and were more apt to tell the truth than tell the future. Even Damiano's father, who had been a witch of great repute, had never tried to summon an angel. Other sorts of spirits he had contacted, admittedly, but of that Delstrego had repented.

At least Damiano hoped his father had repented. It was quite possibly so, since Guillermo Delstrego was a good while dying.

While Raphael played the pastorelle, Damiano attempted to follow him, knowing the music. But soon the angel burst the confines of the French piece, as his student had known he would, and drifted away into melodies and rhythms suggested or invented on the spot. Raphael had a trick of running his lines together until, like the triune Godhead, they were united into a single being. Then, when Damiano had almost forgotten what he was listening for, the different lines sprang apart again. There were four, no five of them. Six?

Soon Damiano was utterly lost, as the angel struck the strings all together in what should have been a dissonant crash but was not. Raphael brushed the strings lightly, as though with his wings, and his left hand fluttered over the smooth black wood of the lute's neck. The sound was no longer music at all—unless water was music or the scraping of wind over the grass.

Damiano heard silence and noticed Raphael's eyes on him. The angel's face was perfect as silver, as a statue, and his gaze was mother-shrewd. He waited for Damiano to speak.

"Am I ever going to play like that?" the young man mumbled, nudged out of a waking dream.

White wings rustled on the floor. Raphael seemed surprised by the question. "You will play like—like Damiano, as you do already. No one can do elsewise."

"That's all? As I do already?" His disappointment dissolved in the intensity of the midnight gaze.

"More and more, your playing will become *Damiano*. As your life takes its form, so will your music."

Damiano pursed his bee-stung lips. His eyes, avoiding Raphael's, slid around the great hall with its cream-colored walls, floor of painted flowers, and assorted alchemy bric-a-brac scattered on the acid-stained oak tables. He focused on the black kettle hanging over the central hearth.

"Damiano jerks and stutters. He has the smooth articulation of a sore-footed cow. And as for his life—well his life is to take lessons: in magic, in music. He has done that for twenty-one years."

Raphael didn't smile. "You are very hard on yourself. Remember that the harshest critic on earth is my brother, and his specialty is telling lies. Personally I like Damiano's playing." He extended the *liuto*. Damiano took it and fondled it absently. He always felt uneasy when Raphael began to talk about his brother the Prince of Darkness.

"If you continue to study," added the angel, "I expect you will develop the ears to hear yourself as I do."

"I knew there was some reason I was studying," he muttered. "So it's just so I can hear myself without wincing?"

His grumble died away, and Damiano lifted his eyes to the echo of siege engines, distant and ghostly, resounding in the hall. The iron lids of the many pots on the hearth rattled in reply.

The angel didn't seem to hear. "I thought that was done with," muttered Damiano, furrowing his forehead. Rough brows met in a straight line. "Last Tuesday the men of Savoy crept out of Partestrada, between midnight and matins. The citizens they abandoned are in no position to fight."

Raphael seemed to contemplate the bare hall. "It's not really . . . battle that you hear, Dami. Pardo's rams are knocking down walls outside of town."

"Walls? Whose? Why?" Damiano shot to his feet

and wedged his shoulders into the narrow crack of a
window. A man of more substance would not have
been able to do it. The wall was almost two feet thick,
for the Delstrego house had been built as a fortress.

Damiano craned his head left and peered along the
main street of Partestrada. From this particular window, if he twisted with a good will, he was able to spy
around one corner to the front of Carla Denezzi's
house, where in good weather she sat on the balcony,
doing her complicated needlework. Damiano was practiced at making this particular neck twist. What it told
him often decided whether he'd bide his time at home
or venture out.

Today the balcony was empty; and its wooden
shutters, drawn. The street below, too, was empty,
totally empty. Not a man or a woman, not an ox wagon
or a wandering ass to be seen. The town didn't even
smell right, he thought as he inhaled deeply through
his nose. It didn't stink of urine, peppers, pigs, sheep,
men's or horses' sweat—none of the comfortable smells
that meant home to him. The streets smelled burnt,
like the air surrounding a forge. He lifted his eyes to
the distant fields and forests beyond the town wall,
which faded from brown to gray to blue in the November
air. Damiano squinted—his far vision was not the best.
Out of habit he reached back along the wall, his hand
scrambling over the slick tiles till he grasped his staff.

It was not the traditional witch's stick, not being
brown, branchy, or picturesquely gnarled. Damiano's
staff was ebony and lathe-straight, ringed in three
places with silver. Knobbing the top was a silver crest
set with five topazes and a rather small ruby (red and
gold being the Delstrego colors). It had been given to
Damiano by his father when the boy was twelve—he
then stood only as high as the second silver band.
Now, nine years later, the staff was still a bit taller than
he was, for Damiano had not grown to Delstrego's
expectation.

The staff was as important to Damiano as crutches

were to a lame man, though young Damiano had two limber and useful legs. It was his spelling-instrument, and upon its black length he worked with more facility than he did on the lute. Also, although he had never worked a spell toward the purpose, Damiano believed he could see better holding the staff. He held it now.

"The wall belongs to a man named Francesco Alusto," answered the angel, his quiet voice cutting easily through the stone wall to Damiano's ears. Damiano weaseled back into the room, his cheeks flushed, his eyes bright with worry.

"Alusto? He owns the vineyards, such as they are. But why? What will they do when they get in? Isn't it enough that they control the town?"

There was an indefinable reproach in the angel's eyes. "Why? Because Alusto became a wealthy man under Savoy patronage. Although his being a wealthy man might be enough. What will they do? Damiano! They will rape and kill, take what they can carry or haul, and then march away. Perhaps they will burn the place as they go.

"But I am not here to instruct you in the customs of war—that would be a bad education, I think, and more easily gotten elsewhere." He spoke without heat, yet Damiano dropped his eyes to the pattern of the floor. Against his better judgment, almost against his will he found himself saying, "Don't you care, Seraph? Don't you hear the cries of men dying? The weeping? It rang in my ears all of last week when they fought beside the city wall. The good God knows that since the Plague there are few enough men left in all the world."

The angel's expression might have been called ironical, if irony were a thing that could be built on a foundation of pity. "I know you hear them, Dami. I almost wish you did not, for when the ears are open, the rest of the soul must follow, to its own pain. But I hear men suffering. I too. The difference between us is that you hear them when they cry out, whereas I hear them always."

Damiano's startled glance flew upward to his teacher's face. He saw the pity, not directed only toward suffering humanity but also toward Damiano himself. He stood confused, not knowing why Raphael should waste his pity on Damiano the alchemist, who was young and wealthy, and in good spirits besides.

"What would you have me do?" the angel continued. His wing feathers gathered up like those of a bird in the cold. "I can't change the heart of man or the history he's making for himself. I am not"—and here he spread his hands out before him and his wings out behind him in a sweeping gesture that took in the entire arc of the compass—"in truth a part of this world. I have no calling here."

Damiano swallowed hard. "Except that I called you, Raphael. Don't—give me up. Please. If I speak offensively in your ears, remember I'm only a mortal man. Tell me my fault. I would take a vow of silence rather than have my words offend you." He reached out and slapped the angel's knee, awkwardly and with rather too much emphasis.

"A vow of silence? That's a rigorous promise, Dami, and there are few people I have met less suited to it." Raphael leaned forward, and yellow hair fell gently curling around his face. "I will not give you up, my friend. Compared to mankind, I am very patient. I have the time, you see. And I am not as easily offended as you might think. But you must not ask me for answers that are not revealed to men." The golden eyebrow rose further, and one wing scraped the flat ceiling. "—It may be that they are not revealed to me, either."

The wing descended, obscuring the window light like a filter of snow. "Besides, Damiano, the important questions involve not the intent of God toward us but the soul's own duty, and you know that clearly, don't you?"

Damiano did *not* know it—not on certain issues, anyway. Behind Damiano's teeth, white and only slightly uneven, trembled the question that had waited in silence for three years, ripening—the terrible question about the necessity of virginity. Surely now was the time to broach it. Raphael had practically asked for such a question—it was not something unrevealed to men, after all, but only knotty. Such an opportunity would not knock again.

He heard a scrabble and panting on the stairs, and his dog tore into the hall, calling, "Master, Master, there's a soldier at the door. With a spear!"

She was a small dog, knee-high, very heavy in the head and shoulders, and bandy-legged. Ugly. Her color was white, except for a saddle mark over her shoulders, and so she was called Macchiata, which is to say, Spot.

"With a spear?" echoed Damiano, feeling the moment for his question dart off like some small animal that, once frightened, will forever be harder to approach. He stood, indecisive, between the angel and Macchiata.

"*Pax tecum*," whispered Raphael. His wings rose and glittered, and he was gone.

Macchiata blinked at the disturbance in the air. She shifted from leg to crooked leg, and her ruddy hackles stood out like the quills of a hedgehog. "Did I scare him away, Master? I'm sorry. I wouldn't scare Raphael on purpose.

"—But there's a soldier..."

"With a spear," added Damiano disconsolately, and he slouched down the stairs after Macchiata.

Chapter 2

The second floor of the house was broken up into smaller rooms. Damiano passed through the vestibule with its florid tiles and heavy, glinting hangings, where the hearth sat smoldering through the short autumn day. The door was made of oak panels layered with the grain in different directions and studded with iron. It stood ajar, as always, for the convenience of Macchiata.

The sergeant watched Damiano advance through the dimness. It was a boy, the sergeant thought—a servant. Beasts with human tongues were bad enough—more than bad enough. That bitch made his honest, though thinning, hair stand on end. He would not now be pushed off on a servant. Not though Delstrego could give a man boils with his stare, as the townsfolk said. Pardo could do worse to the man who did not follow his instructions.

Then Damiano stood in the light.

Not a boy, quite. But spindly as a rail. Girl-faced too.

Damiano blinked against the sudden brilliance.

"I want your master, boy," growled the soldier. He spoke surly, being afraid.

"You will find him in the earth and above the sky," answered Damiano, smiling. The sergeant was surprised at the depth of the voice issuing from that reedy body, and though he did not trust the words, he involuntarily glanced upward.

But Damiano continued, "*Dominus Deus, Rex Caelestis:* He is my master and none other."

10

The sergeant flushed beneath his bristle and tan. "I seek Delstrego. God I can find on my own."

Insouciantly, Damiano bowed. "Delstrego you have found," he announced. "What can he do for you?"

The sergeant's left hand crawled upward unnoticed, prying between the leather plates of his cuirass after a flea. "I meant Delstrego the witch. The one who owns this house."

Damiano's unruly brows drew together into a line as straight as nimbus clouds. "I am Delstrego the alchemist: the only Delstrego dwelling in Partestrada at this time. This house is mine."

Snagging the flea, the sergeant glanced down a moment and noticed a patch of white. That hideous dog again, standing between the fellow's legs and half concealed by the robe. Her teeth shone white as the Alps in January, and her lips were pulled back, displaying them all. Perhaps she would open her mouth in a minute and curse him. Perhaps she would bite. Surely this Delstrego was the witch, whatever he looked like or called himself.

"Then it is to you I am sent, from General Pardo. He tenders his compliments and invites you to come and speak with him at his headquarters." This was a prearranged speech. Had the sergeant chosen the words himself, they would have been different.

But Damiano understood. "Now? He wants to see me now?"

"Certainly now!" barked the soldier, his small store of politeness used up. "Right now. Down the street in the town hall. Go."

Damiano felt Macchiata's rage vibrating against his shins. He restrained her by dropping the heavy skirt of his robe over her head. "All right," he answered mildly. I'm on my way." He stepped out onto the little, railless porch beside the sergeant. A twiglike, white tail protruding from the back of his robe pointed stiffly upward.

The sergeant noted the gold and scarlet velvet of the robe and its foppish sleeves. Inwardly he sneered.

He further noted the black wand, man-high, ornamented like a king's scepter. "Not with that," he said.

Damiano smiled crookedly at the soldier's distrust. "Oh, yes, with this especially. Pardo will want to see this." He spoke with great confidence, as though he, and not the sergeant, had just left the general's presence. Glowering but unsure, the sergeant let him pass.

"Aren't you coming along?" inquired Damiano, turning in some surprise halfway down the stair. The sergeant had stood his place at the open doorway, his ruddy bare knees now at Damiano's eye level. "—To see that I don't play truant by darting over the city wall or turning into a hawk and escaping into the air?"

"I am to guard the house," answered the soldier stolidly.

Damiano stared for a moment, his mind buzzing with surmises, then he continued down the stairs.

Under the arch of the stairway, beside the empty stables, stood another of Pardo's soldiery: a tall man with a scar running the length of one leg. He too watched Damiano pass and kept his place.

The street was not so bare as it had appeared earlier. It was scattered with swart-garbed soldiers, who stood out against the dust and stucco like black pepper on boiled frumenty. Damiano had never been able to abide boiled frumenty. No more did he like to see the streets of Partestrada dead like this. He was quite fond of his city.

Damiano could feel, using a little witch-sense—which was nothing like sight or sound, but rather like the touch of a feather against the face or, better, against the back of the palate—that there was no one at home in any of the square plaster houses around him. He gripped his staff tighter and strode forth, immediately stumbling over Macchiata.

"Get out of there," he grumbled, lifting his skirts and giving the dog a shove with his foot. "Walk before, behind or beside, but not under."

Macchiata laid back her ears, thin, white, and

folded like writing paper. "You put me there, and I couldn't see."

Damiano started forward again, hoping no one on the street had noticed. "That was to keep you away from the soldier. He might have spitted at you in a moment, and there's nothing I could have done about it. Then where would you be?"

The dog did not respond. She did not know the answer.

Someone *had* noticed. It was old Marco; even war and occupation of the city by the enemy could not keep him from his place beside the well, squatting on his haunches with a bottle of Alusto's poorest wine. Damiano, at this distance, could not make out his face, but he knew it was Marco by his position and by the filthy red wool jacket he wore. Damiano would have to pass right by the old man, and he would have to speak to him, since Marco had been one of Guillermo Delstrego's closest friends. Perhaps his only friend.

Marco was, however, insufferable, and as Damiano passed he only bowed in the general direction of the well and called, "Blessing on you, Marco," hoping the old sot had passed out already. Quite possibly he had, since it was already the middle of the afternoon.

"Hraaghh?" Marco had not passed out. He jack-knifed to his feet and strode over to Damiano, holding the wine bottle aggressively in one sallow hand. Macchiata yawned a shrill canine yawn and drooped her tail, knowing what was coming. Damiano felt about the same.

"Dami Delstrego? I thought you had flown to the hills three days ago, just ahead of the Green Count's army."

Damiano braced his staff diagonally in front of him and leaned on it. "Flown? Fled, you mean? No, Marco. You haven't seen me for three days because I've been tending a pot. You know how it is in November; people want my father's phlegm-cutting tonic for the winter, and when I say I'm not a doctor, they don't hear me.

"Why did you think I'd run away?"

Marco waved his bottle expansively, but very little of the contents splashed out. "Because they all have. Every man with any money in the village..."

"City, not village," corrected Damiano under his breath, unable to let the slight pass, yet hoping Marco would not hear him.

"And every young fellow with two arms that could hold a spear, and all the women of any age, though some of those old hens are flattering themselves, I will tell you..."

"Why did they leave, and for where?" Damiano spoke louder.

"Why?" Marco drew back and seemed to expand. Damiano sighed and cast his eyes to the much disturbed dust of the street. Nothing good had ever come from Marco swelling like that.

"Why? You juicy mozzarella! To save their soft little lives, of course. Are you so addled with your books and your devil's music that you..."

"What do you mean, 'devil's music'?" snapped Damiano in return, for nothing else Marco could have said would have stung him as sharply. Macchiata vocalized another yawn and flopped upon her belly on the ground.

"Maniac, pagan... The church fathers themselves called it cursed."

Damiano thumped his staff upon the ground. Its vibration, smooth and ominous as a wolf's growl, brought him back to reason. "They did not. They only said that contrapuntal music was not suitable to be played in the mass. But that too will come," he added with quiet confidence, thinking of the hands of Raphael.

Marco listened, sneering, to Damiano's words. To the deep humming of the staff, however, Marco granted a more respectful hearing. The old man plucked absently at his felt coat, from which all the gold embroidery had long since been picked out and sold, and he raised his bottle.

"Well, boy. You should still get out. You have two

arms and two legs and are therefore in danger of becoming an infantryman. And Pardo isn't from the Piedmont; he may not be intimidated by your father's name."

"I thank you for your concern, Marco. But I am much more valuable as an alchemist than I would be as a soldier. If Pardo is a man of vertu, he will see that."

The bottle did not quite drop from Marco's hand. He stared at Damiano slack-jawed, all the stumps of his front teeth exposed. "You will go over to the monster?"

Damiano scowled. "The monster? That is what for forty years you called Aymon, and then his son Amadeus. He was no friend to Partestrada. He ignored our city, save at tax time—you yourself have told me that, and at great length."

"The old tyrant grew softer once he'd filled his belly from us, and his son at least is mountain born," snorted Marco.

"Perhaps Pardo will be different. Perhaps he is the one who will realize he can ride to greatness along with the city of Partestrada. If he has a mind, and eyes to see, I will explain it to him." Damiano spoke words he had been rehearsing for the general's ears. Marco cleared his throat, spat, and turned his back on Damiano to shuffle toward the sun-warmed stones of the well.

"Wait, Marco!" called Damiano, hurrying after. He grabbed the greasy sleeves of Marco's jacket. "Tell me. Are they all gone? Father Antonio? Paolo Denezzi and his sister? Where is Carla? Have you seen her?"

Marco spun about, vermilion-faced. "Tell you? That would give you something else you could explain to General Pardo." Without warning he swung the clay bottle at Damiano. The staff took the blow, and the bottle fell in purple-stained shards at his feet. Only a swallow had been left in it.

"Your father," called Marco, stomping down the street in the direction from which Damiano had come, "was an honest witch. Though he burns in hell, he was an honest witch."

Damiano stood staring at the drops of wine beading the dust, till Macchiata laid her triangular head against his leg. "He shouldn't have said that about your father," she said.

Damiano cleared his throat. "He wasn't insulting my father. He was insulting me.

"But I can't believe Marco thinks I would betray my friends, let alone my city. He is just old and angry."

Damiano shook his head, took a deep breath, and jerked his sleeves from his hands and his hair from his eyes.

"Come," he said. "General Pardo is expecting me."

Damiano hated being reminded about his father, whom he had last seen dissolving into a green ichor. Guillermo Delstrego had died in pain and had stained the workroom tiles on which he lay. Damiano had never known what spell or invocation his father had been about, for there were many things Delstrego would not let young Dami observe, and that particular invocation Damiano had never had any desire to know.

Guillermo Delstrego had not been a bad father, exactly. He had certainly provided for Damiano and had taught him at least a portion of his arts. He had not beaten Dami often, but then Damiano had not deserved beating often, and now it seemed to Damiano that his father would have liked him better if he had. A mozzarella was what Marco called him. Delstrego probably would have agreed, being himself a ball of the grainiest Parmesan. But after their eighteen years together, and despite Damiano's quick sensitivity to people, the young man could say that he'd scarcely known his father—certainly not as well as old Marco knew him.

Damiano was like his mother, whom Delstrego had found and married in Provence (it was said no woman in the Piedmont would have him), and who had died so long ago she was not even a memory to the boy. He had her slimness, small face, and large eyes. And though his nose was rather larger than hers had been, it was nothing like the strongly colored and very Roman appendage that Guillermo Delstrego had borne. Yet Delstrego had had to admit the child was his, because witchcraft did not run in his wife's family, and even as a baby Damiano had given off sparks like a cat.

Was Delstrego in hell? There was gossip that said a witch was damned from birth, but the Church had never yet said anything of that sort, and Damiano had never felt in the slightest bit damned. He attended the mass weekly, when work permitted, and enjoyed involved theological discussions with his friend Father Antonio of the First Order of San Francesco. Sometimes, in fact, he felt a little too sure of God's favor, as when Carla Denezzi let him sort her colored threads, but he was aware of this fault in himself and chided himself for an apostate whenever the feeling got out of hand. His father, though, who died invoking the Devil, alone knew what . . . Who could be sure about him? When he asked Raphael, he was told to trust in God and not to worry, which was advice that, although sound, did not answer the question. Damiano prayed both at matins and at vespers that his father was not in hell.

It was quite frosty, even though past noon. Cold enough to snow. The sky was heavy and opaque, like a pottery bowl tipped over the city, its rim resting on the surrounding hills and trapping all inside.

Except it had not trapped anyone, anyone but old Marco and himself. Where had the people gone? Where had Paolo Denezzi gone, taking his whole family? It was not that Damiano would miss Denezzi, with his black beard and blacker temper. His sister Carla, however . . .

The whole city was one thing. An undifferentiated mass of peasants and vendors and artisans called Partestrada; to Damiano it was all that Florence is to a Florentine, and more, for it was a small city and in need of tending. Damiano was on pleasant terms with everyone, but he usually ate alone.

Carla Denezzi was another matter altogether. She was blonde, and her blue eyes could go deep, like Raphael's. Damiano had given her a gilded set of the works of Thomas Aquinas, which he had gone all the way to Turin to purchase, and he thought she was the jewel around Partestrada's throat. Damiano was used to seeing Carla at the window of her brother's house or sitting on the loggia like a pretty pink cat, studying some volume of the desert fathers or doing petit point. Sometimes she would stop to chat with him, and sometimes, if a chaperon was near and her brother Paolo was not, she would permit Damiano to swing himself up by the slats of the balcony and disturb her sewing further.

In his own mind, Damiano called Carla his Beatrice, and if he was not being very original, it was at least better to liken her to Dante's example of purity rather than to Laura, as did other young men of the town, for Petrarch's Laura had been a married woman and had died of the plague, besides.

Now Damiano passed before the shuttered Denezzi house front and he felt her absence like cold wind against the face. "Where are you, my Beatrice?" he whispered. But the bare, white house front had no voice—not even for him.

The town hall had no stable under it, and it was only two stories high. It was not a grand building, being only white stucco: nowhere near as imposing a structure as the towers of Delstrego. It had not been in the interest of the council to enlarge it, or even to seal the infected-looking brown cracks that ran through the wall by the door. Except for the weekly gatherings of the town fathers, discussing such issues as the distance of the shambles from the well and passing judgment on sellers of short-weight bread loaves—such were commonly dragged on a transom three times around the market, the offending loaf hanging around their necks—the town hall had been occupied by one or another of Savoy's captains, with the half-dozen men necessary to keep Partestrada safe and in line.

Damiano knew what Savoy's soldiers had been like: brutishly cruel or crudely kind as the moment would have it, but always cowed before wealth and authority. No doubt these would be the same. It was only necessary for a man to feel his own power...

His confidence in his task grew as he approached the open door of the hall, which was guarded by a single sentry. His nod was a gesture carefully tailored to illustrate he was a man of means and family, and a philosopher besides. The soldier's response, equally well thought-out, was intended to illustrate that he had both a sword and a spear. Damiano stopped in front of him.

"I am told that General Pardo wants to see me," he began, humbly enough.

"Who are you, that the general should want to see you," was the cold reply.

A bit of his natural dignity returned to Damiano. "I am Delstrego."

The sentry grunted and stepped aside. Damiano passed through, leaning a bit on his staff, allowing any casual observer to believe he was lame.

"Not with that," spoke the soldier, and Damiano paused again. He could not lie barefacedly and tell the man he needed the stick to walk, but he was also not willing to be parted from it. He squinted nearsightedly at the guard, mustering arguments. But the guard pointed downward. "The general doesn't want to see your dog."

Macchiata's hackles rose, and she growled in her throat. "It's all right," Damiano said softly to her. "You can wait outside for me. And for your sake, do it quietly!" The dog lumbered out the door, watched by the amused guard, and Damiano proceeded into the hall.

General Pardo was the sort who looked good in black, being hard, neatly built, and of strong color. His height was impossible to judge as he sat slumped in the corner of an ornate bench-pew, his legs propped on a stool beside it. He was dusty, and his face sun-weathered. He regarded Damiano in a manner that was too matter-of-fact to be called arrogant. Damiano bowed from the waist.

"You are the wizard?" began Pardo. To Damiano's surprise, the general addressed him in a clear Latin.

The young man paused. He always corrected people who called him witch, though everyone called him witch. No man had ever before called him a wizard. The word was one Damiano had only read in books. It rang better than witch in the ears, but it also sounded pagan—especially in Latin. It did not seem right to begin his conversation with General Pardo thinking him a pagan, and yet it wasn't politic to begin matters by correcting the general. "I am Delstrego," he replied finally, knowing that at least his Latin accent was above reproach.

"Not a wizard?" The question was sharp.

"I am . . . an alchemist."

Pardo's response was unsettling. His mouth tightened. He turned his head away. It was as though something nauseated him. "*Deus!* An alchemist," he muttered in southern-accented Italian. "Just what I need."

Damiano leaned against his staff, puzzled. He also dropped into Italian: the Italian of the Alps, heavily flavored with French. "An alchemist seeks only to comprehend matter and spirit, and to raise each to the highest level, using the methods of Hermes Trismegistus . . ."

"DON'T," bellowed the general, "TELL ME—" He took a deep breath. A soldier clattered into the room, then seeing it was only the general exploding, he backed out.

"—about Hermes Trismegistus," finished Pardo.

Damiano stood pale and staring, like a man who has broken through ice into cold water.

"Why?" he asked in a small voice. "Why not Hermes?"

The general shifted in his seat. A smile spread across his features. "Because, boy, I have heard enough about Hermes Trismegistus and the quest of alchemy to last me three lifetimes. Florence is riddled with fusty old men who claim they can turn lead into gold. Venice is almost as bad." He turned a gray-eyed hawk glance on Damiano. "Avignon...is beyond help.

"You are too young and healthy to be an alchemist, Signor Delstrego. Also too clean. Can you turn lead into gold?"

"Not...in any great quantity," answered Damiano, embarrassed.

"Can you at all?" pursued the general.

Damiano sighed and fingered his staff. It was his burden that many of the goals of alchemy he found easier to accomplish using the tools of his father rather than those of the sainted Hermes.

"My methods are not pure"—he temporized—"and the amount of labor involved is..."

Pardo swung his legs down from the stool and glared at the youth in frustration. "What I want to know, boy, is HAVE YOU POWER?"

Pardo had an immense voice and was used to commanding large numbers of men on the battlefield. But Damiano was no longer used to being commanded. The bellowing raised in him an answering anger. His fingers tightened upon the black wood of his staff.

Without warning the air was filled with booming, as every door and shutter in the building slammed back upon its hinges. Sparks crackled in the folds of Damiano's woolen robe. The light wooden door of the audience chamber trembled for half a minute. A cloud of plaster dust fell.

Pardo regarded it calmly. "I could feel that," he remarked, "in my ears."

Damiano kept his mouth shut, feeling he had done enough, and knowing that slamming doors would not protect him from a regiment of swordsmen. Besides, he was tired.

"That's what I was trying to find out," added the general conversationally, as he nudged the stool in Damiano's direction. "Sit down, Signor Delstrego. I want to talk to you."

"Thank you, General." Damiano lowered himself gratefully onto the cushion. "I also, was wanting to speak with you."

"Ahh?"

Uttered by a Piedmontese, that single, interrogatory syllable would have echoed in the back of the throat and in the nose, like the crooning of a mother cat. At the most a Piedmontese would have glanced at his companion as he spoke to show him it was to him the inquiry was addressed. But General Pardo was a Roman by birth. Both eyebrows shot up and his lips pulled back from his teeth. The intensity of interest revealed by the single syllable of "Ahhh?" seemed in Damiano's eyes excessive: a thing too, too pointed, almost bloodthirsty. It was of a piece with the general's appearance and his snapping temper.

These Italians, Damiano thought—not meaning to include the Piedmontese—they are too hot and too cold together. Passionate and unreliable.

"To speak with me? I expected as much," concluded Pardo, with some satisfaction. "Well be my guest, Signor Dottore. I slept in a bed for the first time in a week, last night, and now am disposed to listen."

Damiano spared only a moment to wonder whose bed the general had slept in, and whether the original owner of it now slept on a straw pile or in the hand of God. Then he put his mind to the task.

He leaned forward on his stool, his legs crossed at the ankles, each knee draped in gold cloth like the smooth peak of a furrowed mountain. His staff was set between his feet, and it pointed at the cracked roof and the heavens beyond. Against the ebony he leaned his cheek, and the wood was invisible next to unruly curls of the same color. His eyes, too, were black, and his mouth childishly soft. A painter or a poet, seeing that unlined face, might have envisioned it as springtime, a thing pretty enough in itself but more important in its promise of things to come.

General Pardo looked at Damiano, but he was not a painter or a poet. He noticed the huge hands, like the paws of a pup still growing, and he saw Damiano, like a pup still growing, as a bit of a clown.

"It is about this city," Damiano began, and was immediately interrupted, as Pardo inquired what city he meant.

"Partestrada," replied Damiano, wondering how the general could be so slow. "Partestrada has been under Savoy governance for many years."

"If you can call it governance," introjected Pardo.

Damiano paused to show he had heard the other, then continued. "In that time the city has grown from a town of four hundred families into the only place of any note between Turin and Aosta."

"Of any note..." echoed Pardo doubtfully.

"Her people are healthy, her surrounding crop-lands flourish. She supports two silversmiths and a..." Damiano decided not to mention the vineyard at this time. "...and she is located on the Evançon, a river that is passable almost its entire length. She has grown like the child of the mountains that she is."

"And you would like her to continue in the same fashion?" asked the general dryly. "Without interference."

Damiano lifted his eyebrows in a gesture that, though he did not know it, was the mirror of that which he had distrusted in Pardo. "No, Signor General, that is *not* what I want for my city. All this she had accomplished on her own, unguided, like a peasant virgin, beautiful and barefoot. What would she be under the protection of a great man?"

Pardo leaned forward, uncomprehending. "I am

not in the habit of protecting virgins, peasant or other-wise," he said simply.

Damiano felt his face growing hot. He had picked the wrong metaphor to use with a soldier, certainly.

"What I mean is," he began slowly. "We need the presence of a man of wealth and culture, in whose house the arts will flourish, and whose greatness of soul can inspire Partestrada with a similar greatness..."

"It's the pope you want," suggested Pardo with a white smile. "Go to him, Signor Delstrego, and tell him to move from Avignon to Partestrada, where the air is better."

Wit is cheap, thought Damiano, yet reason cannot best it. He dropped his eyes, accepting the humiliation as he had accepted it from his father daily in his childhood. This general reminded him of his father in more ways than one.

For the sake of his city, he tried once more.

"General Pardo, it would not be bad for you to join yourself to Partestrada and to grow with her. By her placement and her people she is destined for greatness. You could be the tool of her greatness. She could be the tool of your own glory. Like Visconti and Milan."

Pardo's nostrils had flared, but he had let Damiano continue until he heard the name of Milan. "Milan!" he barked. "When I marry a city it will be one with a greater dowry than Partestrada! Why do you think I am up here, sweeping your little hill towns like a housewife with a broom, if not in preparation for Milan? I need money and power, and my army needs experience. I will get what I can from the crumbling House of Savoy, while Amadeus is busy with his new wife and the stupid wars of Jean le Bon. When that great one turns to bite the flea on his leg I will be gone.

"But I will come again. And again. And each time I will harvest this miserable, cold cloud-land, until I am rich enough and have men enough, and then I will move on Milan. If I cannot buy that city's love, I will take it by force."

Damiano's face tightened painfully, but he spoke what was to him the obvious. "Milan has been in so many hands. You will not be remembered in history by taking Milan."

"HISTORY IS SO MUCH DOG SHIT!" bellowed the general, pounding his fist against the wooden back of the pew. "Milan? That is something else. Passed through many hands? Well the whore is none the worse looking for it.

"Boy, have you SEEN Milan?"

"Many times," answered Damiano, meaning three times, once with his father and twice since, buying books. "It is a beautiful city, although very flat."

Now it was Pardo's turn to lean forward and stare. "I don't want you to take this as an insult, Signor Delstrego, because I think I could like you. You have loyalty and enthusiasm. Also a very useful talent, if that business with the doors was any guide.

"But your provincial upbringing has colored your thoughts. You have read about Florence and Rome, and you think they are no different from your little town in the hills, where your family has a certain . . . reputation. It seems to you better to devote your time to making the little town bigger than to risk all by starting anew in a place where there are more possibilities, but you have no reputation at all."

Damiano frowned perplexedly and shook his head, but Pardo continued. "My advice—and I am a man of some experience—is to risk it all and leap for what you want. Most men are less than they seem. It is nature; their fate is to feed the few who have vision and courage. Most cities exist to be plundered, and it is out of that plunder we create the glory of Rome, of Florence, and of Milan."

Pardo smiled, with a too-knowing smile—with Guillermo Delstrego's smile, in fact. And he was speaking in sly, comradely fashion, as Damiano had often heard his father speak to some low companion, the two sitting side by side in the empty stable, away from the light of the sun.

"Alchemists are all posers," Pardo said. "And real magic—black magic—is very rare. But it exists! I am sure in myself that it exists!"

Damiano shook his head more violently. "Not for me," he protested. "Never black magic."

"Your father was not above cursing an enemy," Pardo contradicted equally. "And I'm told he did it effectively."

"Who told you? That's hearsay. You mustn't believe it!"

"An old man named Marco told me," answered the general. "At the same time that he told me where the inhabitants of the city were hiding in the hills."

Damiano rose from his chair, his face draining. "Marco? He betrayed the citizens?"

With one hand Pardo waved away Damiano's shock. "Don't worry. I'm not going to butcher them all. There's no value in that. It is what they took with them that I want, and any villager who is willing to die over a purse or a ring of gold deserves what he gets.

"But it's what Marco told me about your father and yourself that I found most interesting. He said your father was the most powerful witch—I mean, rather, wizard—in the Italies."

"He was a witch," said Damiano, dully, "and not the most powerful, by his own admission. He always said that Saara of Lombardy . . ."

"Good enough," interrupted Pardo. "He also said you were almost your father's equal in power, though too faddish and delicate-minded for your own good."

"A mozzarella," murmured Damiano, staring at the floor. Marco betraying the city. Soldiers with hairy knuckles ripping the gold from around Carla Denezzi's neck. The gold and what else? He became aware that Pardo was still talking.

"—with me," the general was saying. "I am not proposing a marriage, like that which you were so willing to arrange between this town and myself, but I am not a bad man. I am educated and a Christian. I kill no man for pleasure. Turn your skills to my service, and I promise you I will reward you well."

Damiano stared through Pardo. "What did you give Marco, for his services?"

Pardo's smile was crooked. "I have granted him the vineyard outside the gates," he replied. "But Marco is an old sot and a traitor as well. I could be much more generous to a man of skill, whom I could trust."

Damiano found his tongue. "You will have no need to be generous with me, Signor General."

Pardo rose slowly from his bench. "You refuse me outright?" Like a cat, which begins its attack with a single step, the general advanced on Damiano. "Outright?" he repeated.

"It doesn't even come to that," answered the youth, standing his ground. "You see, I would be of no use to you. The abilities I possess—or even those of my father—do not make good weapons of war. If they had, I think he would have used them so."

General Pardo stood facing Damiano. They were almost of a height. "Explain," barked the general.

Damiano leaned forward upon his staff. He gazed at the red tile floor, thinking. At last he began.

"Works of magic are no different from ordinary labor. One starts with material and adds the strength of one's own power, and in the end you have made something. When I threw open all the doors and windows of the building, I used the air as my tool and hammered it according to a design I had learned. In the end I was more tired than I would have been had I run from door to window and swung them open by hand.

"But the windows in rooms that were bolted you could not have touched at all without wizardry. Am I right?" The general sought in Damiano's face some sign of subterfuge or evasion. Damiano met his glance.

"Ah, yes. But that is another element: the moral element, and that is a very real thing in magic, real and dangerous. If I open a door that you have locked against me, or cause it to open as you are walking by, with the intention of hitting you with it, then my deed is a wholly different thing than a mere opening of doors. Magic worked in malice will almost always spring back against the worker; that is why purity of heart is important in a witch.

"You may well laugh," added Damiano, for Pardo *was* laughing, "but so it is. Being a channel of this power, I must be careful of my desires. If I grow angry with a tradesman and feel in my imagination my hands around his neck, then I will carry the seed of strangling around in my head and may well feel demon fingers at my own neck in the middle of the night."

"Still," introjected the Roman, "curses are pronounced, so someone must dare to pronounce them."

Damiano shrugged. "A witch can be able without being wise. Notice how many with the power are poor and diseased, worse off than the unfortunates they have cursed. Some carry such hatred that they would rather do harm than remain well themselves. Some have learned the skill of putting off all their payment until some time in the future, trusting they will die before the bill falls due."

Damiano sighed deeply. "But I don't think by dying one can escape that particular sort of debt." Again he found himself thinking about his father. "Still, even if I could murder and escape unscathed, it would be a sorry sort of killing, because in the time it would take me to strangle one man through witchcraft—one man, I say, for I don't have the power to destroy a regiment—I could be run through ten times by a simple soldier with neither mind nor magic."

Pardo's gaze was eager and predatory. "This is interesting. Very. And convincing, since it is my intuition that nothing in this life is free. Yet, Signor Delstrego, you are not a military man, and therefore you don't know what things can be valuable in war. You need not kill a regiment to destroy it; merely let them see their commander fall from his horse, gasping and turning purple. Let me tell you what things I have seen ruin an army: flux from bad water, the prophecy of a crazy old whore the night before a battle, three crows sitting on the corpse of a black heifer. Things as silly as this make the difference between loss and victory. And it will always be so, as long as armies are made of men. Think what it will mean to my men to have the wizard Delstrego riding with them into battle. Think what it will mean to the enemy!"

In General Pardo's gray eyes sparked enthusiasm, and Damiano was not immune to it. Certainly no man before had ever expressed exhilaration at the thought of having *him* at his side in battle. The wizard Delstrego. . . .

But even as he felt these things Damiano also felt his staff thrumming quietly in his hands, a private voice of warning. He reminded himself that he had come here to argue for his city, and that Pardo had refused him. And Pardo was a Roman, so obviously could not be trusted. Besides, he reminded Damiano of his father, and what could be less inviting than that?

Suddenly he was aware of noises in the hall outside the audience chamber, and the room itself grew dimmer as bodies blocked the light from the door. Pardo was hedging his bet.

Damiano smiled vaguely at the general, and his fingers tightened over the second silver ring on his staff. He opened his mouth as though to speak, but instead he disappeared.

General Pardo blinked. His eyes darted right and left. "FIND HIM!" he bellowed at the men who poured into the small, square chamber.

For a moment the doorway was empty, and Damiano stepped through on tiptoe, holding the shoe of his staff off the tiles. He paced the hall, trading stealth for speed as he approached the arched door that gave onto the street.

Macchiata sat in the dust with an attitude of martyred

patience. Her nose worked, sensing him near, and her head turned expectantly toward the entryway. The single sentry stood oblivious to Damiano, his helmeted head craned over his shoulder as he attended to the rising hubbub from the general's quarters.

Damiano touched his dog on the back so lightly she did not feel him. He whispered two words. She yelped and started.

"Oh, there you are," she gasped, and her inadequate little tail wagged stiffly. In answer Damiano put his hand to his mouth and gestured for her to follow.

"I am invisible," he hissed, springing lightly along the bare street, where aimless flakes of snow had begun to fall.

"But I can see you, Master," the dog replied following in more cumbrous fashion.

"You are invisible, too." Damiano paused, staring.

Against the well sprawled old Marco, snoring, a powder of snow, like dandruff, across his felt jacket. He looked the same as ever: dirty, slack, disgruntled, even in sleep. Had he really betrayed the people of Partestrada to Pardo? If so, why was he still sitting out here in the snow, instead of throned in relative splendor at the house that until today had belonged to Cosimo Alusto? Pardo must have been lying. Yet what he had repeated concerning Delstrego and his son was every inch old Marco.

What did it matter? Damiano bent down and shook Marco by his greasy ears. "Wake up Marco," he whispered. "Talk or I will turn you into a pig and you will talk no more! Wake up now."

Marco came awake grasping at the air. He gasped, "What? Who is it?"

"It is Delstrego, old man." Let Marco figure out which one himself. "Where have the citizens gone? Speak or be sausage."

Marco clutched at the wrists of invisible hands that in turn were clutching his lapels, slamming his head against the stones of the well. Feeling their solidity did not reassure him.

"Guillermo? Do me no hurt, old friend. They are in the vetch field, where the sheep are summered. Pardo said he will offer them no violence, except, of course, for Denezzi, and I knew he was your enemy, so I told the general he had gold—more gold than he has, you know..."

Marco giggled ingratiatingly. In horror, Damiano stood, letting him drop back against the well. He turned on his heel and darted off. Behind him came a snap and a yowl of pain, then he heard Macchiata panting at his side. "I always wanted to do that," she growled contentedly. Damiano only hushed her.

The tall, scarred soldier still stood beneath the arch of the Delstrego staircase. Peering upward, Damiano could see the door was open. He stopped and pulled off his boots. His breath was beginning to steam; he hoped it was not obvious. Barefoot he climbed the stairs, with Macchiata behind him. Her nails clicked against the stones, and he glared back at her.

In five minutes he was out again, still invisible, with an invisible sheepskin sack slung over one shoulder and the *liuto* over the other. In the sack he carried wine, cheese, money, and phlegm-cutting tonic. In his heart he carried purpose. He lifted his eyes to the northern hills, where the sheep pastures flanked the Alps.

Damiano padded noiselessly past the guard and down the open stairs. Once at the bottom he turned and looked about him, missing Macchiata.

Where was the bitch? Surely she knew better than to wander off ratting now, in the middle of their escape. And it was costing him energy to keep her invisible.

He hesitated to call out for her, because invisible was not the same as inaudible. Painfully, Damiano squinted up the stairs into the darkness of the house.

There came a scream, followed shortly by a curse, and then the guard at the door fell flat on the stucco landing, bellowing. Macchiata's squat form scuttled down the stairs and past Damiano. He had to run to keep up.

"I bit them both, Master!" she panted, exultant. "I bit both soldiers and old Marco, too! Three in one day." Suddenly she came to a stop, turned, and threw herself, slobbering, upon her winded master.

"Oh, Master, I have never been so happy! This war is wonderful."

Damiano could not spare breath to disagree.

Chapter 3

The moon rose just before sunset. It hung as invisible behind the slate clouds as Damiano had been to old Marco at the well. But Damiano knew where it was, out of a knowledge so accustomed he didn't know whether it was his father's blood in him or his father's training. He always knew where the moon was; he could have pointed to it. The five planets came harder, but he had a feeling for them, also. Even with peripatetic Mercury he was usually right.

Though Damiano's eyes were faulty in daylight, he had a compensating ability to make use of moonlight, even moonlight behind clouds. For most of the month he could read without candlelight and could perceive things in the dark that most people could never see at all (nor did they want to). The full of the moon also tended to sharpen his other senses and put his feelings into a roil.

Guillermo Delstrego had liked to say that male witches were like women, with their monthly cycles. It was a joke Damiano had found in the worst taste.

Tonight the moon was at her third quarter, waning. Damiano felt as dull and heavy as a water-soaked log. For the past three nights he had tended the batch of tonic, sitting on a hard-backed chair so that he could not doze off for more than an hour at a time. The mixture had been ready this morning, and Damiano had bathed and gone immediately back to the workroom for his lesson with Raphael. He would not be able to walk the night through.

Besides, to the vetch field it was two and a half days' march. How did the citizens do it, with old women and babies, and Alfonso Berceuse with his one leg?

The road into the hills was also the road to Aosta—good and wide, open almost all the year. Why hadn't he heard? Why hadn't someone told him? It was sad that they would all go off and not think of Damiano, alone without family or servants, sitting up and brewing medicine for their sakes.

Damiano was swept with self-pity. He hated to be forgotten. And he couldn't bear the thought they had left him behind on purpose. And now three toes on his right foot had no feeling at all.

But Father Antonio would not have left him behind on purpose. Since Delstrego's death Father Antonio had been very kind to Damiano and had spent long evening hours with him in the parlor of the rectory—the good father felt constrained to avoid the Delstrego tower, though he knew Damiano worked no impieties there—drinking spiced wine and talking about sanctity and Holy Mother Church. It was a subject about which Father Antonio seemed to know much more than anyone else Damiano had met. More than did Raphael, for instance. Father Antonio was the sort who never forgot anyone—not the least of his parishioners, in their good fortune or bad. If he had left without Damiano, it was because he had believed Damiano to be gone already.

And why not? Damiano hadn't set foot outside for three days, nor let a candle shine, nor lit any fire save that under the caldron. There was no need for him to feel neglected.

Still, forgotten or no, he had to sleep. Damiano lifted his eyes to the rounded hills on either side of the

road. Immaculate, white, they seemed to give off their
own faint light. Damiano knew this landscape with a
child's minute memory. He remembered that the hill
with a lump on the side of it, three back from the road,
concealed a long, skinny cave, dry for most its length.
He remembered also that from the top of that hill one
could see Partestrada down in the cup of the valley,
where the Evançon ran under this road. He had stood
there in summer twilight and watched the lamps twin-
kle through the soft air.

Plunging into the snow-sprinkled gorse at the side
of the road, he looked at his footsteps behind him.
There was no need to concern himself with covering
them over. The wind was doing that. The tiny toe-
dimples of Macchiata's progress were half obscured
already.

A good thing, too. Damiano wasn't sure he had
the strength left to work a wind spell. "How are your
feet, Macchiata?" he asked the dog, his words coming
slurred through frozen lips. She replied that she couldn't
remember, which was probably meant as a joke, although with Macchiata one never knew for sure. He
heard her behind him, bulling her way through the low
shrubbery.

At the top of the hill he stood and looked down,
gripping his staff as tightly as his clumsy hands allowed. There was a light in the valley: one smoky
firelight where there should have been dozens. The
wind billowed his mantle out before him, and the
ermine lining glimmered brighter than snow. There
was no sound but the wind and the crackle of his
breath, along with the heavier, warmer sound of the
dog's breathing.

Already he felt removed from Partestrada, both in
distance and in time. His removal had been surgically
quick, but as he considered now, quite thorough. All
the strings that bound him to his home had been cut:
Carla was gone ahead, and both Macchiata and the lute
were portable. Damiano felt an unwarranted lump in

his throat—unwarranted because, after all, he was not
leaving Partestrada forever, but just for so long as it
took him to find his people, and to do something about
this General Pardo. Perhaps two weeks, he estimated.

He clambered down from the crest of the hill,
poking amid the dry growth with the heel of his staff,
looking for the mouth of the cave he remembered.

It was still there. Crouching down he crawled into
it, his hands smarting against frozen earth.

Inside there was no wind, and the rivulet that had
created the cave was frozen on the floor of it like a
broken silver chain. He inched over it. Macchiata slid
behind.

There, as he remembered it, was the hole in the
wall: an egg-shaped chamber that had been the perfect
size for a boy alone to play in. It was tighter for the
grown Damiano and his lute, and tighter still when
Macchiata squirmed in, curling between his nose and
knees. The staff would not fit in at all, but he laid it
along the lip of the chamber with its silver head hanging in. He touched this, mumbling three words in
Hebrew, and it gave off enough light for him to arrange
the furry mantle between his body and the stone.

"This is not too bad," he whispered to the red spot
on Macchiata's withers. She grunted in reply.

He let the light go out. "Tell me, little lady, did you
see anyone come near the house while I was tending
the kettle? Did anybody perhaps stop and look for a
light in the windows, and then pass by?"

Macchiata squirmed sleepily. "I saw many people
go by, and horses and carriages, too. All the dogs of the
city, I think. They wanted me to come with them; they
said it would be fun. —But of course I didn't.

"Also somebody knocked on the door one day. Not
today. I don't remember when."

"Ahh!" Damiano lifted his head. "Father Antonio?"

Macchiata yawned. "No. That Carla with the blond
hair."

Damiano's skull struck the stone roof of the chamber, but that didn't distract him from his joy. "Carla Denezzi, at my door? Why didn't she come in?"

"Because I didn't let her in," explained the dog. "You said you were not to be disturbed. I offered to take a message, like always, but she just stared and ran off. She's timid as a cat, that one."

Damiano's happiness was such that he had to hug someone. Macchiata gave a piglike grunt. "Timid? Ah, no, little lady, she had courage, or she would not have come at all. If that lout Denezzi knew she had come alone to the house of Delstrego, he would . . . well, I don't exactly know what he would do, but he would be very angry. And she must have had endless matters to attend to: sorting and packing and settling with all the tradesmen. Oh, don't say she is timid, Macchiata."

The dog stuffed her nose down among her folded paws in meaningful fashion and said nothing at all.

When Damiano awoke, the cave walls were chalky with diffuse sunlight. He was warm, but very hungry. Macchiata was gone, but he heard her at the entrance to the cave, snuffling among the shrubbery. Rolling onto his back, he dug into his sheepskin bag and found the waxed wrappings of a cheese, which emitted a tiny crackling.

Along the path of the rivulet he heard a frantic scrabble, and Macchiata slammed her broad head smartly against the end wall.

"Mother of God, what is it?" demanded Damiano, blinking down the length of the tunnel.

"Breakfast. Maybe?" she answered, wagging everything up to her shoulders.

Damiano laughed. "Maybe," he admitted.

He divided the cheese expertly in half, as was his custom, knowing that although she was much smaller than he was, he had never had an enthusiasm for eating that could equal Macchiata's. (It was for this reason that Damiano was thin while his dog was fat.)

He washed down his bread and mozzarella with

wine. Macchiata lapped snow. Gathering his gear and cradling the lute against his stomach, Damiano crawled out of the cave.

It was a beautiful morning. The sun beat gloriously over snow a foot deep, and the occasional pine trees wore blankets and hats. Not a print marked the road, which ran smooth as a plaster wall upward toward the north. In the distance, beyond the foothills and even beyond the black band of forest, a jagged rim broke the horizon.

The Alps, clean and sharp as puppy teeth. Even Damiano's eyes could distinguish them.

"By John the Baptist and by John the Evangelist and by John the Best Beloved!—if they are indeed three different Johns—this is magnificent!" He clambered down the slope, showering snow. "A good night's sleep, a full stomach, and the road spreading before us like a Turkey carpet! Were it not for the plight of the citizens of Partestrada, I would have nothing else to desire."

Macchiata peered up at Damiano, her brown eyes puzzled, a lump of snow on her muzzle. "But you could have slept in the cave anytime, Master. You didn't need to be thrown out of your house to do it."

Damiano grinned from ear to ear and sprang over the little valley where the stream ran down from the hill. "You're right, little dear. And you know what? I think you are very wise."

Macchiata's ears pricked up. It was not a compliment she had known before.

"We live our lives bound by our little tasks and possessions and never know how free we could be unless God sees fit to pry us away from them. You know who knew true happiness? I'll tell you—Giovanni di Bernardone, whom our Holy Father has sanctified under the name of Francis. He had nothing in the world, and the world had nothing in him, and he used to walk barefoot in the snow, singing."

Damiano himself began to sing, though he was not

barefoot but instead wore soft leather boots with wool-
en linings. He found it difficult to sing and climb at the
same time.

"You have a lovely voice, Master," said Macchiata,
feeling that one good compliment deserved another.

"Eh? Thank you, Macchiata, but it is nothing special."

"Say, you know what I think I'll do?—after finding
Carla, of course. If the soldiers have robbed her, I'll
give her my money, and for those who catch the
flux...

"Anyway, I think I'll cross over the Rhone to
France, and maybe after that to Germany, for there is
the heart and soul of alchemy, you know. Why not? I
am young and strong."

And he did feel strong—strong enough to bend
down a young bull by the horns, as the burly peasants
did to show off during the harvest fair.

"I have an intellect, too, and have studied hard."
Suddenly Damiano remembered that Carla Denezzi
would not be in Germany but at home in Partestrada.
"And then," he concluded more soberly, "when I have
a name and my words mean something to men of birth
and education, I will use my power for Partestrada. I
will return."

Macchiata had been listening with some concern.
"What about me, Master?" she whimpered.

Damiano glanced down in surprise. "Why you will
be beside me, little dear. While we both live on this
earth, we will not be parted!"

After this promise they walked some while in
silence. Macchiata's robust little heart was filled with
happiness and touched by the importance of her com-
mitment to Damiano. He, at the same time, was busy
with thoughts and plans. He would lead the people of
Partestrada into the Valle d'Aosta, for Aosta was many
times larger than Partestrada and also much closer to
Chambéry and so to the Green Count of Savoy. There
Pardo would not dare follow.

Then Damiano would go on to France, where he

would write a poem about the Piedmont and Partestrada. It would be called "The Sorrows of Exile," and it would burn men's souls. He could feel it within him now, stirring like a chick in the egg. It shouldn't be a poem only, but a work of music, like the ballades sung by the old trouvères, and Damiano would play his lute as Raphael had taught him—France was far more musically liberal than Italy—till hearts bled for Partestrada as Dante had made them do for Florence, with its confusing lot of Guelphs and Ghibellines. Was not art, after all, the greatest weapon of man?

Damiano considered, as his boot soles crunched down on snow. It was great, yes, but tardy, and Dante had never returned to Florence. Damiano sighed and shook his head, for the first energy of the morning was gone and so was the warmth of the wine. The snow was deepening as the road climbed; Macchiata cut into it with her breastbone as she trotted beside him, holding her head up like a nervous horse. The risen sun glinted in the corner of Damiano's right eye.

Perhaps Germany was a better goal. In Germany there was at least one emperor, and emperors can afford to be generous. But Damiano was not a fool; he knew what it meant to allow the ass's nose within the tent or to ask help of a foreigner in settling a local grievance. It would be no great sort of fame to be known as the man who invited the northern wolf over the Alps.

In Nuremberg there were said to be many scrolls written by Mary the Jewess, and students of the great Hermes Trismegistus himself, and in Nuremberg now dwelt the sage Nicolas, who was called the prophet. Though Damiano did not know what help the art of alchemy had to offer defeated Partestrada, he would like very much to visit Nuremberg.

"Master," began Macchiata, as she leaned her shoulder against his calf.

"Uh. What? Macchiata, little dear, am I going too fast for you?"

"No," she replied, with a dog's inability to recognize weariness until it has throttled her. "But I was thinking... If I am your little dear, and we'll never be parted until somebody dies, then why do you send me away all the time?"

"I don't!" cried Damiano, stung.

"Yes you do. Every spring and every fall, for two weeks."

"Oh." Damiano's eyebrows lifted and his tangled black hair fell over his eyes. "That is necessary. It is not something I want to do, but you are a... female dog, and such have their times when they must be alone."

"But I don't want to be alone. Ever," she said simply. "Nothing is different then, except that I feel... friendly, and then I hate most to be in a pen."

Damiano stared stolidly up the road. The wind blew over his uncovered ears, which had gone very red. "It is the things you say," he admitted. "During those times you are not yourself."

Beside him Macchiata gave a whuffle and a bound to keep up. "What do I say? I don't remember a thing about it."

"I know. God be praised for that!" He marched on in a businesslike manner and would discuss the subject no further.

Forest grew up around them. By midday they were in a dark hush of pines. Here the air was still and smelled somehow ecclesiastical. They had seen no one and passed no one.

This was not surprising, since even in times of peace, travel between Aosta and the south slowed to a trickle after snowfall. There was another road ahead, which creased the base of the high hills from west to east, and which would intersect the North Road some ten miles ahead. Less than a mile along the right-hand path of that road stood a village of a dozen huts. It was called Sous Pont Saint Martin, which was a French name and longer than the village itself. Damiano assumed that it was as deserted as Partestrada. But it would shelter him at least as well as a cave, and there might be food. If the sky was clear, however, he would walk through the night.

Contemplating an all-night journey made the young man's muscles ache with weariness. It was now as near midday as no matter. And weary legs on numb feet made the army of General Pardo seem a more serious problem than it had after breakfast. Certainly he couldn't trot off to Nuremberg or Avignon while Pardo ravaged the hills. Damiano gave a large, round sigh.

He had outdistanced all his solitary childhood rambles an hour ago and stood in a brilliant, wild landscape unknown to him. Damiano noticed a rock standing ten feet from the road, sparkling in the sunshine with mica or ice. He squatted against it, wondering how many travelers it had sheltered since the six days of creation. Its cracked face was the color of honey, and Damiano leaned his cheek against it, half-expecting it to be warm. The snow swam before his eyes, as though moles or tunneling rabbits were disturbing its surface. He rummaged for the wine bottle.

"I hope you de-tuned your lute," said Raphael. Damiano realized that what he had taken for snow were the outstretched wings of the angel, who was sitting motionless on a rock not four feet away. Raphael's robe was whiter than the white ground and without ornament. His hair shone as colorless as sunlight.

Damiano's grin spread slowly, because the skin at the corners of his mouth was cracked. "Seraph! O spirit of fire! How do you like the snow?"

Macchiata ploughed over from whatever private business she had been on. "Raphael! You found us!"

"Yes! Yes, I found you!" replied Raphael, in tones of enthusiasm that he reserved for the dog alone. He rubbed the sides of her head till her ears snapped like leather whips. Damiano felt a slight pang of jealousy.

Raphael turned back to him. "I like the snow very much, and the mountains. I think they have a beautiful voice."

Damiano gazed at Raphael until his eyes smarted. He was so glad to see him he could think of nothing to say, and his mind filled with inconsequentials.

Had Raphael skin beneath that lustrous garment, or was he no more than face and wings—an illusion worn so that Damiano could understand him? And why, since angels were immaterial and sexless, did Raphael seem to Damiano entirely male? All the painters gave their angels the faces of women.

Had Raphael seemed a woman, Damiano, easily swayed by such things, would not have been able to bear it. He would have made a fool of himself, for certain, and perhaps sinned in his heart. Perhaps, Damiano reflected, that was why Raphael did *not* appear so, since the good God did not offer a man temptations he could not possibly resist.

The chiseled face tilted sideways, almost like that of a curious bird, and the wings swept snow into the air: snow that broke the light like a thousand prisms. "Why are you looking at me like that?" asked Raphael.

Damiano swallowed; he realized his hand still clutched the neck of the wine bottle. "I had forgotten how amazing you are, Raphael. Seeing you under the sky, like this . . . is very beautiful."

The angel's face remained unchanged, as though the compliment had gone through him. "The blue sky is very beautiful," he agreed, tilting his head upwards. "But then so it is in the rain, and the snow."

Damiano's cold and nervous hands fumbled under the folds of the mantle and found the pear-shape of the lute. He brought it out. "You see, Seraph. I loosened all the strings, knowing the cold might have snapped the neck."

Raphael knelt in the snow and took the instrument in both his hands. One by one, he adjusted the eight strings.

"This is as loose as they need to be," he remarked. "Unless you are going to the top of a mountain."

Damiano sighed, thinking how much there was to

explain. "Only as high as the summer pastures, where the people of Partestrada have fled. Then...I don't know, Raphael. Perhaps France, or Germany, but not until...tell me, what should I do for my city?"

Raphael gazed at Damiano until the young man felt he were standing alone beneath hosts of stars. Had he known how, he would have laid open his soul to the angel, with the history of his every thought, and let Raphael judge him and decide his path. No matter the pain, weariness, or worldly shame, Damiano believed, he would have done Raphael's bidding.

But he did not know how to bare his soul, and he was certain that Raphael was not about to tell him what to do with his life, so instead Damiano dropped his eyes to the cork and the green glass of the wine bottle. Consequently Raphael's words caught him by surprise.

"Pray, Damiano! Pray for the people of Partestrada, and pray for yourself; for guidance. It may be you will need it." The angel spoke with a clear intensity, and Damiano flushed at his own omission.

"Of course, Seraph. Since yesterday...all has been topsy-turvy, and I have forgotten. But aren't you my guidance?"

Raphael laughed and Damiano, too. It always worked that way. "No, Dami, I'm not here as a messenger of the Highest. It was your will that first called me and my own will that chose to come. I am not your guide but your friend."

Damiano bowed his head to follow the angel's advice, but immediately he raised his eyes again and saw Raphael sitting before him, wings folded back. Macchiata lay curled on the angel's lap like a white piglet, slightly soiled. "Don't go," begged Damiano. "I'm afraid when I look up again, you'll be gone, and you just got here."

Raphael took Damiano's hand and held it.

The mortals ate while Raphael looked on. They didn't speak of Pardo or Partestrada or the horsemen who even now must be combing the uplands for the city's unfortunate people. In fact, later, when trudging the road that afternoon, Damiano looked back upon their conversation, and it seemed they had talked about nothing at all. Raphael had turned down Macchiata's invitation to walk along with them, saying he was not much of a walker.

The afternoon clouded up, and the snow that the sun had softened began to freeze. Black walls of evergreens now were not such an inspiring sight, for the travelers had seen nothing else since morning. The climb continued.

By the time the shadows covered the road it had become slick, and Damiano began to fear for his lute. If he fell on the little instrument, which was only the size of a toddler's potbelly, that would be the end of it.

He did fall, injuring his right hand but not the lute. As he was a witch, and therefore left-handed, he thanked God for small favors, but the fall let him know he could not go on through the night.

The sun had failed when Damiano saw a wink of yellow light at the top of the slope to the right of the road. In his state of weariness he stared dumbly at it. "What could that be?" he mumbled to the world in general.

"It's sausage," answered Macchiata promptly. "And three people. Men. With an oil lamp. And wine."

Damiano gaped in amazement. "You learned all that by smelling?"

Macchiata wagged her tail, but her nose pointed like a lodestone toward the glimmer of light. "My nose gets better when I'm hungry.

"Can we go say hello, Master?"

Damiano chuckled at her greedy eagerness, but he didn't feel so different himself. It was the thought of fire, however, that drew him. He found himself shivering under his wool and fur. "They may be Pardo's soldiers," he said uncertainly, but he stepped toward the light as he spoke.

"No. Not soldiers," answered Macchiata with authority. "They don't smell like soldiers."

Damiano didn't question her statement. He followed the dog up the slope, climbing with his toes and one bruised hand, while his left hand dug the staff in behind him.

He came close enough to recognize the stone hut that marked the meeting of the North Road and the west, and which had held a guard in his great-grandfather's day, before the house of Savoy had made the land safe. Then it had become a traveler's shelter. Now, perhaps the new ruler of the Piedmont would open the guardhouse again, at least until Amadeus VI drove him away.

Damiano stepped closer, brushing snow from his trousers as quietly as he could.

There were two windows overlooking the North Road. One was dark, being stuffed against the cold with rags and scraps of firewood, along with a single, soleless leather boot. The other window was smaller and had panes of cow's horn. It was through this window that light was pouring.

In the amber glow Damiano stood, gripping his staff in both hands. "Mirabile! Videāmus," he whispered. "Let us see."

And he saw three men, as Macchiata had said. All of them were his age, or thereabouts. They were not soldiers; they wore clothes of fashion, though these were time-stained and not of the best. From their belts hung the jeweled, effete daggers of the young bravo, yet all three had taken the clerical tonsure. Damiano smiled, hearing French laced with Latin: the speech of students. Damiano spoke a passable French.

The staff throbbed in his hand—a reminder from his instincts to himself to be careful. These were not three Poverelli of Francesco, to be sure, whatever their clerical bent. Since the Holy Father had moved to Avignon, it seemed all of Provence had adopted the styles of the Church, saints and sinners alike. And these fellows had been drinking.

But still, they were students, and what else was Damiano? The brotherhood of students was as close as that which existed in any cloister, and more entertaining besides. Damiano knocked his damaged knuckles against the wooden door, while Macchiata whined in her most placatory manner.

What had been boisterous conversation became silence. "Qui?" called a voice, and then in broken Italian, "Who there?"

"Naught but a traveling student," answered Damiano in Latin. "And his dog."

More silence followed, and then a scraping. The door opened, revealing the scene Damiano's craft had shown him before. Three men, a smoky hearth, and a tin lamp set on a table strewn with food. Damiano blinked against the beauty of the sight.

"Enter then and be welcome," said the fellow who had opened the door. He was moonfaced, plump, and balding, despite his youth. The two others regarded Damiano from their places at table. One was dark and square, the other towheaded with a long face. This last mentioned student held a greasy spiced sausage in his lap in a manner most proprietary.

"My name is Damiano Delstrego," Damiano said, bowing. "This lady is my dog Macchiata. We thank you for your courtesy on this icy evening."

The dark youth rose, smiling slightly. The bow of the fellow at the door was a marvel involving three separate movements of the foot. "Signor Dottore Delstrego. Let me present our small company. This one standing, with the shoulders of Hercules—he is Paul Breton, and he is a poet. The blond without manners is called Till Eulenspiegel. We are golliards, the impossible children of Pierre Abélard himself."

"Till Eulenspiegel!" Damiano burst out, involuntarily.

Slyly the blond looked up. "What's wrong with that?" He spoke an egregious Italian.

The first student stepped between them. "You see, Dottore, we believe that a name chosen oneself or by those who know one is more meaningful than the one chosen at birth. It is the custom of golliards to forego allegiance to country, town, and family for the highest fidelity to learning itself. Therefore Jan Karl is Till Eulenspiegel, and world watch out.

"I myself," he concluded, "have the honor to carry the name of Pierre Paris, because that is the place I like best."

A chair was sought for Damiano, to no avail. He who called himself Pierre Paris offered his own, but Damiano chose to sit on the table. From his pack he took the remainder of his bread and cheese, pulled off portions of both for Macchiata, and put the rest on the table. The dog wolfed what she was given and retired to the space beneath Eulenspiegel's chair, where she lay consuming the aroma of sausage.

"Delstrego," drawled the Dutchman. "Doesn't that mean 'of the witch'?"

"Yes it does," admitted Damiano. He had become impatient waiting for someone to invite him to eat and so had begun unasked.

"Is it also"—the blond ran out of Italian and switched to French—"a title self-chosen?"

Damiano shook his head forcefully. "Definitely not. It was my father's name and his father's before him for I don't know how long." He continued in Latin, for he was quite at home in it, having the advantage of being Italian. "If I took a name to myself it would be Damiano Alchemicus."

"Not Damiano Musicus?" asked Pierre Paris, as with lightning speed he whipped the long sausage from Eulenspiegel's grasp and cut a section for their guest. The blade of his dagger he wiped on the hem of his black overshirt. "I was hoping we would hear that lute you have cradled so carefully in the corner.

Damiano followed his glance to where the lute rested, wrapped in the white fur of his mantle. "Perhaps later, Signor Clericale, once it's warm. But I'm not very good." Half the thick slice of sausage disappeared into a wet mouth waiting under the table. The other half Damiano held between his fingers, nibbling.

"Good students," he said, "for such I see you are—though I had thought that war and pestilence had ended the golliard's jolly times—I am a student also, both of science and spirit. Why do you travel weaponless through a land devastated by war?"

Paris stared owlishly at Breton, who in turn looked toward Eulenspiegel, who kept his eyes fixed on Damiano. "Who would devastate the barren mountains, and how would one be able to tell they had been devastated?" inquired Paris, who in all matters seemed to be the spokesman of the three.

Damiano felt a variety of envy for them, whose lives had not yet been touched by the present troubles. He assumed that because his troubles were not theirs, they had no troubles. This supposition on his part was a human error, certainly, but it could have been dyed a much deeper hue had Damiano felt contempt and alienation from the three because of their fortune.

Instead he wanted to help keep them safe and carefree, and to that end he said, "Believe me, Signori Clericale: we are little more than a day's travel from what was a thriving city and is now abandoned to General Pardo's soldiery."

"Pardo?" spoke up Eulenspiegel, who seemed to have a quick ear, though a slow tongue. "The condottiere in the service of the pope? He was at Avignon a few years ago."

Damiano peered stricken at the blond at the other side of the table. He was just at the limit of Damiano's close sight, and Damiano could not be sure Eulenspiegel was joking. "You mean . . . It could not be that the Holy Father is sacking the towns of the Piedmont?"

Paris broke in smoothly. "It could be, but I think it isn't. The condottieri serve contracts, not men, and I remember hearing when I was at the papal court last

that Pardo's time was lapsed, and either he or the Holy
Father did not renew.

"And, my dear brothers, what is a condottiere
without lands or employer, but a brigand?"

"They're all robbers, anyway," sneered Eulenspiegel,
glaring dourly into the distance. Damiano reconsidered
his conception of this man; there was doubtless sorrow
in his past.

"Nonetheless, I beg you to beware, Signori. Do not
follow the road down from the hills or you may find
you have walked into trouble. And if you hear the
sounds of many horses on the road, then leave it
quickly and hide where you may."

"Would in any case," growled Eulenspiegel, while
the poet just sighed.

"Ah! I thank you, friend Delstrego," said Paris,
placing both the basket-covered wine jug and a husk of
bread in front of Damiano. "I drink to your health, for
you have cared for ours." He picked up Damiano's
green bottle and did as he had promised. "Now you
must drink too, or the toast will be invalid."

Smiling sheepishly, Damiano drank their wine. To
his surprise, it was as good as his own. He complimented
them upon it.

"Should be good," said Eulenspiegel, showing his
teeth.

Paris cleared his throat. "I appreciate your advice,
Signor Dottore Delstrego, and believe we are all grate-
ful. Yet our path was decided for us before we left
France, and to veer from it would destroy the meaning
of our journey.

"Let me tell you, friend in the wilderness, that we
three are retracing the steps of the great Petrarch from
Avignon to Milan, seeing every inch of the countryside
about which he wrote.

"Ah, the verse!" cried out Breton, the poet. "Im-
mortal verses, wild as the god Pan!"

Damiano started. It was as though a dog had
talked—another dog, not Macchiata.

"I saw him, in Milan," ventured Damiano. "He was very gracious, and let me copy four of his poems into a book. I dared not ask for more, for I was sitting in his office where the window looked out onto il Duomo, and he sat across from me, asking which parts I liked. It was a great moment for me. Yet I don't believe Petrarch rode from Avignon in the beginning of winter, did he?"

The poet opened his brown eyes very round. "He has spoken with you? The laureate himself. You sat in his house?"

Damiano shrugged in a self-deprecating manner. "Only for an hour. I doubt he would remember my name."

"Delstrego would be hard to forget," remarked the blond. "I've been looking at that," he added, pointing at the staff, which rested like a baby in the crook of Damiano's left arm. "You use it just to walk?"

Under the combined stares of four pairs of eyes the black wood hummed. Damiano stroked it, embarrassed, as he was at any mention of his witchhood.

"No, although it is very useful and sturdy in that way. I use it as a focus for my concentration, because otherwise the—power—roams free in the body and clouds the mind."

"You're a witch?" breathed Paris, and the room froze.

"A wizard," contradicted Damiano, immediately wondering why on earth he had said that. The three students huddled like birds before the eyes of a snake, and Damiano blushed harder.

"*Domine Deus*, my friends, there is no need to be afraid of me for that! I am a scholar and a Christian!" But still they sat, and they sat very still. In a moment Damiano was sure someone would say "but the devil can quote Scripture," a proverb that always made him wince. He groaned deeply and rose from his chair, placing his staff by the wrapped lute in the far corner of the room from the fire.

"There, Signori Clericale. My power is there and I

am here. I cannot hurt you now even if I would. Is that enough?"

Till Eulenspiegel relaxed, wiping the sweat from his pale forehead. The poet sighed once more, and Pierre Paris reached for the green wine bottle, a conciliatory smile on his round face.

The staff boomed a warning, alone and helpless in the corner, as Paris lifted the bottle and brought it down with force on Damiano's head.

Chapter 4

Damiano awoke to cold and pain and a feeling of being stifled. This last was due to Macchiata, who was lying on top of him, her nose anxiously denting his face. "Master, Master. Get up and move!" she crooned. "Or you'll die and freeze and leave me alone always!

"Please!" she cried, her voice like the neighing of a horse, in his ear. His arms moved to placate her, to ward her off.

"Can't breathe," Damiano gasped, and the effort of this sent waves of nausea through his body. His eyes closed again.

"Master!"

Damiano turned, bringing his hands under him. He remembered the golliards and the bottle against his skull. His head rose and his poor eyes peered through the little hut, at the table, with its remains of bread and cheese, the hearth, where the fire still blazed (thanks be to God), the shape in the corner that must be his lute. That glint of silver along the floor meant his staff was intact; had any of them tried to touch it, woe unto them. His mantle lay upon him where Macchiata had dragged it, off-center and with the lining upwards.

"Where are they?" he asked the dog, his voice as shaky as that of an old man. He sat up and wrapped the mantle about him. Her response was a growl as preternaturally ominous as the sound of an avalanche in the distance. Damiano turned his head with difficulty and looked at Macchiata, who stood stiff as wood and spiney all over. All her teeth showed, as yellow as the tushes of a boar, and in her eyes was a rage he had never seen before. He began to shiver.

"They are far away, Master. So far I can't hear them or smell them. They will never hurt you again."

Through his haze of misery he tried to understand. "Did you . . . kill them, Macchiata? All three?"

"They were not dead when they ran down the hill and down the road. But there was only one of them without a hole in him." The ugly dog softened. She lifted one paw up to Damiano's shoulder and licked his eyes, one after the other.

"Go sit by the fire, Master. It will make you feel better."

Pulling his garment tighter, Damiano obeyed her, but first he fished across the floor for the length of his staff. With this in hand, he sank gratefully down on the ashy stones of the hearth. In passing he noted that the firewood that the three "students" had been burning was composed of a splintered chair and a heavy oak footstool, as well as half a shutter. He sighed: their behavior was all of a piece. But why had he not noticed this last night? Macchiata clambered onto his lap.

"Master no more, dear one," he sighed. "Say rather I'm little Dami, your foolish pet. Imagine what my father would have said, if he had seen me put my staff aside in a room full of strangers." The grown witch had tried to make his son careful. In Damiano's mind came the vision of his father snatching the black wood from the dozing boy's hands and simultaneously giving him a cuff on the ear, while he laughed, laughed, laughed . . . The memory gave him the added warmth of shame, but it made his head ache more.

Macchiata snorted, piglike. "Of course you are my Master. Only you are too trusting for your own good."

Damiano's brows drew together, which brought lancing pain along his scalp. The fire, however, was helping him.

"It was Pierre Paris's fear that caused him to strike me. Had he not known I was a witch, it would not have happened."

"You are wrong, Master," said Macchiata, quickly but diffidently, for she was not used to contradicting Damiano. "I'm sorry, but it's true. The one with the pale hair tried to stop that one. He said he'd be sorry for it. Then the one with no hair on his head asked what was the difference: a knife in the back at night or a wine bottle at dinner?"

"They were robbers? They meant to kill me in my sleep?" asked Damiano, incredulous. "What else did they say?"

Macchiata's skinny tail slapped his leg: once, twice, then rapidly. "They didn't have time to say much. I was asleep, but the sound woke me up."

"The sound," repeated Damiano. "The echo of the blow resounding in my braincase. That's what woke you up."

She licked his hand. "But I cursed them for it, and I bit them. I bit the black one on the thick part of the leg, but on the blond my hold slipped, so I made a big rip in his shirt, and bloodied where he would sit."

"So the one you missed altogether was the one who hit me with the wine bottle," remarked Damiano, not meaning to denigrate her victory.

"Yes, because he tried to beat me off with your staff. It bit him."

Damiano felt the blackwood beneath his fingers. "Signor Paris may never have use of that hand again," he said.

"Both hands. But it was my curses that chased them out the door without their packs. I got the words from your father." Macchiata wrapped her tongue around her muzzle, then smiled till her bristly muzzle resembled a cat's face.

Leaning on his staff, Damiano rose to his feet. "Packs?" he murmured, and shuffled off to see. "And curses? I only hope, Macchiata, that you didn't compromise your soul with evil wishes. They are very deadly."

"Have I a soul, Master?" She asked in a tone of casual interest. "I never heard that before."

There were two bundles under the table, besides his own sheepskin bag. A third huddled against the hearthstones. "Of course you have a soul, Macchiata," he answered, and although he knew himself to be on shaky theological ground, still he believed that anyone who liked Raphael as much as the dog did, and who was so liked in return, had to have a soul. "And a great spirit, besides. . . .

"Now let's see what the three scholars have left us."

Within the packs was an assortment of trash, along with a few objects of peculiar meaning and value. The first sack dumped on the table offered a lady's hairpin in gold and pearls, along with three silver florins in a needlepoint pouch. The second bag held a double handful of walnuts, together with a bundle of faded letters written in a script that was not quite German. Out of the final bag dropped a squarish parcel wrapped in linen and tied with twine. Damiano undid the tiny knot with a tiny loosing spell.

"*Domine Deus!*" he breathed, as a book in vellum, bound in both wood and leather, flapped onto the table. "So they weren't totally false!"

It was a volume of the poetry of Petrarch, copied in painful, schoolboy script. The premier letter of each verse was illuminated in the old manner, with awkward care and much gold paint.

These items were heavy, and he did not really want to be reminded of their former possessors. Yet books were like children; they could not be abandoned to the snow. And he did appreciate Petrarch.

In the end Damiano decided to take all but the clothing as spoils of war.

Their fire, too, was his by right. And their food. He felt almost well enough to care about that. His eyes scanned the table.

"What became of the sausage, little dear? Did our friend the German carry it with him out into the snow?"

Macchiata's tail and ears stood up. She dashed to the corner and nuzzled under Damiano's lute, backing out with something black and dirt-covered in her mouth.

"No, he dropped it," she mumbled, placing an irregularly shaped piece of greasy meat in his hand. "I saved half for you."

In the first light Damiano woke once more and spent a few minutes playing his lute. He had a headache and a spot of numbness on his scalp. Further, his eyes refused to focus on the strings. Raphael did not appear, but then the angel would scarcely have fit in the hut, and besides, Damiano had no time to spare. He took a swig of the wine in the basket-jug, and for luck, another of his father's tonic. Then he stepped into the cold.

After a half-mile's march the headache had grown to fill the world, and the light of the new sun on the snow pierced his eyes. Tears ran along his cheeks, and even the dog had nothing cheerful to say. Damiano was not too far from wishing he were dead, but the alternative of every person in the winter wilderness—curling up in the snow and sleeping—had no attraction.

"We shall be there today, and early," he muttered. "Except for the weather, we might have reached the pastures by yesterday nightfall." He watched for the cluster of huts that housed the shepherds of the mountains and a small number of hunters whose livelihoods kept them in the heights all winter. The nearest real

village was Pont Saint Martin, on the North Road two
miles from the spot where Damiano had turned, which
was the reason this poor assembly was known as Sous
Pont Saint Martin. Damiano had been there only once,
in July, when his father had been called to treat the
sheep for a bad flux.

The road had been swept by wind and the abrasive, frozen snow of the night before. In rare spots the
wind had come again and shaved the earth bare, leaving
only the strange, reversed prints of men and horses,
made of pressed snow and glistening white against the
black earth. Who knew how old these were?

The slopes dropped away on either side of the
road, and the travelers came to a river: the Lys. It ran
wide and violent, though ice crusted each bank like
sheets of shattered glass. Across the river a stone
bridge led. It was wide and smooth, with waist-high
guardwalls on either side. It was the sort of craftsmanship
the country people dismissed as Roman work, heavy,
useful, built to last. There was no evidence it was old
Roman, except in the fact that no Piedmontese was
likely to take such trouble on a mountain bridge. Roman work was like the hills themselves: whether or not
men could make such things today, they were there for
free and so not to be admired too much.

As he crossed over the span the wind hit him and
turned his head to the left, from whence the river
flowed.

His left foot trod on his right, and then Damiano
stopped stock still. "Mother of God! Can it be?" he
cried and sank down on his knees in the wet snow.

There stood peaks ranked against the sky: an awesome white phalanx, blinding bright from the teeth of
their summits to the green cloaks that wrapped their
feet, which were banded with silver rock. They were so
tall they crowded the sky, and they grew taller as they
seemed to rush at the kneeling youth. In their silence
were all the voices of an infinite, inhuman choir.

Two presences dominated. To the left sat the highest

peak in the Valle d'Aosta: Mont Emilius, whom the peasants called Grandfather. Rugged and glistening, it had roots reaching almost to the road. To the right, far away and behind a palisade of mountains, out of a shimmer of light rose a single white fang, sharp as the tooth of a dog, and crooked at the tip, like a dog's tooth, but unearthly clean. Damiano did not know it was Mont Cervin: the peak called the Matterhorn.

As he stared, kneeling, he wept, knowing the beauty he saw must be like that of Raphael, if the archangel were to fling aside his little human cloak and appear as a flame of divine love. This the angel would never do, of course, out of a concern for the limits of man. The mountains, however, were less merciful. Damiano's ecstasy bid fair to do him damage.

"Master! Get up! Please, your knees are getting soaked. Master! Damiano. What is the pain?" Macchiata danced a circle around him, nuzzling his hands with her warm tongue and her cold nose.

"Little dear, I see a beauty fit to kill a man! Can't you see the . . . thrones of the ages?"

"Thrones of who?" She prodded him to his feet.

"Of the . . . the mountains. Mont Emilius and another. Doesn't their loveliness pierce you?"

She snorted. "I see nothing. The wall is too high. But if piercing is what loveliness does to you, I want no part of it!

"Come, Damiano. You can't stop here, in the wind, and now wet besides."

Docile, made meek by so much splendor, he allowed her to lead him forward. In a few minutes the village of Sous Pont Saint Martin peeped out between two hills. Damiano passed between them into a natural rock shelter, where the wind swirled aimlessly, carrying snow spray in a high spiral into the air.

The west side of each square hut was braced with a flying buttress of white. The patch of ground blocked from the wind by each building was scattered with bootprints, along with the prints of shod hooves. Many riders had been here recently.

But were not here now. The village was desolate. Silence rumbled in Damiano's ears. Or was that Macchiata, growling?

Damiano glanced down at the dog in surprise. Her hackles were up, her squat legs braced. Nervously, her eyes met his. "Let's go back to the road," she suggested.

"Why, Macchiata? Here is shelter, and my feet are frozen. What's wrong, little dear? Do you smell soldiers?"

"Yes. No. No soldiers now. Just blood. Frozen blood."

Damiano took a wary step forward. Macchiata scrabbled in front of him and stood barring his way. "No, Master. You are too sensitive; looking at mountains hurts you. This will hurt you worse!

"Let's go back to the road. Our people aren't here."

Damiano's easy color rose to his cheeks, and he gazed resentfully down at her. "Love of beauty is not the same thing as cowardice, Macchiata.

"Wasn't it I who found my father perishing in torment? And have I not grown up hearing Father Antonio remind us that all flesh is the food of worms— flesh of both dogs and men, little one? Dead men hold no terror for me."

The dog dropped her head and Damiano swept by.

In the circle formed by the huts was a little meadow, which in the summer was browsed by chickens and the occasional hobbled goat. Now it was swept by wind and ice and snow, with the gray stubble of grass exposed where the wind had scraped most deep. In this field lay the broken bodies of three men and an old woman, frozen clean and uncorrupt. The edges of their many wounds were fresh and sharp: the color of good pork.

At Damiano's feet lay the severed head of one of the men: a young peasant with a reddish beard. The skin was blue and white and waxlike. The neck was chopped neat. With the hollow windpipe arched through it and the spine running through the back, the neck looked like a slice cut through a fish. Ice crystals had grown from the edges of the empty veins. The head wore an expression of slack bewilderment as it stared at the sky over Damiano's shoulder. One eye was open wider than the other.

Damiano thought he was doing very well until he tried to move. The horrid field reeled, and only his staff held him to his feet.

He shuffled from one body to another, mouthing an incoherent prayer for the dead that was also a plea for Christ to sustain him through this nausea. He dared not look at Macchiata.

The head was the most horrible, but the old woman was the saddest, for she had been trampled and her fusty black skirt torn off. Around each of the forms the snow was tinted a faded ruby, much like the color of the stone at the tip of Damiano's staff.

He raised his eyes to the sound of rhythmic lapping. A dog was licking at the bloody snow by the severed head. For a terrible moment he thought it was Macchiata.

It was not, of course. It was a shaggy herd dog, doubtless belonging to some man of the village. Perhaps the beast's master lay dead here before him. Whatever, it could do these poor figures no hurt.

Macchiata noticed the cur at the same moment. With a bull bellow she flung herself upon the stranger, who offered no fight, but tucked tail and fled.

"Come back, Macchiata," called Damiano, as the red spot that was all he could see of her bobbed into the distance behind a row of huts. "There may be more of them. Come back!"

A human voice answered his with a cry shrill and weak. Damiano's hair prickled. He stared around him.

There was nothing to be seen: an ox wagon, its tongue buried in drifts; a stack of brushwood for burning; a pitchfork, wooden tines protruding from the

snow like bird claws; the imperturbable gray stones of
the huts. No more. But the cry came again, from across
the expanse of wind. Damiano sprang toward it, plunging knee deep. He leaped over a dimple in the snow,
not knowing it was the village well and twenty feet
deep. The row of buildings greeted him with silence.

"Hello!" he cried. "Who's there?"

"In here!" came the answer from behind a door.
He put his shoulder to it.

The door sagged in, hanging by one hinge.

The darkness within took his sight, and he gagged
at the smell. "Speak!" Damiano commanded, swaying
in the doorway. "If there is a Christian soul within . . ."

"Here," she replied, and he saw her: the pale spot
of a face in the corner by the door. She was covered in
blankets and the skin of a cow. One hand held the
wraps under her chin. That and her face was all he
could see. He knelt beside her.

Damiano's eyes saw her young face waver as though
seen through the steam of a boiling pot. She was taut
with agony. She stared at him. He pried the covers
from the grip of her hand, and he dared to pull them
back.

She was naked. With her other hand she was
holding—like a woman with an apron full of peas—
Mother of God, it was her guts she was holding,
spilled out of the rent in her belly and sticking to the
coarse wool of the blanket.

"Lord have mercy," whispered Damiano, letting
her pull up the blankets once more. "Forgive me,
Signora." Somewhere a dog was howling.

"We're all dead here," she said quite calmly.
"Ernesto. Sofia and her brother. Me. My little 'Lonso.
Renaud. We are only six and had nothing, and the
soldiers killed us all. I am the last, but I'm dead
nonetheless. Give me water."

"Ahh?" Damiano felt about reflexively and realized
he was still carrying his sheepskin bag. His cold hands

dug into it. "I have only wine," he told her, and heard his own voice trembling. He held the bottle to her lips.

She drank greedily, and Damiano tried not to think of the red wine trickling out of her belly below. "Thank you," she gasped when the bottle was empty. "It will do me no good, but thank you anyway.

"Renaud threw a pitchfork at the first soldier to stick his head between the guard hills. They cut his head off and killed us all, and I don't even know who they were or from where. It does not matter from where. I curse them. I curse the women who bore them and the man who sent them here. I curse the place they came from and the place they will go to.

"I curse . . ." And she stopped for breath. Damiano could feel the curses hanging in the air, like thunder on a still day. They stole the mutilated woman's strength, and she flickered before his eyes. As his father had flickered: a dying fire on the tiles of the workroom. The dog howled. Was it Macchiata?

"No more, Signora," he whispered, stroking her black hair back from her face. "Pray instead. For peace. For forgiveness."

The woman cried out in sudden pain and rocked back and forth on the straw bed. "Forgiveness? I have done nothing, not even to throw a pitchfork at the pig who tore me open! And I forgive no one. Least of all God, who let this happen."

Damiano knew something of healing, but he also knew that for death there was no remedy. He tasted in his mouth the salt of his own tears and could think of no way to help.

Except for a little charm, not a witch's charm but a child's, to steal the pain of boils and bruised fingers. He took the dying woman's right hand in his right hand and hugged the black staff with the left side of his body.

"Charm, charm
Cure the harm.

Tell the pain
Be gone again."

This he repeated over and over, with great concentration, till he felt himself no more than a black hollowness, like the length of a flute, through which the invisible passed. He played the charm like a tiny song along the length of his mind's body, opening certain passages to the power and stopping others. With what small part of his mind was not involved in the spell casting he prayed that this little charm might grow into one large enough to shroud the pain of a deadly wound. Meanwhile, the moaning of the dog went on and on.

Her hand softened its grip on his. Damiano opened his eyes.

The woman gazed steadily up at him. Her breathing was easy. "The pain is gone," she said, and sighed. "But you ... have a palsy. Your hand shakes."

He shook his head. Exhaustion nearly toppled him onto the blood-soaked pallet. The woman patted his hand.

"I see, you are a witch," she said. "Like the man who came when the sheep were sickening. He shook like that and then slept an hour in my brother's bed."

"My father ..." began Damiano, but she wasn't listening.

"If I were a witch, I would not be lying here with my bowels torn. If I were a witch, I would have justice."

Struggling, she raised up on one elbow. "What right have you to live?" she asked him, her voice rising shrill again. Her image wavered like sun on water. "Give me justice."

Damiano caught her as she fell back. Her slight weight almost overbalanced him. He found himself shouting "Raphael! Raphael! I can't help her. Help me, Seraph! Help me!"

And white wings filled the squalid hut.

Damiano took the archangel's perfect fair hand
and laid it upon the woman's. Raphael glanced down,
a distant pity in his eyes, then looked again at Damiano.

The woman's gaze had not moved. "Witch, give
me justice, or have my curse too." Her words came
faintly through dying lips.

"Raphael?" The angel merely shook his golden
head. "Raphael, comfort her, give her peace. I cannot!"

"Peace? I forgive no one, least of all God," she
stated. Her light flared and was gone.

Damiano covered his face with one hand. He turned
away from the angel and barged into the light.

"I'm sorry, Damiano. She could not see me."

Raphael also wavered in Damiano's sight, through
a haze of tears. "Couldn't you have spoken to her—
told her something of God's goodness—if not to stop
the pain at least to sweeten her bitter heart? She has
gone to judgment with a weight of curses on her back."

". . . neither see me nor hear me. Dami! I could not
touch her. And if I could have, what would I dare say?"

Puzzled by the angel's words, Damiano blinked
his eyes clear. Vaguely he noticed that Raphael stood
on the dimple in the snow that he had leaped over in
his dash for the hut. The angel left no mark in the
snow. Damiano walked around him.

"Damiano, my dear friend. I am spirit and cannot
die. Likewise I cannot understand death. What comfort
do I have to give a mortal, who is in love with what
seems to me a trial and a bondage? You are earth itself
that has been given the nature of the Father: God in his
most infinite humility.

"I am . . . only a musician. Even less, I am only
music. Your pain is so far beyond me . . ."

I should have closed her eyes, Damiano thought.

"I don't understand what you are saying, Seraph.
I'm too tired. I'll think later on your words."

"But do not forgive me later, Damiano. I know I
have failed you. Give me your hand."

Raphael shone like ice in the sun as he extended

his hand. Dull from too much crying, Damiano squeezed it. Then he turned again to face the crazy-doored hut. "If there is failure here, it is mine, no doubt. I'm going to bury them now."

The bodies in the meadow were frozen stiff as wood. He dragged them over to the body of the young woman, not forgetting the grisly head of Renaud, who threw a pitchfork at a soldier and so destroyed six lives.

Six? He had only four. There were two more to find. He raised his head and listened to the dog's moaning. Was it Macchiata? He called her name.

The howl cut off abruptly. "Master!" came the yip from the slope behind the village. "Here! It's here."

He forced his feet to move.

Macchiata lay curled at the foot of a dead man. The thin howling escaped her as though she had no will in the matter. "It won't get warm. They threw it in the snow and it won't get warm."

"He's dead, Macchiata," said Damiano, wondering at her. "Like all of them, killed by the soldiers."

"This one too?" The dog uncoiled and stepped back, exposing the stiff, blue body of an infant. "It isn't bloody or anything, and it's so little! Can't it be alive?"

Damiano stared and blinked. "No," he answered, feeling nothing through weariness. "No it can't." He picked up the tiny corpse and dragged the man by one rag-wrapped foot.

When all the bodies lay in the fetid darkness, Damiano braced his staff on the hard earth outside. Using his horror and the last of his strength as tools, he shivered the stone walls from top to bottom. The hut fell into rubble, burying the dead beyond the reach of weasels and starving dogs.

Raphael was gone. Damiano had not seen him depart. He had more to say to the archangel, but it would have to wait. He turned back to the road.

Chapter 5

The road remained empty and the countryside bare, but this need not have been due to war or the passage of soldiers. Only fifteen years previously the pestilence had swept up from the south, and within the space of a year the population of these hills had been cut in half, and many towns and villages disappeared entirely.

Partestrada had escaped the Death entirely, some said through the influence of Guillermo Delstrego, while others claimed it was because they had locked the gates of the town and posted archers to slay any who tried to get in.

Damiano, who had been six years old, did not remember much about it except that it had been a hungry time. But he had grown up knowing that the world had been better, once, and that men died easily.

Now he plodded through an empty landscape, and hummed a sad trouvère's tune.

At last he found footprints, on the path that snaked down from the West Road to the mountain meadows. Here, where time or some cataclysm had shattered a rock wall so that it looked like brickwork, was a small lap of ground protected from the wind. The snow lay only inches deep, old and crusted. Were these the prints of the refugees from Partestrada, or were these marks left by the pursuing soldiers? Certain of the imprints were soft edged, either weeks old and sun softened or left by the rag-wrapped feet of the peasantry.

Damiano bent on one knee. Inches from the face of the wall was a soft print that seemed to overlie the

clean print of a leather boot. That was a good sign;
infantrymen did not wrap their feet in rags.

"What does your nose tell you, little dear?" Damiano
asked of the dog, who sat beside him, her thin-furred
belly steaming in the noon sun.

"It tells me that men have been by this way, and
that the black man is near." She spoke without dropping her muzzle to the ground.

"The black man?" For a moment he wondered
whether she meant the Devil himself. Absently, his
fingers traced the metalwork on the staff, which had not
left his hand since his waking that morning. It, too,
spoke of a visitor, but not a supernatural one. His lips
tingled, along with the fine hairs inside his nostrils.
Damiano rose and strode forward along the path.

Where the rock wall ended, a white glare filled the
path. Damiano stopped still, for in the middle of the
light stood a figure black as night and obscured by the
brilliance. Something sparkled: a sword.

"Who hides in the shadows?" spoke a voice Damiano
recognized.

"Denezzi? Paolo Denezzi? It's I, Dami Delstrego.
I've been looking for you for two days. Is Carla..."
Damiano stepped into the sun, expecting Denezzi to
give way for him, but the heavy figure stood like the
rock wall behind.

"Delstrego," echoed Denezzi, in tones of contempt.
"I should have known." The sword slid into its sheath.

Damiano had not expected such a greeting, but
though his feelings were wounded, he was in no mood
for an argument. Damiano stepped around Denezzi.
"For two days I have followed after... Why didn't you
stop and tell me you were evacuating the city?"

Paolo Denezzi was a bull-faced man with a full
beard and as dark as his sister was fair. He snorted,
looking more bull-like than ever. "I had thought it was
fairly plain, to anyone who looked out his window in
the last week."

Reluctantly he met Damiano's look of reproach.

"We didn't leave you behind on purpose, Owl-Eyes. It seemed that you left before us."

Damiano flushed at the hated childhood nickname and at all implied by Denezzi's words. It was on the tip of his tongue to tell Denezzi that Carla, at least, had known where he was, but discretion curbed him.

"Where is . . . everybody, Paolo, and how did you evade the soldiers?" Only a narrow path marred the white: a path such as a single walker might make, breaking the thigh-deep snow. But greasy smoke hung in the sky ahead.

"What soldiers?" Denezzi glared as Macchiata, huffing and panting, squeezed between his legs and trotted off. "Pardo's men? They don't know where we are. I made sure of that."

"He does. They do. They left the day I did, but earlier."

Suspicion and confusion played a dangerous game on Denezzi's face. "What do you know of this, witch?"

"Pardo told me, and he told me he had sent a party of soldiers after the citizens. Not to slay, but to rob. He wants money to finance an attack on Milan." Damiano saw Denezzi's hand move and heard the terrible slick sound of steel. He stood motionless, holding his staff in both hands.

"It was not I who betrayed you. I've come to help."

Silently he added, "Through cold and peril, you obdurate black donkey."

Denezzi drew his sword, but let its tip drop into the snow between them. "What were you doing, sharing words with the general himself, eh? And who betrayed us, if indeed we have been betrayed?"

Damiano paused for only a moment. Marco's deed could not be hidden, not after the gift of the vineyards. "It was old Marco who told. He has been given the Anuzzi property. I spoke to Pardo to discover his intention toward the city."

Denezzi's small eyes were lost in wrinkles of doubt.

Fur of black martin rustled as he shrugged his huge shoulders. "If I could believe you, Delstrego, I would be sure you are a fool. But as it is, no soldiers have bothered us." He turned on his heel. "You had better go back the way you came." As Denezzi walked he sliced with his sword into the snow on either side.

Damiano took one step after the man, when he heard Macchiata lumbering back along the path toward them.

"Master, I have found them," she called. "All the men, Master."

In a fury of irritation, Denezzi raised his sword above the dog, who gaped upward in stunned surprise.

"No, Paolo. You will not touch her!" The lean form sprang forward. Paolo Denezzi felt himself in the middle of a cloud like a promise of thunder, which stole the warmth from his heart and the air from his lungs. His hand slipped on the leather sword-hilt. His anger grew as his strength lessened.

"What will you do, Owl-Eyes? Squinting in the sun, you can hardly see me."

Damiano was indeed almost blind. His brown eyes were sore from glare and from weeping, and at distance they had always failed him. Yet he knew where Denezzi stood and how the sword hung in the air, as though that figure were mapped within his brain, and he saw Macchiata inching backwards down the path, though a wall of snow lay between dog and master.

"Whether I see you or not, Paolo, if you strike Macchiata you're a dead man," he stated. In pure fury, he was willing to commit the violence that Pardo's threats could not force from him.

Slowly the dark man lowered his sword, eyes fixed on Damiano. The dog was long since gone. "This is a silly quarrel," he grunted, turning back along his footsteps. "But may God curse you if you've betrayed us, witch."

Damiano followed without speaking.

It was a shelter thrown together out of brushwood

and brambles and waxed cloth, piled between a cliff
rise and an old, dry rock wall. Smoke runnelled upwards through the twigs and dead leaves, and the feet
of men and horses had trampled the snow of the
pasture.

Macchiata nosed between Damiano's legs, her belly to the ground like a cat's. Her tail thumped hopefully, but she kept her nose on Paolo Denezzi.

Damiano approached the rude shelter, aware he
was the focus of dozens of eyes. Covertly, he kicked the
dog away. "Now would be the time for me to fall flat
on my face, you idiot," he hissed. She whined an
abject apology and leaned harder against his leg.

The men of Partestrada huddled like rooks on a
tower. Over a hundred men shared the ghost of warmth
between the cliff face and the ancient wall. They had
strewn the snow with pine boughs and dead bracken,
which they now fed bit by bit to damp, unwilling fires.
Even in the open air, the smell of hot wool was
overpowering.

Macchiata had been exactly right. They were all
men. Every face that met his grew, or was capable of
growing, a beard. The response to his greeting was a
spiritless mumble, more wary than hostile.

Belloc, the blacksmith, and two pot-bellied burghers edged aside for him, and Damiano sank down
beside the most flourishing of the fires. His staff rested
in the crook of his elbow, but the lute he wrapped in
his mantle and set behind him. Heat beat against his
face, potent as the grace of God.

"You really shouldn't keep the fires going in the
daytime," he remarked, watching the gray smoke sail
out into the air, roiling, bending east. "You are visible
from a distance."

Belloc raised one shaggy eyebrow. "Not all of us
are as well clothed as you are, young Signor." He
stared pointedly at the ermine.

Damiano flushed. He had always liked the blacksmith, who once had sealed his father's caldron so that

the elder Delstrego had never known that Dami had
allowed it to break. With guilty haste he pulled the
instrument from its wrapping.

"I don't need it." Belloc half smiled, looking away
from the offering. "But there's some that might."

Damiano flung the mantle onto the piled branches.
He didn't look to see what hand plucked it up.

"Besides," continued the blacksmith, and he sighed,
"no one is looking for us."

"According to him, there are soldiers on our trail,"
said Denezzi, from behind a pile of embers that seemed
to be his alone. All faces turned to the new arrival amid
a sudden silence.

"Where are the women?" demanded Damiano.
"And the old men and children? Surely there is no
cave, or concealment nearby, that . . ."

"The women are in Aosta," answered Belloc, with
a dour satisfaction. "Along with the children, the lame,
and those men born under a lucky star. Also in Aosta
are the money, the carriages, most of the clothes and
food . . .

"We sent them straight on, while we came to this
forsaken rock covered with frozen sheep dung and
hungry sheep lice."

"Why?" Damiano looked from one uncomfortable
face to another. "Why didn't you follow them to Aosta?"

Denezzi broke the silence. "If we abandon our
homes, Owl-Eyes, we will return to find them occupied." Other men grunted assent, but Belloc spoke
again.

"That was your reasoning, Signor Denezzi. But I
left little I can't do without. My tools and my anvil have
gone up the hills in an oxcart. Still, it is important we
hang together, if we're ever to be a town again." His
sighs were deep, as befitted the size of his ribcage.

Damiano was at first heartened by the news that
the most delicate part of the city, at least, was safe. But
then his mind began to turn over Belloc's words.

"Signor Belloc," he began, sliding his hands

absentmindedly in and out of the flame. "Your news troubles me."

The blacksmith stared fixedly as orange flames licked Damiano's fingers. "I could use hands like that," he muttered. "I wouldn't need the tongs."

Shyly the youth pulled back. "It will burn me too," he admitted, "if I leave them there."

"The Devil takes care of his own."

Damiano swiveled at Denezzi's remark, but the black beard was cut by a toothy smile. "I am not serious, Delstrego. All the world knows you're the first in line at the communion rail."

"Listen to me, Belloc, Denezzi, all of you. I know there are soldiers after you, for your money. The whole town is to be squeezed dry. You especially, Paolo..."

Denezzi scowled. "Why me?"

"Because Marco told Pardo you were very wealthy."

The big man's cry was pitiful. "Aaii! No! Why did he say that! It's a lie!"

Belloc chuckled.

"Because he doesn't like you, Paolo. I can't think why not." The laughter that greeted Damiano's sally raised the effective temperature inside the shelter.

Damiano continued. "If you haven't seen them by now, it means they either passed along the West Road unnoticed..."

"We've kept a sentry at the road," interjected Belloc.

"That's how I found you," added Denezzi.

"Worse and worse." Damiano rubbed his face with palms hot from the flames. "Then Pardo's men must have turned back and headed north, either by mistake or intent, and come upon the carriages of the women."

The shelter erupted in noise and movement. Half the men cursed, while the other half rose to their feet, knocking snow-damped wood into the fires.

"Impossible," roared Denezzi, then added in calmer tones, "When would they have passed the fork in the road?"

"On horseback? Two days, perhaps. I know they stopped at Sous Pont Saint Martin."

Cries, sobs, and gasps followed one another down the huddled line, as Damiano's news was relayed.

"God . . . help us. They may have caught them," whispered Belloc, and Denezzi stared dumbly into the fire. "Perhaps they will only take the money."

"Will they resist?"

The blacksmith did not understand.

"Signor Belloc, this very morning I buried those who dwelt at Sous Pont Saint Martin. A peasant threw a pitchfork at a soldier, you see . . ."

Muscles tautened in the blacksmith's massive jaws. "Jesu! Boy, do you come to kill our hope?"

"I've come to help, if I can," said Damiano.

Denezzi stood, and all eyes looked to him. Damiano felt a hot pang of envy toward this man, whose strength and brute temper had won him more respect among his fellows than had Damiano's selfless dedication. "We'll have to take the chance he's right. I will lead a party of horsemen back to the North Road.

"But tomorrow. There's little light left today." He glanced down at Damiano. "For men's eyes, anyway."

"In the meantime, if you want to help us, then find us food. Else we will have to draw lots to see whose horse is butchered."

Damiano glanced sharply at him. "What do you expect of me: loaves and fishes? I have a jug of tonic in my bag; it's the reason I missed the evacuation, you know. I was minding the pot."

Despite the worry in his face, Belloc grinned. "Ah, yes, that pot."

"What did you expect to eat," continued Damiano. "Coming out here with little more than the clothes on your backs."

Denezzi growled, throwing tinder into the flames. "We expected to go home!—when Pardo had passed through: perhaps a week's time. And I expected the

shepherds to drive the flocks home as soon as they
heard of the advancing army.

"But they never showed, though I held up the
march a day and a half to wait. Probably they are long
since in Turin, and have sold the sheep as their own."

"Give them the benefit of the doubt," grunted
Belloc. "They may have been overrun, and all our
mutton sitting in the bellies of the southerners." Denezzi
was not comforted.

"You gave the order to march?" mused Damiano,
idly fingering the slack strings of his lute. "Yourself,
not the mayor, or the council?"

Denezzi gestured as though to brush away flies.
"I'm on the city council. My opinions are heard. Besides, most of the councilmen are not of military age;
the mayor himself went to Aosta with the women."

Damiano peered through the lacework of the ivory
rose that ornamented the lute's soundhole. Was there
dampness within? "I have neither meat nor bread,
Paolo. Nor can witchcraft create them. You'll have to
kill a horse, I'm afraid."

"That will be a sore burden on some poor fellow,"
replied Denezzi. "And unnecessary. I think you can
help us, Damiano."

"How?"

"You can call us meat from out of the hills."

The young witch's head snapped up in startlement,
but Denezzi continued, "I have seen you do it, when
we were both boys, calling rabbits from the fields and
dogs from their masters' kennels. And my horse: I
remember how he threw me and ran to you, pushing
his black nose into your hand. Oh, yes, I won't forget
that."

"I didn't ask him to throw you, Paolo. That was his
own idea." Damiano had his own memories of the
episode, foremost of which was the bloody lip Denezzi
had given him in consequence of the fall. This had
occurred when Damiano had been nine and Denezzi
thirteen.

The young witch furrowed his brow, trying to explain a thing that was not easily put in words. "You see, Paolo, I can... tempt the beasts to come to me, for bread or a pat on the nose. But I can't force them. And if I call them saying, 'Come to me and be slaughtered,' well I think I'll be calling a long time."

"Just say come," suggested Denezzi. "I know how little you like the sight of blood, Owl-Eyes, so you just pat the goat or whatever on the head, and we'll do the rest."

Damiano dropped his head again. "That's betrayal." He heard a man snicker on the other side of the fire.

The witch ground his teeth together. "It's very hard to lie, Paolo, without using words."

Denezzi rustled beneath his black pelts. "It's very hard to go hungry. It's either a wild beast or a horse, Owl-Eyes. You can at least try."

He could have pleaded weariness as an excuse; in truth he was swimming with fatigue. But he felt eyes on him, and he had offered to help. What was more, Damiano knew most every horse in Partestrada by its simple, unspoken name. He rose from the fire.

He passed through a gap in the brush pile, and a chill hit him. "I'll need my mantle back," he mumbled sullenly. There was no response until he turned his black eyes into the crowd. Then the fur-lined wrap was handed out.

"If I bring in a goat," he said to Denezzi, "you must give me time to get out of it." The big man turned his face away.

Damiano trudged through crackling slush to the middle of the pasture. Shadows were growing, striping the field with blue. Tucking his mantle under him, he sat down on a hummocky stone. The shoe of his staff was braced between his boots; he leaned his face against the staff's lowest silver band.

For half a minute his mind floated free. Then he spoke a silent "Come," and unbidden to his mind sprang the image of a sword. He heard it snick free of the scabbard. By willpower he burst the image, only to see it reform in the shape of a pitchfork, tines protruding through the snow.

He was very tired. He tried again, and his call carried the odor of an abattoir, of a hut filled with dying. Mother of God! He didn't want to do this. He wanted to sleep, here in the sun, if no better place offered.

In the emptiness of his mind he saw how lovely it would be to rest. He remembered the honey-colored rock where he had eaten and talked with Raphael—only yesterday. He felt the heat of the hearth, where a chair was burning. How wasteful, but how warm.

His mind was flooded with the memory of this very pasture in the green of summer, when his father would treat the sheep with tar poultices and incantation. Grass up to his half-grown knees, except where the flocks had cropped it. It had been cool then, in the mountains, but pleasant. Sheep's milk. Napping at midday, surrounded by curious, odorous, half-grown lambs.

All the while Damiano dreamed, his call continued, rising into the air, growing, following the wind like smoke.

He remembered waking up with nothing to do all day, a condition he had experienced as recently as a week ago. He remembered the warm flood of sound Raphael pulled out of the lute. He remembered Carla, sewing as he read to her from the gilt-edged volume of Aquinas. (Her little brass needle caught the sun. She made only the gentlest fun of Damiano's squint as he read the fine script.) He remembered how quickly and quietly the days had passed before this war.

A shadow fell across the sunlight, and his drowsy eyes opened. A face stared down at him: Sfengia, the cheesemaker. The man's eyes were wet with longing. He was not alone, for Damiano sat at the center of a circle of silent figures that was even now increasing.

They came for the sunshine, for the summer, for the memories of August and the dusty roads that caked a boy's bare feet and legs. They came at Damiano's call.

He felt their minds around him, open to his. There was Sfengia, afraid for his three daughters, and Belloc, heavy and mild. Behind them all, drawn but unwilling, Damiano sensed the brittle presence of Denezzi.

The witch smiled wistfully. He had never compelled such rapt attention. It was very pleasant to sway men's minds. Let Paolo equal this.

Suddenly Damiano knew how to fulfill his task. It was all very easy. He imagined himself an animal, a hoofed beast: a sheep or a cow or maybe a goat. He allowed his dreams to shift in consonance with his animal being, though the call continued.

Green grass. That was good. Tall dry grass, with grain spilling out of the head. Free water running. Sun.

No halter. No wire twitch against the tender lip. Damiano touched the mind he had been seeking, the warm, wordless brute mind. It was tame to him and unafraid. It answered from very near. Unsuspicious, it opened to him and let him in. His meadow visions it made its own, improving them in the process. Salt. A warm back to rest one's head upon. Sage in the wind.

The old stable, out of the wind, and the smell of mash in the pail.

Once more the sun stroked Damiano's face; this pastoral rhapsody was losing him his human audience. But he scarcely noticed, for he was sharing the eyes of the cow that passed down into the dell along the lee of a cliff face, seeking summer just ahead. It was no wild beast, but lonely, lost. Its udder was shrunken, and its dappled sides gaunt. It stopped and looked around. Damiano saw the meadow and himself in the middle of it, motionless on the rock like a dark tree stump.

Summer was calling. His mind shouted it. Grass, crackling hay. The cow trotted forward.

She smelled man and stopped—curious, innocently wary.

When the first watcher beheld the spotted cow ambling down the hill toward them, he hissed a warning. All the townsmen froze. Those who had swords put their hands to the hilt. Belloc hefted his blunt hammer.

The cow stopped, her conviction failing as Damiano's did. Her ears revolved, and she peered over her shoulder at strange movement. One dainty foot was raised.

"Take her," shouted someone, and a half-dozen swords caught the light. Belloc raised his hammer.

Damiano saw the blow descending. "No!" he cried, or tried to. "No! Let me..."

The cow fell to its knees, and Paolo Denezzi opened its brown and white spotted throat. It died in the snow without a sound and was butchered where it lay, steaming in the air like a kettle of soup.

Carlo Belloc plunged his bloody hands into the snow and turned away from the carcass. He was most surprised to see young Damiano face down in the snow; a splash of gold and scarlet. Denezzi was looking down at him.

The blacksmith hurried over. "What did you do to him?" he snapped at Denezzi.

"Do to him?" Denezzi shook his head. "I did nothing. I'd pick him up, but that bitch of his..."

Macchiata's bent legs straddled her limp master. Her mouth was a rictus of hate, dripping slaver. Belloc regarded her earnestly, from under beetling brows.

"You can talk, can't you dog? Tell us what's wrong with your master?"

She licked her lips, and her fury was extinguished. "I don't know. He fell down when you hit the cow." Her nose burrowed through the hair at the back of Damiano's neck, to assure herself he was still alive. "He's very sensitive," she added.

Denezzi bit off his laugh at Belloc's warning glower.

"Allow us to pick him up and carry him to the fire, puppy," said Belloc. "If he has taken hurt, we will help him. We're his friends."

The blacksmith lifted Damiano easily and set him over one huge shoulder. The staff lay where it had fallen until Macchiata, seeing her master laid gently before the fire, returned. Taking the brass foot in her mouth, she dragged the stick to Damiano's side.

The men she passed got out of her way.

Time was a trickle of chilling blood. Red went brown. Brown went black. Memory fell apart. Sense fell apart. He saw nothing, heard nothing, felt nothing, and knew nothing except that he saw nothing, heard nothing, and felt nothing.

Hope fell apart.

Damiano's eyes were open, staring blindly at the fire. When Belloc spoke to him, he made no answer. He neither stirred nor spake the night through, nor did the smell of roasting beef rouse him. Macchiata lay by him, equally quiet. She, however, ate her fill.

At dawn the light of the rising sun stole his gaze from the fire. He propped himself on his elbows, and Macchiata uttered a whinny of glad relief. She smothered with kisses his dull and unprotesting face.

"Eh, boy? Are you with us again?" murmured Belloc, who had watched half through the night and finally pitched his blankets next to the tranced form.

Damiano slowly turned his face to Belloc. "How long?" he whispered.

"Have you lain there mazed? All yesterday evening and night. It's dawn already, Dami Delstrego. Where have you been?"

The answer was halting. "I have lain trapped in the body of a dead beast. Dead. Knowing myself dead.

"Was it only one night? I thought it was decades. I thought my time had passed. I thought there would be no escape until the last day, and judgment." His eyes were still very wide, brown and soft like a cow's, and his face expressed nothing.

The blacksmith sighed. "If you were trapped within

the cow yesterday, then you spent the night in a
hundred stomachs. I think you're still not well, Damiano,"
said Belloc. "Stay here for today, while a party rides to
Aosta. There's plenty of firewood left, and I saved you
some meat."

Damiano had started to rise, but at Belloc's last
words his stomach rebelled. He gagged but was empty
as a dry bucket. "No," he panted. "I'm riding with
you. You will need me, should you find what you are
looking for. And I—I am beginning to see what must be
done. I'm riding with you."

Chapter 6

The procession wound down and east, past the abandoned village, where the ruins of one hut were already
softened with a cloak of blown snow, back over the
river Lys, and toward the crossing of the roads. They
were a somber line of men, and they pushed their
horses, but they were not soldiers.

Damiano rode one of Paolo Denezzi's geldings,
with a leather strap for a bridle and no saddle at all. It
was a black horse; all of Denezzi's four horses were
black. The witch reflected on what Denezzi had said
the previous afternoon—how hard it would be on some
poor man to lose his mount to the knife. And here was
the rich man with one to ride, two for pack, and an
extra. Damiano smiled grimly.

The horse was nervous bearing him. Well it might
be, for Damiano's mind was filled with cold and weeping blood. The call that he had begun the day before
could not be utterly silenced.

Bored with the slow pace, he turned his horse's
head once more to the straggling tail of the company,

where men rode on cart horses and hinnies. There was
even one fellow, Aloisio by name, who sat astraddle an
ass, his bootless feet dragging in the dust. He was a
tanner by trade and carried neither sword nor spear.
But he had a long hide-splitter, razor sharp, and a
young wife in the train to Aosta.

"Aloisio, can't it move any faster?" asked Damiano,
looming over the man from his seat on Denezzi's lean
horse. He had intended his words to sound warmer.

The tanner raised his head, wary but unafraid.
"No, Signor Delstrego, it cannot. Not unless I get
behind and push."

Damiano nodded in resignation and tried to smile.
Dryly his lips slid back from his teeth. He fell in place
beside Aloisio, at the tail of the line, where he could
make sure no one became lost.

The tall peaks, crystalline now in the easterly sun,
stood in the distance at the right of the road. Damiano
squinted and wondered what he had seen in them,
only the day before. They were unscalable stone, as
they had always been, and they harbored neither food
nor beauty.

Thinking about the peaks and his previous intoxi-
cation led him to think about Macchiata. He felt again
her wet, impertinent nose against the palm of his hand
and heard again her fluttering worry, like that of a hen
as she prodded him from his knees in the slush. In the
universe of ash in which he found himself, the little
dog could spark a tiny flame of gladness.

She scrambled at the proud horse's feet, pottering
into every mark and blister of the snow at the side of
the road, panting very hard. A few days like this and
she would not be so ridiculously fat.

Damiano placed his hand on the horse's knotty
head and without words suggested that it trot back to
the head of the line, to Denezzi's side. The animal
started and plunged at the contact, almost costing
Damiano his seat.

Very soon the crossroads came into view. Damiano

led his mount to the snowbank where his own trail from the guardhouse broke onto the road. He gave the reins into the hands of his nearest neighbor and leaped down. His lean legs disappeared into the trail, stepping high and storklike. The procession slowed to a disorderly stop.

He emerged from the shelter bearing three soft bags. "Clothing," he said. "Not very good. Not clean. But for any man who needs it. And for any man who needs a hair pin." He held up the jeweled ornament. Two dozen eyes stared uncomprehending, before he slipped the pin back into his belt pouch. As he climbed onto the horse's back Damiano rustled like dry leaves or paper, and a flat weight hung forward inside his woolen tunic.

The North Road was a steady climb, slick as wellstone. Some of the heavy steeds at the rear of the line, especially those without shoes, had trouble. Damiano noticed with dull amusement that Aloisio's ass was doing very well under the new conditions and was climbing toward the front of the company.

Damiano turned to Belloc, who had ridden silently on his gray gelding since breaking camp. "I learned to play the lute from an angel," he said. "An archangel, to be exact. No one can see him but me—and Macchiata." Belloc turned on him a slow, suspicious eye.

"Doesn't that sound silly, Signor Belloc? Until yesterday, it seemed quite natural to me. My lessons were, perhaps, the most important things in the world. As important as the quest of alchemy. Now . . ."

He turned his head in a circle, peering around with eyes that could not fathom distance or endure the sun. Belloc stared at him with a sort of stolid, masculine pity. "Now it seems very irrelevant. Both the angel and the lute. And alchemy as well.

"It was spending the night in the dead body of a cow. That puts a different perspective on things. It makes one see life as it really is, in all its misery. Or possibly it only makes one sick."

"Sickness plays tricks on the mind," rumbled Belloc in reply, not sure whether by sickness Damiano meant seeing angels or not caring to see them. "I told you you should have stayed back at the pasture."

"Eh? Why? We're not going back there, you know. If we find no one on the road all the way to Aosta, there'll be nothing to do but stay in the city. Most of us, anyway. If we catch up with Pardo's soldiers, then either they will kill us, or we will kill them, or we will all kill each other. If it is we who survive, then we'd better keep going—for Pardo's men have many friends, and Partestrada has none. Unless the Green Count comes to avenge us. In the spring, of course."

Damiano's eyes shone dry like polished stone. His skin was white. Belloc shook his head. "When did you eat last, boy?"

Damiano shrugged without interest.

Paolo Denezzi, who was riding a few feet in front of the two, as though he were a commander and the others his lieutenants, peered back over his shoulder. After a weighty silence, he spoke. "We will go to Aosta," he conceded. "Those with friends or family there may stay. Or those with money to buy. The rest I will lead to Donnaz, where we will prepare our own vengeance."

Damiano felt a challenge rise up in him. When had these plans been adopted? When he had shown up at the camp no such idea had existed in the men's minds, and he'd heard no talk since. . . .

But then for many hours he had not been listening. And could he provide any better destination? Denezzi at least had the good of the city in mind.

Besides, Damiano did not believe events would pass so smoothly. A troop of hardened cavalry did not disappear into the hills forever.

Belloc cleared his throat. "You have property in the town of Donnaz, Signor Denezzi?"

Denezzi nodded, distrustful. "What of it?"

"I was wondering where you would put our home-less neighbors."

"They will pay me back," stated Denezzi. His thin mouth was dour, and his moustache bristled.

Suddenly Damiano could stand it no more: the interminable, straggling march, the presence of Denezzi, even Belloc's taciturn kindness. He called Macchiata, ordering her to stay by the blacksmith until he returned, then he kicked his mount forward.

"Where are you going, Delstrego?" demanded Denezzi, rising in his saddle.

"Ahead," answered the witch.

The dark man opened his mouth as though to forbid him. He remained that way for a moment, uncharacteristically indecisive. Finally he said, "If you break my horse's leg, boy, I will break your head."

Damiano smiled thinly. "You're not even four years older than I am, Paolo. And as for breaking my head..." He swiveled front again, and the black horse sprang forward as though whipped.

Alone was much better. His head was clear, with that peculiar ringing lightness that comes with fasting. The horse climbed energetically, in a dumb effort to leave its rider behind. Damiano felt some pity for the beast, but not much. Pity was deserved all around and could be spread much too thin.

His tall staff passed under his belt and lay against the horse's flank like a sword. Damiano secured it with his right hand, so it would not slap with every iron-shod step.

In a short time he left the clatter and creak of the citizens behind. Up here the road wound the shoulders of a peak like epaulets and crossed two great chasms, one on a bridge of rough wood, and the other on a splendid stone arch twelve hundred years old.

The North Road was deceptive, folding back upon itself, taking whatever path or purchase it could, so that Damiano once found himself staring across a sheer

drop no wider than a snowball's throw, at a length of
snowy road he was not to touch for half-an-hour's
climb.

Sound was deceptive too, for now he heard the
speech of men again, together with the blow and
whinny of horses. He looked below, but could see no
sign of the ascending company. He turned a corner and
looked ahead.

It was the troops of General Pardo, displayed against
the smeared white cliffs like chessmen. They rode in
order, two abreast. There were fifty of them, and behind them lumbered five ungainly wagons. Damiano
stared wide-eyed at the wagons.

Four were heavy laden, covered in waxed linen,
pulled by four oxen apiece. The last wagon was open,
and packed with...women. Damiano blinked and
clutched at his staff. He was sure they were women,
wrapped in shawls and blankets, mostly black. But
these were not all the women of Partestrada, by no
means. There could not be more than twenty in that
sad, paintless farm cart. What was this? Was Carla
among these? He did not know whether to hope she
was or to pray she was not.

Damiano heard a stentorian cry. As he watched, so
he was being watched.

Though he sat in hailing distance of Pardo's cavalry, a large loop of road lay between them. A single
soldier broke from the head of the line and drove his
mount back against the direction of their march, between the third wide wagon and the empty edge of the
road. The beast was frightened; its legs splayed stiffly
against the slick road, and it backed against the wood
of the wagon, its brown eyes rolling at the sheer drop.

The horseman peered over at a figure gorgeously
dressed in scarlet and gold, its hair in wild black curls
that obscured half its face. It rode a fine horse as a herd
boy will ride a cow: bareback, sitting the withers, legs
bent and feet gripping the beast's ribs. Unaccountably,
the soldier's neck prickled.

Damiano perceived less about the soldier because he could not see as well.

"You!" shouted the soldier. "You are to come here!"

Damiano barked a laugh. "Why?" he replied in more normal tones. "Very soon you will all be over here."

The horseman scowled. "What? I don't hear you. Don't you hear me, man? Come here!"

Damiano didn't want to shout. He didn't want to talk to the fellow at all. He turned his horse's head and started back down the road, not daring to canter him on the bend.

Another cry split the air, sharp and shrill: a woman's cry. Damiano twisted from the waist to peer behind him, and at that moment something hit him on the breastbone, with a blow no harder than that of a hard snowball, well thrown.

His shock sent the black gelding skidding into a gallop that quickly put a wall of granite between Damiano and Pardo's men. Damiano let the horse run while he blinked down at the shaft of the arrow protruding from his clothing. Then with one hand he reined in the horse, while the other very calmly worried the arrowhead from the wood and leather cover of the works of Petrarch. Further examination found that the arrow had penetrated quite half of the vellum pages and left a clean incision through an entire packet of letters written in an unknown, Germanic tongue.

"If I live," he murmured to the wind on his face, "this will be something to talk about."

When Paolo Denezzi spied his black horse hurtling down the North Road toward him, bearing its light burden clinging about its neck, he cursed foully. But before he could gather his breath to release his roar of anger, Damiano had slid from the horse's back.

"Off your mounts," he cried to the company. "Every man on his own two feet and forward with me."

"No such thing!" bellowed Denezzi. Men paused,

one foot in the stirrup, as authority flew confused. Denezzi, however, sprang down to confront the witch.

"What is this, Owl-Eyes?" Without thinking he grabbed for the chain of Damiano's mantle. The silver head of the staff flashed across his knuckles, and he drew back a bleeding hand. "Don't touch that," snapped Damiano. "If they'll obey you, then help me save their lives. Get the horses away from them."

Denezzi's face was wine purple. He sucked his damaged fingers. "Why? What's coming—the soldiers you prophesied?"

"Yes, and either they will kill us all or terror will. Off your horses to save your lives," he repeated, shouting at the top of his lungs.

"Asses too?" drawled the tanner Aloisio, but as he spoke he lifted his weight on his toes and allowed his little beast to walk out from under him. Ten men laughed, but fifty dismounted. Belloc got down from his gray.

"They are not twenty minutes behind me," announced Damiano. "They can't move fast, because they are leading wagons—ox wagons, Belloc, and one of them was once yours."

"Catarina?" gasped the blacksmith, but Damiano raised his hand. "There are a few citizens with them, but I couldn't pick them out at the distance.

"Listen, my friends. I am going up there..." and he pointed along the sloppy road whence he'd come. "To conceal myself, if I can. When the soldiers ride by, I will...surprise them. Be ready to take back our wagons. And be ready to run." He turned and in half a minute had vanished from sight.

"Do we do as he says?" asked Aloisio, standing behind Denezzi with the halter of his ass in his hand. "I'm afraid young Signor Delstrego is a little bit...disturbed."

"I will, anyway," responded Belloc. "I can't speak for any other man."

Denezzi suffered no such limitation. "We will. If

these ghostly soldiers of his really exist...well, he seems to have a plan. If not, I swear I will bury that foppish simpleton by the side of the road." He strode forward, dropping the reins of his horse, trusting someone would mind the beast. Aloisio wordlessly did so.

Damiano huddled behind a hummock made from the roots of a tree and the few hundred years' worth of soil it had collected. He waited to hear the jingle of the cavalry harness. Behind him the ground dropped abruptly away, farther than he could focus on.

He felt Macchiata beside him, worming her way into the scant cover. "Macchiata, no!" he hissed. "Get out of here. Don't be near me!"

"Don't be near you?" she repeated in accents tragic. "Don't be *near* you, Master? How can you say that? I have already been parted from you for hours today, and we were never to be parted while we both live; you said so..."

Damiano was unmoved. He crouched close to the earth, his eyes fixed on the upper road. "Yes, little dear, and if you don't get out of here and down the road very fast, one of us will not live much longer. GO!"

Macchiata went.

The men of Partestrada were assembled a few hundred feet to Damiano's left, in a spot visible from behind the trunk of the pine, but concealed from the upper slope of the road. They milled about, swords and cleavers dragging. They did not resemble soldiers, but at least their horses were nowhere in sight.

Damiano saw the head of the column, with his swart uniform and dull brass, at the same time he heard the ring of shod hooves on ice. The captain was the same who had spied Damiano and ordered him to stop. Damiano peered behind him, to see which of the men carried bows.

The captain passed before Damiano's earthy concealment. He led fifty men: twenty swordsmen, twenty spear, five archers, and five more to mind the booty.

They passed so near Damiano he might have swung his staff and brained one.

Instead he stood up, filled with grave excitement and a thrill of dread. The nearest soldier leaped back in superstitious fear, to see Damiano appear as though he'd floated up the sheer cliff.

Damiano took his staff in both hands. Its ebony length filled his mind, and he allowed his dark, invisible power to flow into the wood. With perverse satisfaction he let free the deadly refrain that had stifled in him since the cow went down.

"Come!" The terrible call rang against rock, out of hearing, impossible to ignore. "Come! Come and be slaughtered!" it shrieked.

Every horse pitched in blind hysteria, and every man clapped his hands to his ears.

The screams of the beasts were one with his, as Damiano made them believe in death. Men, who already believed, fell from their saddles and lay in the mire.

In front of the women's wagon the oxen were thrashing, kicking the air uselessly. One of the bullocks gored his yoke-mate's face, and the bellows of the wounded animal punctuated the cacophony. The women themselves were screaming. Damiano opened his eyes in time to see a horse leap blindly over the edge.

It was all wreckage. No rider controlled his horse; few sat mounted. As he watched, the oxen of the front goods wagon broke the wooden brake lever and plunged from behind the company, careening forward, trampling men and horses alike. Tall, brightly painted wheels left tracks shining red.

The men of Partestrada stood plastered to the inner cliff wall; Damiano could scarcely see them. The ox wagon swung wide at the bend. The outside wheel spun in emptiness, then the wagon tipped. Frenzied bellows rose into shrieks that grew thin and keen, as though the beasts were singing on their way to the ground.

Damiano contemplated the destruction. Men crawled on hands and knees, like horses, their swords abandoned. A chestnut gelding lay flat on the ground before him, crying like a man. A few soldiers had risen and stood propped against the face of rock. One held a bow. With clumsy, clattering movements the archer raised it, pointing it at Damiano.

Without haste, indeed without enthusiasm, Damiano propped his staff between the archer and himself. It drew the arrow, as Damiano had meant it should. The limber feathered shaft broke in pieces.

But the archer had not acted alone. A man staggered forward, leaning, his head lowered, as though he breasted the wind. It was the troops' captain once more. His belt still carried a sword, and as he approached the heart of his terror he unsheathed it and stood upright.

"So," thought Damiano, looking into the face of the man before him, seeing the gray metal unveiled.

He knew nothing of fighting, with swords or without. Even had he the strength to run, there was nowhere to go except to follow the oxen. And as it was his strength was used up, along with all his caring.

"So," said Damiano to himself, and he waited for what would happen.

What happened was that the captain swung his sword back over one shoulder, aiming for a decapitating blow, and then Belloc's great hammer came down on the man's head. Beneath the helmet of leather and iron, the captain's skull splintered. Damiano looked away, to encounter Belloc's square head and ashen face. The blacksmith's lips were gray with horror, but he was not looking at the bloody ruin he had created. He was staring at Damiano. Then Damiano watched the death of Pardo's captain with his strange sight. Light flickered green and golden over the still form, like rags soaked in oil and burnt.

Then the fire departed and the man was gone.

Gone. Escaped. Not here in this ruined shape at all. Damiano blinked at this; it was death and yet not what he had thought he knew. It was cold and terrifying, like a night of no stars, but it was not the mindful death he had known, despair in rotting flesh. It was not what set him screaming. Damiano's hideous call was cut off sharp.

Belloc took a deep, shuddering breath. "Boy," he gasped, "are you Satan himself? Or how is it you have not burst, doing this?"

Damiano heard the voice, but not the words. His ears were ringing with silence. His gaze slid wearily from Belloc's face to his black, brain-spattered hammer.

"Ah! The hammer. Yes, Belloc. That was very fitting." He smiled at Belloc, or he tried to.

The citizens of Partestrada scrambled heavily up the road, their rude weapons in their red-fingered hands. They fell upon the dazed soldiers like men threshing wheat. Damiano walked toward the two remaining ox wagons, where one beast hung dead in the traces. He did not look back at the carnage.

The women were still in the middle wagon: they had been tied there. Damiano looked at faces he knew.

Old Signora Anuzzi was there, stuffed in a corner like a black sack. And Lidie Polsetti, and Vera Polsetti, and little Françoise. And Signora Mellio, the widow who looked after Father Antonio. And Bernice Roberto. They were all crying at once, faces striped with tears and noses slimy. Damiano could hardly blame them; he had worked this misery himself, and though he was not tied, he felt much the same as they. Still, he could get no sense of them.

He hauled himself up and into the wagon, groaning with effort. As he lay on the wooden boards, his eyes closed, he heard the only voice that could have pleased him.

"Dami! Damiano, are you wounded? Were you hit by the arrow up above? Dami, speak to me?" He looked up into Carla Denezzi's frozen, wind-chapped and fear-whitened face.

"O Bella! Bellissima!," he whispered, and he smiled at her as though the two were alone.

Wonderingly, the blond girl extended her bound wrists. She touched his breast awkwardly, where the arrow had left its neat cut: a slice no longer than the last joint of a finger. He took her hand in his, grimacing at the ropes. An instant later, every binding in the wagon took life, and like snakes, wriggled free. The wagon tongue dropped to the road and a dozen women shrieked at sudden freedom and missing laces.

"Damiano!" hissed Carla, who either wore no lacings or did not care about them. "I prayed I would see you again, but I had little hope. How did you get through? I think the Devil himself has flown over us. Could you feel him?"

"Eh?" Damiano turned his face away. Though a bare two minutes ago he had stood between life and death, indifferent, Carla's presence had revealed his own face to him again. The Devil himself? He was ashamed, not knowing quite why.

Meanwhile, murder was running like a flame all over the snowy mountain road. Damiano didn't want to look upon that, either, so he regarded the rough wooden boards.

"The children," he stuttered. "All the rest of the women and the old men. What happened to them? Father Antonio . . . Did they . . ."

"Everyone of them is in Aosta," spat Signora Aluzzi, who had always felt herself to be a class above any mere artisans like the Delstregos. "They went under a guard of soldiers, all very proper. As though the poor scum were royalty! Only those of us who are worth something have been tied up like pigs to market!"

"The soldiers . . . offered no violence?" Damiano blinked stupidly from one face to another.

Signora Aluzzi snorted. "We haven't been raped, if that's what you mean, you young gutter rat!"

He scratched his head in simple puzzlement. "But . . . ." He glanced again at Carla Denezzi. "They're all being killed," he said, and then fell silent as though awaiting confirmation of his words. She regarded him soberly and silently, her hand resting lightly upon his. "The soldiers are all being killed, for revenge of their crimes against you. And it is I who have made that possible," he concluded.

"God be praised!" grunted the old signora of the vineyards.

Carla felt Damiano start. She caught his stricken glance and held it. It was only her perfect understanding at this moment that kept Damiano from being swept away, blown into tears or madness.

The wagon tilted. Paolo Denezzi was climbing aboard. "It is done," he announced, and he saw Damiano and Carla.

"You don't touch my sister!" he roared, throwing half the women back into quaking hysteria. "She is a pure dove! And you . . . you, Delstrego, are a monster!"

"Paolo!" shouted Carla, in anger and indignation. But Damiano very slowly drew his hand back. He said nothing and slunk out of the wagon. He picked his way amid the graceless figures on the road, which lay so still they might never have known life at all.

Chapter 7

Aosta was a larger and more prosperous town than Partestrada, since it lay at the most pleasant dip in the only road entering the Piedmont from the north. Damiano had often thought this an unfair advantage for a city that did not have much else to recommend it. It shared with Partestrada a rushing river, which was named in the mountains the Evançon, though at the feet of the hills it changed its name along with its tempestuous personality and was called the Dora Baltea.

Much of the gold Damiano had brought out of the Delstrego tower had gone to buy shelter for the poorer refugees, and even so these would have to find work quickly or move on. Had the burghers of Aosta known that this ill-timed influx of business had left fifty soldiers and eight horses buried in the snow of the passes, their welcome would have been short indeed. The Valle d'Aosta, feeling some protection from its mountains but not much, had no desire to involve itself in battles that ought to have been fought by Amadeus himself.

As it was, there was no need for the Aostans to know. General Pardo himself would be slow in finding out, for not a man would return to him.

Still, find out he would. Now that the matter of the citizens had been cleared up (or at least Damiano felt no further responsibility for them), he had time to reflect.

It was strange to realize that he had no more virtue than Pardo, no more than the soldiers who put a tiny hamlet to the sword because one peasant showed fight. Damiano had killed fifty—he did not allow the knives and hammers of Partestrada credit for the blood—in revenge for that six. Or perhaps it was a revenge for the soldiers' crimes against the women of Partestrada— a meaningless revenge for crimes that had never been committed.

Whatever—Damiano had not felt wicked in action. He doubted General Pardo did, either. "Man is born in sin, and his nature is evil." Father Antonio had announced that from the pulpit, though it was not a subject upon which the good priest had dwelt in his leisure time. Never till now had Damiano thought about it.

Were the peasant woman's curses now satisfied? Would she rest peacefully, now that her murderers were all dead?

And while he was asking questions, where was Father Antonio, anyway? Damiano needed direction (the sort of direction Raphael would never consent to give). And he needed it immediately.

The dank common room of the inn where Damiano sat, though warm and crowded with his companions, was sullen and quiet. Damiano rose from the crude table of wooden slats, leaving behind him crumbs of bread, the wax rind of a cheese, and an untouched length of sausage. A whine beneath the table prompted him to throw the meat to Macchiata.

Carla was unreachable, in the house of friends and guarded by her villainous brother, but Damiano could at least go looking for his friend the priest.

The basilica of San Sebastiano at Aosta was really just a small round church. Damiano stood at the door, certain he would find the priest nearby, but feeling a stiff, unreasoning reluctance to enter. As he stood undecided, Carla Denezzi stepped out.

"Damiano!" she gasped, and caught him by the hand. "Step in here, quick." He let himself be dragged into shadows smelling of wood smoke and incense.

Left of the door was a baptismal, separated from the vestibule by a lacework of wood. As though this offered concealment, she sat him down.

She was wearing a cream-colored shawl. Her face was clean and rosy, and the sight of it brought the past once more to life for him: warm, filtered sun threading through the pales of the loggia, and bright threads lying on a basket, neatly sorted, and ideas neatly sorted, and laughter. Damiano wanted to tell her how glad he was to see her, and how he had missed her, and sought her, and thought of her as he lay curled in a black cave in the hills under snow, but the very cleanness and rosiness of her face stopped him. It made Damiano shy.

"I shouldn't have my staff here," he murmured. "It isn't right."

She had reached out her small hand, meaning to lay the stick aside, when she remembered and drew back. "Ah! I forgot one mustn't touch it."

Smiling with an odd sadness, Damiano took her hand and touched it to the ebony wood. "Signorina," he whispered, "nothing of mine will ever hurt you. I promise that. You could put your hand on my beating heart, and it would do you no harm."

She chuckled at this fervid gallantry, wondering how such a deed could hurt anyone but Damiano himself, but with a reawakened memory her hand went to the breast of his tunic—to the hole. "Your beating heart," she echoed. "How is it—by what miracle, Damiano . . ."

"The miracle of a book." He laughed in return and slipped out the volume to show her. "The miracle of Petrarch's poetry."

With a small cry of wonder, Carla took the book. She gave his hand a tiny squeeze. "Oh, Damiano, I thank God for that. When I saw the man raise his bow I screamed aloud, for I knew by your colors it was you across the gap. I prayed that he had not hit you, but I feared every moment we would pass your body in the snow."

"It must be that I owe my life to your prayers," he said sincerely. There was a moment's happy silence.

Then Carla sighed. "Your soul and mine comprehend one another, dear Damiano. I wish you were my brother instead of Paolo."

This, although it denoted affection, was not the sentiment Damiano wished to hear from Carla. He caught his tongue for a moment, rehearsing words. Of course he would tell her how he loved her, but how and to what end?

Should he say, "Carla, beloved, I am going to Provence where my music in your honor will make you famous. Wait for me"? Or was it to be, "Carla, best beloved, I am going to Nuremberg, where my alchemies in your honor will bring you glory. Wait for me"? It was certain he could not say, "Carla, little dear, friend of my childhood, come with me to Provence or Germany and starve."

But it was Carla who spoke. "My brother is not pleased with me, old friend. You alone in the world, Damiano, have the soul to understand why I have applied to the convent La Dolerosa at Bard."

Damiano gazed blankly at the pink marble christening bowl, lily-shaped and smoother than flower petals in the faded light. "Why you what? Say again."

Carla leaned forward. Her hands folded together on her lap. "I have applied—and been accepted—at the cloister of Our Sorrowful Mother at Bard. I will enter on my birthday, next month. Paolo would stop me if he could, having plans to marry me to a cousin in Donnaz, but by law he cannot stand between me and the vows."

His ears rang. The font, the lectern, the marble leaping fish, all stood out in impossible relief. "Carla? You are going into the cloister? You will become a nun?"

She nodded, slowly and fervently. "I will become one of the sisters of Saint Clare. I will dedicate my works and prayers to the poor and the suffering." Something in Damiano's expression daunted her. "You...aren't happy for me, Dami?"

"I will never see you again!" cried the youth, his voice rising to a wail. Carla put one finger very near his mouth, darting a glance left and right.

"Hush, Damiano! My brother rarely sets foot in a church, but...If he found us, he would come at you like a bear—he is so furious."

Unable to restrain himself, he took her hand and kissed it. "Carla, *cara*, my dear, my Beatrice. Don't leave me and hide yourself behind stone walls forever, or I will die!"

Her little chin dropped in surprise. "What are you saying, Damiano? Am I going mad?"

"Please!" he implored. "When the soldiers marched into the city, all I thought about was you, and when I knew that you were gone, I feared for you. I marched through the cold and snow and was assaulted by thieves. I spent a night of death alive in the torn carcass of a dead cow, and then I sinned, killing men to save you . . .

"Mother of God, Carla, don't leave me! Let me serve you instead. All I have. All I am. All the days of my life. . . . I will not touch you, if it is your will that I do not. Though I hope fervently that is *not* your will! Please, it must be the will of God that I want you, for I could never want anything so much by myself!" His words broke off in a sob.

Carla sat still. Damiano, suddenly abashed, released her hand. Slowly she began to shake her head.

"Damiano. Where did this speech come from? In all the time I have known you, our conversation has been of God and of the sciences. You introduced me to the philosophers of the Church, whom I might never have known. You read to me interminably—I mean at length—from blessed Hermes, whose name I could never find on the list of saints, and taught me the elementals and how they combine, and the orders of the angels. . . .

"But you never spoke to me of love—worldly love. I had thought you would scorn such a feeling!" Her eyes wandered hidden in the darkness.

"Eh? God. Study. Love. Is there a difference among them?" he blurted. Damiano no longer knew quite what he was saying. He shrugged spasmodically. "I love you, Carla. I swear to God that I love you."

"I didn't know that," she said simply, shifting on the stone seat.

"Perhaps because I didn't either. Please, Carla, believe it now. Pretend you have always believed. Let it make a difference to your decision. Can't you?

"Can't you?" He stroked the air above her knee, not daring to touch her.

Her slow denial was inevitable and crushing. "No, my dear Damiano. I can't."

"This is a world of much bitterness; you have seen that as I have. Life is wracked with pain and cut short by war and pestilence. The weak suffer under the strong, and the strong, like my poor, fearsome Paolo, suffer under their own passions. Seeking after happiness itself leads to sin and greater suffering. We were not put here to be happy."

"That's good then," Damiano said, putting his elbows on his knees and his head in his hands. ". . . because I certainly am not . . . happy."

Reluctantly, knowing she shouldn't, Carla stroked Damiano's black hair. "We who are allowed to see this, my brother, my dear brother, brother of my soul . . . we are not given the choice of whom to love—for we must act love toward all, even the most repellent—nor whom first to serve. It is God himself whom we must serve. But for the rest, it is as you say—it must be with all we possess, and with all we are.

"And I am called by Him to prayer." Her smooth brow frowned momentarily. "I believed that you were, also, Damiano. It is from you I have learned my lessons, and I brought with me to Aosta the big book of Thomas Aquinas you gave me, and also the poems of Brother Francis that we read aloud together and were so beautiful. Can't you also feel your vocation?"

He lifted his head with a brief, choking laugh. "Me? A bastard, you know, cannot become a priest, but even a bastard is more welcome than I. A witch is barred from religious life: even from lay orders. They think we are not quite right, you know. Some say we are even damned."

Damiano's shoulders twitched, but he immediately straightened and wiped his tunic sleeve on his face. "Forgive me, Signorina. I am weary and . . . not pleased with myself. I will offer you nothing more to sour your resolution. I do understand it, though it . . ."

He took a deep breath and started again. "Believe me, Carla, if you wish to be a sister to me, I will be a brother to you. If you disappear behind the stone walls

of La Dolerosa, and I never see you again, then I will
still love you and be glad to love you, for it is better to
love than not."

She stood beside Damiano, her blond hair escaping the confines of her shawl. He turned stiffly, lest
motion should make him cry once more (which would
be too many times in too few days). He strode out of
the baptismal and through the vestibule. At the arched
doorway Damiano winced and turned his face from the
cold light of the sun.

Night fell early in the valley now, at the end of
November. Aosta sat in shadow, in the cupped hands
of the hills. The air was filled with wood smoke.

Damiano had paid a townsman to take him in that
night—him and Macchiata. If he went within now,
there would be a fire and hot soup, no doubt. (To
stretch one's dinner to feed a stranger, one always
made soup.) But instead Damiano sat on a log in the
meadow, where the banks of a frozen stream hid him
from the wind. He had wound his ermine mantle close
around him, and his booted feet were buried beneath
the mass of a warm dog.

The sky had faded, like violets pressed in the
pages of a book. The ice of the stream was gray.

"With all we possess. With all we are." She had
thrown his words back at him, and they scalded. What
Damiano had, money and property, had been quickly
dispersed. What he was, seemed nothing worth the
gift.

He shivered, and Macchiata shifted on his boots.

Still, anything could be turned to use some way. A
chair that could not be sat on could be thrown on the
fire. A man whom no one needed, whose actions
turned to harm, could serve a similar purpose. Damiano
had a sudden, dreadful idea that fit his mood. He rose
and started back toward the street.

An hour had passed. Macchiata had been put to

bed at the landlord's hearth. She had not objected. "Raphael," he called, sinking once more onto the lonely log.

"Raphael. Seraph. If you can spare a minute..."

The archangel sat himself gracefully on the frozen water.

"I can spare eternity," said Raphael. His smile was filled with that potent sweetness that man can appreciate only from far away. It gave Damiano unexpected pain, that smile, though he had seen it so often before.

"I would like..." He stopped, not knowing what to say. "Raphael, sit with me awhile, because I may never see you again."

The angel fluffed his feathers, and his eyebrows rose in a gesture as simple and dignified as that of an owl.

"Don't say 'never' to me, Dami!" Then Raphael's smile returned. "It's a word I cannot understand." Reflectively the angel added, "—though I understand 'forever' quite well. The two words are very different in quality, I think."

Damiano did not reply but clutched his knees to his chest. Slowly Raphael reached out a hand, and then a wing, taking the young man into his circle of light.

"Shall I play for you, Damiano?" he asked, as minutes passed.

"The lute is in the cabinetmaker's house, with Macchiata." Damiano's voice was phlegmy. He cleared his throat.

"I have my own instrument," said the angel, diffidently.

Damiano's eyes flickered briefly with curiosity, but that brightness failed.

"Thank you, Seraph, but I can't afford the peace such music would bring to me. There's something I have to do, and I must remain strong for it.

"Please sit beside me, Raphael, and don't ask me to talk."

To huddle in the compass of the angel's wings was

like sitting on the disk of the full moon, except that the moon was both more gaudy and more tarnished. Damiano was no longer cold. "You must continue to believe, Raphael, even if it becomes difficult... you must believe that I love you."

Raphael's black-blue gaze was beyond surprise or judgment.

Young Carla Denezzi walked the dark streets from the basilica to the inn, chaperoned by the Signora Anuzzi. They had passed the evening praying for the souls of the dead. The old signora's prayers had been specifically for her nephew Georgio Anuzzi, the owner of the vineyards, who had refused to abandon his holdings before the influx of soldiers and was now presumably among the departed. Any spiritual benefit that overshot this target would presumably go toward the souls of the two Partestradan men slain in the battle of the road.

Carla's prayers had been less exclusive. She had prayed for the souls of all who lay dead in the mountain snow. In fact, she had disbursed her prayers among some who were not dead at all, but only unhappy.

The sky was starless, and the women picked their way with worried care, fearing a fall on the frozen mud of the street. Signora Anuzzi muttered hard words to the air. At last they stood at the iron-bound inn door. Carla looked along the street to its ending, and she spied an angel in the fields beyond.

It was white and beautiful and unmistakably an angel, with huge wings folded forward and down— wings like a girl's white woolen shawl. It sat motionless on the earth, praying. It must be praying, for what else would an angel be doing alone at night, when many men were new dead?

"Signora, look!" she whispered, pointing into the darkness. "Do you see?"

"See? Child, I can scarcely see your finger, on a

night like this," the old woman snorted. Abruptly she turned away and went through the door.

Carla Denezzi bent down on her knees in the cold. With the angel for company, she uttered a silent prayer that all men and women, live or dead, should know peace.

Chapter 8

The night was black with no clipping of moon. Damiano stood alone in cold that made his ears ring, and his breath crackled against his face like a tiny fall of snow.

And he was afraid, though not of the cold. His staff stood braced before him, unfelt by frozen hands, and he whispered words he did not remember learning—unless he had heard them in sleep, from his father. With a prickle and thrill the young man intuited that his father had spoken these words at least once.

"Sator arepo tenet opera rotas. Ades, Satan!" he pronounced, but at the concluding word *"Dominus"* he choked and the word went unsaid.

The omission was meaningless, for a sheet of blackness disassociated itself from the night and flung Damiano into the air—or into the ground. The young man could not tell the difference, for both air and earth had gone suddenly impervious and malevolent. His limbs were stiff in an uncleanly paralysis, and Damiano had no breath to scream. He sailed through winds that were eddies of pain.

This was hell, he thought, and he had not needed an interview with the Devil to find it. He mouthed the words "O God!" not knowing what he said.

The darkness broke under an assault of noonday light. Damiano put his hand to his face and in wonder noticed that he was still on his feet, that his blind, sweeping passage had not disarranged the folds of his mantle.

Under his feet was rock, round and hollowed like a riverbed but colored carnelian. Around him curled huge tines of the stuff, taller than his head. In the distance rose a cliff wall, taller than the Grandfather itself, and within it an enormous arched opening, like a window. Beyond that . . .

With simple, terrible understanding, Damiano realized that the arch *was* a window and the cliff wall *was* a wall, and the rounded, fleshy rock he stood upon, miles above the ground, was an open hand. He swiveled so quickly he fell down, on a palm that was easily as hard as river rock.

The face of Raphael leaned down over him, beautiful, pure and clean-chiseled. It was the angel's face, but it was hot and ruddy, mountainous in size. "Mother of God!" yelped Damiano in terror.

The face instantly retreated. "Would Father Antonio appreciate such language?" it asked. "Common politeness itself forbids . . ."

The voice that spoke these words, though naturally enormous, was civilized in expression and modulated in tone. But still, there was something about it of the dry, abrasive sound of a shovel cutting through ashes, and it was not Raphael's voice at all.

Nor was the face quite as much like that of the archangel as Damiano had first supposed. The lean cheekbones arched out below the eyes in more aggressive fashion, perhaps more barbaric and perhaps also more interesting. Raphael's hair, though fair enough, was reduced to a childish flaxen next to the gold that curled fastidiously over this enormous head. It was a gold that deserved to be minted in coin.

Then Damiano remembered that Lucifer, too, had begun as an archangel, and Damiano knew he was in the presence he had summoned. The witch sat on the

Devil's palm, his staff across his thighs, toes pointed to the unimaginable ceiling, and he continued to stare.

The terrible eyes narrowed, as a man's eyes will narrow when he tries to focus on the form of an insect he has captured. "Well. What is the problem, my friend? Did you not expect that little voyage? Did you think I would come to you, when it is so much easier, and more fitting as well, to bring you to me?"

Damiano's ears were buzzing, and his head was filled with woolly numbness. He dared not open his mouth, for he had no idea what sounds would come out of it. Yet he spared a glance around him.

The view was endless, and the young man's vision was not, but he saw enough to convince him that he was in a room of some sort. Four flat walls, chalky white, supported hangings indistinguishably embroidered in red. There was an enormous expanse of polished, tile floor on which stood a table the size of a cathedral, supporting a bowl filled with tawny grapes. Four windows looked out in four directions, displaying respective cloudy vistas of blue sea, green fields, icebound rock, and featureless sand. Though these views were incompatible, and for the most part uninhabitable to man, as Damiano peered from one window to another he felt a keen longing to be in any of them, flying through the sweet, free air (flying? Why flying? Damiano had never in his life flown anywhere). In freedom, true freedom, under sunlight or shadow, answerable to no one, not even to . . .

"It is my audience chamber. A pleasant place, is it not? Merely to sit in it and breathe the air calls forth the best qualities in a man. And it is convenient to all places and times. I too have spent many hours gazing out at my dominions."

Damiano nodded absently, thinking that the attraction was more out the windows than in the room itself, where the air smelled flat, like a dead fire. He wondered if perhaps that was how Satan himself felt, and whether that was not the reason he spent hours staring out at the places where he was not. Also, if these vistas were like others the youth had seen, then they were a cheat, for once one had labored toward them, one invariably found one was still standing on soil that was similar in looks and feel to that of home, breathing and rebreathing the cloud of one's own breath. Damiano could understand if Satan felt that frustration when he gazed out his windows, for the great demon's breath was particularly stale. In fact, for one brief instant he felt he understood the Devil very well, but then that moment passed.

Satan cleared his throat. "I think you requested an audience, Dami?"

Hearing his name spoken, Damiano shivered uncontrollably. Delstrego would not have been so bad to hear, though any evidence that the Devil knew one was unpleasant to the ears. To have Satan call him by his Christian name would have been understandable, since most everyone in Partestrada called him Damiano, having known him since a child. But to be called Dami, as Carla and as Raphael called him Dami, by these lips that were only too massive to be Raphael's, and in that scraped-ashen voice . . . that was worse than having the Devil reprimand him in Father Antonio's name.

Yet he planted his staff and climbed to his feet again. "I did," he answered, his voice sounding unexpectedly steady. "If you are Satan, that is."

The fair brow shot up in a gesture distractingly familiar. "I am," whispered the gray voice, "Lucifer, the ruler of the earth and of mankind. I heard you, and since I try to be open and accessible to all my subjects, I have helped you hither to me."

Damiano's gaze of confusion continued, and at last the huge face flushed. The effect was like sunset on the mountains. "You speak of audacity! You act as though you don't believe I am who I say!" Fingers curled around the young man, threatening to shut out the light.

Damiano recalled how Father Antonio had once

said that no man is as offended at doubt as is the habitual liar who has for once told the truth. Though he stood in a dread so thick as to be indistinguishable from despair, this small observation comforted him. "I believe you, spirit. I believe you because you look so much like the archangel Raphael, whose face I have seen and whom I know to be related to you. But still that paradox astounds me, that you should look so much like an angel."

The once-highest of the archangels went redder than beets, until his face had the look of flayed flesh. His fingers curled around the tiny figure of gold and scarlet until it seemed he would crush it.

But Damiano stood braced, and the huge embrace halted, with a perfectly manicured thumbnail resting against the young man's throat. "There was," admitted Satan, "a litter of creatures spawned, with a superficial resemblance to me. Imitation, no doubt. But I am by far the greatest."

Damiano nodded, feeling the cold horny nail against his adam's apple. "I was told you were greater than they," he replied. "I only brought it up to explain why I was staring." He coughed, backed away from the thumbnail and felt the end of a hard finger between his shoulder blades.

Satan smiled, thereby destroying the last resemblance with Raphael. "Who," he crooned, "gave you such good information? One of my lieutenants on the earth, I presume. A murderer, or the pope at Avignon?"

Damiano glanced up sharply. "Raphael told me. He said you were always the greatest of the angels."

Rude laughter barked and boomed, till Damiano swayed on the palm of the Devil's hand, his own hands over his ears and eyes. "Humility!" roared the red face. "I love it!" Then, with whip-crack speed, it was sober. "And I am gratified to find a man without an exaggerated respect for that twittering crew."

Damiano stiffened and set his jaw. He had not come to get into an argument with the Devil, like the one he had been dragged into by General Pardo, but he was an Italian born and could not hear his friend so demeaned. Not by any man or devil. "Power is not everything, Great Lucifer," he stated. "I don't think it means anything, to Raphael. Not like music does. And though he may be less powerful than you are, he is still far above me."

Satan set his eyes on Damiano as a wolf might have set its teeth in his neck. He could neither move nor look away.

"He *is* far above you, boy, because he has made you believe it. Be aware that spirits are very subtle and they say nothing by chance.

"I have a certain reputation in that direction myself, Damiano, but I swear to you that I am forthrightness itself, compared with the spirits who bow to the Beginning."

"The Beginning?" echoed Damiano.

Satan sighed and his face knit into lines of pure philosophy. "All things, and spirits, came out of the Beginning. Exploded from It, you might say. It had no choice in the matter and would certainly have maintained us all as part of Itself, if It could have.

"But It could not, for freedom is as old as the Beginning, if not older. Ever since all of us, spirits and creatures alike, escaped and became ourselves, It has been trying to cozen us into returning, so It can consume us again. With that in mind It spread the tale that It transubstantiates into bread, to be consumed by man, so that man will feel less objection to the truth that It consumes man, like bread.

"To be dissolved into another! That is the antithesis of freedom."

It was God he was talking about, Damiano realized.

"In fact, Damiano, though I am the lord of the earth I am also the one apostle of freedom upon the earth, and those who serve me know the gifts of liberty, for there is nothing I will deny a man. I will not even deny him the intellectual pleasure derived from

bowing at the alter of the Beginning, if that is his
desire, though that Other does not extend such courtesy to me.

"In fact I have many who worship me in such
part-time fashion, some of them worthy men in cardi-
nal red. I . . ."

Damiano had lost the thread of Satan's conversation, for he was still trying to understand how freedom
could be both natural and a gift. Perhaps his lack of
attention was written in his face, for the Devil stopped
in midsentence.

"But here now. You didn't come all this way to
discuss histories, or to tell me that that fluttering limpid
brother of mine knows his place. What do you want of
me, Damiano Delstrego? What is your desire, my dear
brother witch?"

Damiano filled his lungs with dry air, more deadly
than fumes of sulfur. "A bargain," he announced.

"Of course. A bargain," echoed the red angel, and
his smile held a languorous ennui. "Everyone wants a
bargain from me. You'd think I were a tradesman,
instead of only the inventor of trade." He dandled
Damiano gently between his fingers, knocking him to
his knees.

"All men lust after my bargains, little friend, though
some pursue them harder. It seems to run in families,
for you are not the first Delstrego with whom I have
spoken . . ."

Damiano made no reply, though the blood in his
heart congealed. Still he knew better than to trust the
Devil concerning his father. Raphael had said to have
hope, so he cast his eyes down at the immaculate
ruddy palm.

"Bargains . . ." Satan ruminated, and he sat back in
his gilded throne, which was the only chair in the
room. "I am sempiternally bored with striking bargains
with mortals. They never have anything interesting to
ask, or anything worthwhile to give." He sighed like a
gale in a cave.

"I think you want what I have to give," began Damiano, grimacing as he spoke, but the Devil cut him off.

"That comes second, little witch. First is the matter of what *you* want."

This was simple to say and not frightening. "I want peace," stated Damiano.

After a moment's pause, Satan grunted. "There are many avenues toward that goal, Damiano. I could build you a castle in a green valley where no man has ever set foot. Obedient demons would do your will and never say no to you. Succubi, too. Unrest is a product of your interaction with other mortals, believe me. With no human company, you would be sure to have peace.

"Alternately, I could provide you with one hundred years on the oil of the eastern poppy, with never a bad dream. That is peace, and poetry, too. I recommend it over my first proposal.

"Then I could make you my vassal over all Europe, of course. That is a popular request, since many men have come to the realization that power is freedom and freedom is happiness." Cold gray eyes regarded Damiano, eyes much larger than platters. "And what is happiness, but peace in action?

"You would make a comical emperor, Damiano Delstrego. You have a kind heart."

Damiano frowned and sat back on his heels. He struck the shoe of his staff against the devil's palm. "No. No, Satanas, I want peace, not for me, but for all the Piedmont. One hundred years without war."

Satan peered closely at the tiny thing in his hand. "With you as duke, of course?" he drawled.

Damiano shook his head. "I can't...I mean I thank you for your confidence in me, but my talents don't lie in that direction. Only once have I been able to unite and fire men's minds, and that time I...No, I don't want to pay that again. I am a man of the arts: an alchemist, a musician, maybe a poet, too, though I have not much experience in that, as yet."

At a thought his tongue thickened and he grew visibly paler. "Or at least these were the things I had planned to be." Then he flipped his sleeves and hair back and began afresh.

"With any suitable man as a duke. Or without a duke, as one grand republic with Partestrada as capital. Or eight little, quiet republics, with Partestrada as the largest."

"That is imp . . ." The Devil cleared his throat, and Damiano seemed to see a cloud of ash spread from his well-molded lips into the room. "Your love for your city does you credit, Damiano, but let's talk concretely. I can give you General Pardo's head on a pike."

Damiano had expected this offer. "That's no good. Pardo alone isn't the problem, for there will always be another wolf to raven the fold. I want a respite from wolves. I want peace and prosperity for the Piedmont."

"Before you said only peace, Damiano. That was bad enough, but now you've added prosperity."

Damiano squinted at the looming face. "I mean peace, but not the peace of devastation and pestilence, when all the people are dead. I mean a thriving peace."

"The head of Pardo plus the head of Paolo Denezzi." Damiano swallowed, abashed at how intimately the Devil had read his worst desires.

"No," he replied weakly.

". . . And I will burn down the convent of La Dolerosa at Bard before the month is out," concluded Satan. "That will change many things, my eager young lover, and you may return to your own tower with a beautiful bride."

Damiano's eyes stung, and his cheeks flushed, though nowhere so red as those on the elegant face of the Devil.

"No." He was scarcely audible. "Do nothing to touch her."

The angry trembling of the great hand ran through Damiano and made his teeth vibrate.

"I find your bargaining to be rather of the take-it-or-leave-it variety, little witch," Satan rasped, and he laid his hand down on the table. Damiano stared, fascinated, at the pond-sized shallow bowl that he had thought to be filled with grapes. "You ask more from me than any man in a handful of centuries," snapped the beautiful red mouth. "What on earth or in hell do you have to give in return?"

Damiano blinked three times and then was certain that the objects in the bowl were fresh human heads. This knowledge, rather than frightening him, gave him a certain hopeless courage. "Myself," he said. "My life. My soul. You can have it now without waiting."

The next instant found him tumbling across the polished wood surface of the table, his staff tangling with his legs.

"Your soul? Damiano, why don't you try selling me this throne, or my own left hand?" As Satan leaned over the table Damiano felt the wood creak complaint and the air grow very hot. "Boy, don't you know what it means to be born a witch?"

Damiano lay flat on his back with his eyes closed. Panic brushed his face. "I know no man is born damned," he hissed. "Father Antonio has said it, and my heart tells me it is true!"

The deadly ire subsided into irony. "To be what they call damned is only to be free and to declare you are free, shaking your fist at brute authority. I will give a lot to free a man, Damiano, but you're right; I can't do it alone. Each man chooses his own 'damnation.' And you"—the fiery face turned away—"chose the black path to my door."

Damiano waited for flames to take him, but after ten seconds passed uneventfully, he opened his eyes.

He lay under the rim of the pottery bowl, which was the color of dried blood. One of the heads brimming over the edge stared down at him. The slack features were those of the captain of cavalry whom he had seen brained by the butcher's hammer not one day ago. That spotted thing behind it: was that a cow's head? Damiano closed his eyes again. He became aware the Devil was speaking.

"You are a fool, and you have wasted my time, boy. But as you are a witch and a freethinker and so have some call on me, I will be very generous. I propose a bargain that will almost exactly suit your needs.

"I will arrange what you call peace for Partestrada. Not the entire Piedmont, mind you, and not for one hundred years, but just for the lives of the present inhabitants. You will be the mayor—simply because you are the only man who will be able to understand your perverse motivations in this matter. Partestrada will happen to lie outside every path of conquest from Italy, France, and the north. Harvests will be adequate. Not ample, perhaps, but adequate. No plague will touch the city. Is that not a good approximation of peace?"

Damiano gazed up fixedly, as though engaged in colloquy with the head of the dead captain. "Possibly. What do you want for it, if my soul is of no value?"

Satan chewed his lower lip and peered out his southern window at endless sand. "I?" He spoke slowly, dreaming. "I, like you, am an altruist. I ask nothing for myself. But the situation imposes its own restraints.

"You are right, little witch, in supposing that the town of Partestrada contains the seeds of greatness. Its location on the Dora Baltea, three quarters of the way between Turin and Aosta . . . its salubrious climate, nurturing grapes yet in the shadows of the Alps . . .

"But I tell you that fifty years of unexceptional peace will kill Partestrada. She will fade and mummify, and her young men depart for Milan and Turin, violent cities of more promise."

Damiano sat up. "That isn't the way it has to be."

The Devil raised one eyebrow in the familiar gesture of Raphael. "Let me finish, please. Not only will Partestrada fade and be forgotten, Damiano, but you yourself. All you have done and dreamed. The alchemical discoveries you are destined to make, the music that even now your unfulfilled love is awakening in your bosom, all your wisdom, your easy gift of friendship, your very name and your family name and your house and the place where your house once stood and your face . . .

"All will be lost and forgotten. In a century you will be a man who might never have existed from a city with a forgotten name."

Damiano put his head between his knees. "No!" he said, and repeated it stubbornly, his voice shaking in his throat. "No. That's not the only way to get peace for my city."

The Devil seemed to shrug. "It's what I offer," he replied. "I can see no other way. Greatness, in man or nation, is incompatible with that emptiness that you call peace."

Damiano rose slowly to his feet, using the edge of the bowl of heads for support. "You can *see* no other way? Raphael can't see into the future. He says no created being can . . ."

Harsh laughter boomed out, along with the odor of a wet fire. "Raphael? My little brother has a long history of confusing dare not with cannot!

"Believe me or doubt me, boy, but you came here to bargain. This is my offer, and if you were the . . . the saint you seem to be, you would snap it up. Even Raphael couldn't fault such a bargain; it reeks of yielding resignation. *And* humility. What do you say, little witch? Will you take it?"

"No," answered Damiano. "The more I talk to you the more I believe in Partestrada. Decay is not the only way to peace!"

The Devil snorted in jovial contempt. "Fine words! But you are a hypocrite, after all," he said. He smiled as though he had just won a hand at cards. "Or a coward. Either way, you're no better than I thought!"

Then the bitter wind took Damiano again and flung him at the wall.

Chapter 9

Damiano spent the next morning lying motionless on a pallet on the floor of the cabinetmaker's house, Macchiata curled beside him. When he woke, his interview with the Devil might have been a dream, except that his knees were bruised from falling on that stony red hand and his nostrils were caked with ash.

At intervals during the morning, the dog left Damiano, only to return and find her master as dull as before. At last she inserted her damp nose between Damiano's stubbly chin and his neck.

"Master," she began, her voice muffled by the contact, "Master, are you sick?"

"No, little dear," he answered slowly. "I just want to stop the sun for a while." Then, remembering Macchiata's literal mind, he amended his statement. "I needed time to think."

The dog sat placidly beside him, her brown eyes a few inches from his. As he watched, a flea crawled out from behind her ear and disappeared among the white hairs of Macchiata's muzzle. "And did you think?" she asked. "I mean, are you done thinking? What *did* you think?"

Wrestling with the heavy felt blanket, Damiano turned onto his back. "I think...there's got to be another way. For both my city and myself."

"I'm sure there is," said Macchiata staunchly, "if

you think so." And she scratched the side of her face with the stubby nails of her back foot.

It didn't bother Damiano that the dog should express her agreement with him without knowing the subject matter of that agreement; he was as used to Macchiata's loyal ignorance as he was to Raphael's smile.

"I need help," he continued, thoughtfully glowering at the black beams of the ceiling. "I need advice."

"Certainly." She sat, ears pricked, and waited.

Damiano bent his head toward her, and a snort of laughter escaped him. "I meant—and I hope you will not be offended, Macchiata—from someone wiser than I."

The dog grinned lazily, and her tongue slid out the side. "Not at all, Master. I know I am only four years old, whereas you are one and twenty. But where are you to find one greater than you are—that I don't know."

Damiano's grin matched hers. The dog's ludicrous flattery never failed to amuse him, because he knew it was sincere. He sat up, throwing the weight of covers aside. Beneath the blankets he was wearing his ermine mantle and nothing else at all. Limberly he twisted right and left over the floorboards, fishing for his tunic and trousers among the tangles of cloth.

"Unless it's Raphael, Master. He must be very wise, because he never gets upset. Perhaps he is even wiser than you."

"Perhaps," Damiano agreed, and his grin grew rueful. "But I know his advice in any case; it is not of the world, as he is not, and unfortunately, our difficulty is very worldly. I can't sit back and pray.

"Besides, if the archangel discovered what I did last night, likely he would never speak to me again."

"Last night when I was asleep, Master? What did you do?"

"I had a chat with the Devil, little dear. And he threw me out."

Macchiata thought. "Is the Devil wiser than you? Did you go to him for advice?"

Damiano pulled his trousers up, wondering how many of Macchiata's fleas were hiding in them, and how many of his own. "I guess I did—go to him for advice. But that doesn't mean I have to take it."

He knelt to fold the blanket. His knees were very sore. "You know, little dear, it feels good to be thrown out by the Devil. Not as good, perhaps, as being welcomed in by the Father himself, but then, after the latter experience one is not usually walking the green earth. I think I know what I shall do next."

"What *we* shall do next, you mean," replied Macchiata, standing unconcernedly in the middle of the blanket her master was attempting to fold.

"What we shall do, then. We are going to take a trip. A very pleasant trip into a beautiful land. Just the two of us."

Macchiata cocked her head to one side, and the tip of her tail began to wag. Slowly the wag gained both speed and mass, until her body was still only from the shoulders forward.

"To Provence, Master, as you said last week?"

Damiano threw the blanket into the corner and stood. He thrust his head out the single small window the room possessed and took a chestful of clean air. "No. Last week I was dreaming childish dreams. I was dreaming of my own happiness. But still, where we are going is more beautiful than Provence. We are going to Lombardy, little dear. To find the witch my father said was the most powerful in all the Italies: Saara the Fenwoman, whose dominion..." and then his tongue clove to the roof of his mouth, as he remembered where last he had heard the word "dominion." "Whose power is over both snow and sunlight. She *must* help us.

"—For I don't know anyone else to ask."

The parting with Carla Denezzi was hard. It seemed to Damiano he had never known how he loved her until

she was lost to him. If he had been more forward . . . but
then he had not suspected there would be a limit to their
time together, and feelings, like fruit, ripen slowly in the
high air.

Damiano bought the black gelding from Paolo Denezzi,
who was more than willing to help Damiano on his way.
The last of his coin was spent on food and warmer
bedding than even his closet at home had provided. Was
General Pardo now storing *his* garb in the Delstrego
wardrobe? It was quite possible, since the tower was
nearly the best house in Partestrada, and certainly the
most defendable.

Now that Damiano stopped to think about it, the
general would be running quite a risk if he did plant
himself in Damiano's house. A man could come to
harm, nosing about in the Delstrego tower, even
though Damiano had quenched the fires in the workroom before leaving. There were still the chemicals,
and the elementals . . . Damiano entertained the possibilities. A problem or two would be solved if Pardo
exploded along with a sealed retort. But it was an
idle notion: there was nothing the witch could do at
this distance to encourage an explosion, and besides,
he did not know for sure that Pardo was staying in
his house.

Damiano rode back along the road south out of
Aosta. He rode bareback because that was most easy
for him. Guillermo Delstrego had never kept a horse;
animals hadn't liked him, and he had returned the
feeling.

Or perhaps it had happened the other way around.
In either case, Damiano had not learned to ride along
with the other boys of family in Partestrada. He had
not learned most things along with the other boys,
but he had learned quite a few things by himself, and
among them was bareback riding.

And the horse liked him much better, now that
Damiano's madness had burned itself out. The gelding stepped easily down the packed surface of the

road, where a warm day had thawed the brown ice and
hollowed it, making sheets brittle and thin like isin-
glass. Shod hooves ground the stuff into slush.

Macchiata pattered about, behind, before, and beneath, interfering in a hundred ways with the patient
steed's walking. Occasionally the horse put its head to
the ground or thrust its lippy muzzle into a crack of the
rock wall, in the forlorn hope of grass. Damiano did
not correct it because he had no rein on the animal,
and also because he had not the heart.

They passed the spot where Damiano had first
been hailed by Pardo's captain and then the bend in
the road where Damiano had destroyed the soldiers
with his memories of a butchered cow. Finally they
passed beside the small crevasse where fifty-two men
were buried beneath snow and branches. For Damiano
this journey was another form of the stations of the
cross. He said nothing, nor did Macchiata, though her
nose had a long memory of its own.

The horse, who had memory but no words, rolled
its eyes, and the hide over its withers twitched.

A mile south of this point, as Damiano stopped to
take a pull of wine from the bag at his left side he
heard a quick clatter of hooves. With his heel he
prodded the horse to the side of the road and called
Macchiata to stand beneath. Then he pulled his staff
out from his bedroll and spoke the spell; it came easily,
for he was both rested and in practice.

When the goatherd passed with his tiny flock, he
did not notice the prints of shod hooves that led onto
the smooth snow of the shoulder of the road and then
stopped abruptly. The goats were more observant. They
stared with their crazy yellow eyes, pupils rectangular
as money boxes, and the witch didn't know whether
they could see him or whether they knew he was there
by other means.

When almost all had passed, one weatherworn
buck halted before the horse, examined them sagaciously

and urinated into his own beard. Macchiata growled at the insult. The goat presented its horns.

"Don't get involved," hissed Damiano helplessly from above. At that moment the goatherd stalked over, and with his supple leather whip, sent his charge bawling up the road.

"Well," said Damiano, when they were alone again. "It might have been soldiers."

By midafternoon Damiano had passed the fork in the road where the stone hut stood abandoned and empty, passed by the shoulder hills that concealed the dead village of Sous Pont Saint Martin, and left behind the footpath where the bones and raw hide of a cow had been tossed to rot in the first thaw. Thus all the tragic histories of this past week were behind him.

The sky was streaked with fairy clouds of ice that scattered the sunlight. He felt warm under his furs, warm and sleepy. "Let's start again, little dear," he murmured to Macchiata. "No more of the Devil. I went wrong somewhere—I don't know where, exactly, and I have no one to ask, but it doesn't matter. Maybe Saara can tell me, eh? She's been round awhile and must have seen much of life, traveling from the Fenland down to Italy."

He waited for an answer, because Macchiata always replied to his questions, even the rhetorical ones. After a few seconds of silence, he looked around, then leaned over to peer under the horse's belly.

"Macchiata?"

When was the last time he had heard from the dog? Sighing, Damiano slid to the ground.

To the left of the road rose hills, more rounded than the peaks visible from the crossroads, pocketed with green-black growths of pine. To his right the land hollowed out, and standing water had turned to sheets of ice. He squinted at the bright white road behind him.

A tiny speck of russet was bobbling in the distance. It became recognizable, and Damiano relaxed, leaning one arm over the black horse's back. As Macchiata galloped she rolled like a small but heavy-laden ship, and her tongue lolled in desperate manner.

"Why didn't you tell me you couldn't keep up?" asked Damiano. Macchiata looked up at him, pulled in her tongue, and then all four of her bandy legs gave at once. As she hit the packed snow of the road her jaws clashed resoundingly. Her inadequate little tail lay flat out behind.

She was hot as a bed warmer when Damiano scooped her up. "That's terrible, Macchiata. Your pride might have gotten you lost! Now lie there a minute and don't move." As he spoke he deposited her across the withers of the horse, where she lay as limply as the goatskin of wine. Damiano leaped up next to her.

"This poor horse," he began, as he clucked the gelding to a walk. "Two riders, two bags, a bedroll, a wineskin, my staff, and the lute besides. It's lucky for him neither of us weighs too much!"

The dog only groaned.

"Do you wonder," asked Damiano, when a few minutes had passed, "why I should care about Partestrada so much? To go running hither and thither, fighting battles in the snow?"

"No," answered Macchiata, and she clambered precariously to her feet on the horse's back, her blunt nails digging in for grip. Damiano had barely time to grab her middle before the twitch of the black hide sent her slipping. He sat her on her tail before him, one arm holding her around the middle. Her back legs lolled in the air.

"No, Master. Partestrada is our home."

"But some might question whether she is worth it. After all, Partestrada isn't the largest city in the area, and she hasn't produced any great poets or philosophers—yet."

"Partestrada is our home," repeated the dog, as though there was nothing more to be said.

But Damiano was not listening. "I think . . . it may be the fruit vendors that make it so special. The way they push their vans down the alleys bawling, 'rubies, rubies, red rubies' when all the world knows they have only apples for sale.. Or it may be the way the sun seems to roll along the crest of the mountains at midwinter, and the dawn and twilight colors last half the day.

"Of course, it could be our wool, because the sheep get to stay cool both winter and summer and yet get enough to eat. We all get enough to eat, as a matter of fact, unlike cities like Florence, where bread might as well be wrapped in gold leaf, for what it costs, and I'm told a man may have a house of marble and yet eat bread laced with sawdust and bran.

"Or it may be the fact that we make our own wine, though frankly, Macchiata, it isn't good wine—not made from the grapes they use in the south." He slapped the gurgling sack smartly.

"And then again, little dear, though they make fun of us Piedmontese because we are so mixed up between France and the Italies, I think this mixedness makes us flexible. No one is as proud as an illiterate Tuscan peasant, though he has naught to be proud of except a field of sunbaked clay! A man with a Lombard father and a Rhenish mother-in-law must develop a sense of humor—to survive.

"But all in all, I think it is the vendors."

"I'm mixed," introjected Macchiata. "My mother is a ratter and my father . . . I don't know, exactly."

"Certainly! And see how fortunate you are in that? Strong, enduring, and, though you are not the largest dog in the Piedmont, fierce enough to put three highwaymen to flight." He squeezed Macchiata till her breath squeaked out her nose.

Then Damiano's dark eyes grew somber and earnest. "Though I know that the highest love asks nothing, still I would like . . . little dear, I would like Partestrada to know me before I die. To know how I have cared."

"We know." Macchiata squirmed around to lick her master's bony hand. "All your friends know."

Damiano flinched, for he had just been reflecting that, although he was very friendly, he had not many friends.

By the early dusk they had reached a region of upland hills similar to those of home. Grass and wild corn stood exposed in sodden patches, and the steady north wind had bent the stalks of the corn until they trailed the ground like willow. Here the road widened. Damiano spied a shape trudging through the distant, soggy fields, bent almost double beneath a load of faggots. Whether this was man or woman or child he could not tell, and he did not hail the creature, for it was enough to know there were people in the world who had nothing to do with war.

"The road tends south," he remarked to the dog, who sat awkwardly and stiffly before him. "We've climbed almost out of the snow."

Macchiata snuffed. "There are too many mountains, Master. And they are too high."

Damiano laughed. "We barely touched them, little dear. The Alps continue northward, far beyond the most distant peaks we could see, where burghers perch their houses in valleys higher than the tops of our hills, and they speak not only French and Italian, but German as well. In the west the mountains continue into France, while in the east . . ."

"I'm tired," said Macchiata.

He hugged her in quick contrition. "I'm sorry, Macchiata. Both you and the horse deserve a rest. But I wanted to leave memories behind.

"And we've done so, for I don't know where we are at all. Let's find some brush out of the wind and make a real camp; it'll be our first!"

Damiano snarled pine boughs into the living branches of a berry bush, and over this he flung a length of smelly oilcloth. He wove more of the slender, resinous evergreen as a mat over the half-frozen earth. He gathered a tinder of dry oats and sparked it between his cupped hands. The fire he nurtured was more suitable for a harvest bonfire than for the night's camp of a single traveler, but Macchiata appreciated it, and even the black horse sidled in toward the warmth.

He picked through his sizable store of cheese, bread, dried meat, fruit, and fish. He could afford to be choosy. He picked out an apple, pink and withered like an old woman's cheek, a hard Romano, and a strip of salted pork. He shredded a bite of the pork and found himself controlling his stomach with effort.

"Gah! I can't eat flesh! I shouldn't even try." He flung the entire strip to Macchiata, who looked quite sorry for him as she gulped it.

"Monks survive without it," mumbled Damiano. "Or they are supposed to. And after all, how is my life different from a monk's? I have no money, no home, no family . . . and no mistress."

"You have me." The dog's tail punctuated her statement.

Her master blinked. "True, Macchiata, and that's quite a bit. Remind me again if I forget." He divided the cheese in two.

After dinner, Damiano took out his lute and examined it by firelight. The finish had gone milky over the inlay of the back, but that always happened in the dampness. A good dry day would cure it. All the strings were sound. He plucked a sad melody he had made up himself a year since.

He was out of practice and his fingers stumbled.

"This won't do," he said to the basking dog. "It is a musician's duty to find time daily for his instrument."

"You've been busy." Macchiata yawned, already half asleep.

"I'm always busy," answered Damiano. "That's no excuse." And he practiced the modes till his own yawns screwed his eyes shut.

*   *   *

The weather in and around the Alps is unpredictable, and it tends toward small pockets of virulence. In
the middle of the night the sky assaulted the travelers
with hail that spat in the fire and drove the gelding
whinnying out of sleep.

"Dominus Deus!" grumbled the witch. "One thing
after another!" He hadn't the heart to resist as the
horse bent its legs and hunkered into the lean-to,
though neither horse nor shelter had been constructed
with such an end in mind.

Soon the hail turned to sleet, and the fire died of
the insult. The framework of branches and cloth lost its
mooring and fell on the horse's back, which Damiano
didn't mind as long as the beast didn't move, but the
corner of Damiano's mantle was soaked.

"After last night we must be very good friends, eh,
Festilligambe?" Damiano said to the horse, fixing it
with soft brown eyes much like its own. (*Festilligambe*
means *sticklegs* in Italian.) "I think I felt every one of
those big feet of yours against my back. And with the
grass you've been grabbing by the road, your digestion
is none too good! So you get us to the vales of Lombardy
the quickest way you know." The gelding nodded as
though it were about to speak.

And given enough time alone with Damiano, it
might have. But Lombardy could not be far away, for
the travelers were entering more populous country,
leaving the realm of white winter behind.

That swath of broken soil to the left, for instance,
lying on the slope of a hill like a tossed blanket. It had
known recent tillage. And unless Damiano's eyes were
failing him (a distinct possibility), ahead of them, at a
hump of the winding road, was a house.

It was a house, but it was the merest hovel, with a
thatched roof rotted black in places and walls built of
mud as much as stone. Two toddling children peeped
out the door at the passage of the magnificent stranger
and his dog. They were scantily clad for the weather,

and one was barefoot. Damiano brought Festilligambe to a halt and regarded them with the attention he reserved for small wild things. There was a stir in the darkness of the hut, and a girl appeared behind the children. Tawny-haired and plump she was, with a face as round and innocent as a dirty flower. Her dress was patched gray wool, and it was pulled off one shoulder. In her arms she held an infant that she was nursing from one bare, ample breast.

Though women had to nurse their children and did it how and as they might, still Damiano sat abashed before so much revealed femininity. This girl had hair like Carla's. And these blue eyes that stared shyly into his were the eyes of a May bunny: the eyes of a child. She was much younger than he.

Before the silence had time to become unbearable, Damiano heard Macchiata growl. Startled, he glanced around to see a lean figure running full tilt across the bare field toward him. The girl noticed at the same time and took a single step back into the hut. The children scampered right and left and were gone.

The peasant was only as tall as Damiano but much wider. He wore nothing but his long woolen shirt and the rags on his feet. He, too, was very young, but he wore at his belt a knife with a blade as long as a man's forearm. He placed himself between the black horse and the door and, still panting from exertion, looked Damiano up and down.

"The Monsignore desires?" he asked, in a patois so thick even Damiano had trouble understanding.

"Eh? Well," replied the witch from horseback, "we request of the other Monsignore to tell us if we will find a town up ahead."

"We are not an hour from San Gabriele," answered the peasant reluctantly. Then, as Damiano moved to go, he added, "The Monsignore does not wear a sword?"

Damiano turned and glowered at the man. "No. I have no need for one. My pure heart protects me." He clucked the horse to a canter, thinking with some satisfaction that his virginity must not be perceptible to the casual observer.

San Gabriele. That was a good sign. Though Gabriel was not Raphael, he was still an angel.

"I didn't know that," said Macchiata, huffing along at his left side, "—that you don't need a sword because your pure heart protects you. I thought you didn't carry one because it got in the way of your staff."

The rider sighed. "That was a joke, Macchiata. The real reason I don't wear a sword is that if I wore one, I would eventually have to use it. That is the way with weapons. Besides, my big flute, here," he said, patting the stick of black wood, "is a hundred times more useful."

The surly peasant hadn't lied; they were approaching habitation. More sheds and hovels sprang up among the rough and borderless fields. On their left they passed the rickety structure of an irrigation pump, an affair of spokes and buckets abandoned for the winter. Next they overtook a goat cart, drawn by a rotund nanny and filled with baskets of squawking geese. Damiano gave the gawky lad who led the boat a pleasant salute.

Macchiata snorted and snuffled in pleasant anticipation, and soon Damiano's nose, which was more acute than that of an ordinary man (though not of canine quality), picked up the odors of dung and garlic.

The town of San Gabriele had been built in a dry scoop in the hills, forty feet above the highway. The rutted road that led into town was littered with wains, carts, and barrows; the oxen that had pulled the wains wandered hobbled in the ploughed fields at either side of the road, still keeping to their pairs. With an outsize thrill Damiano realized that it was market day in San Gabriele. He dismounted and led Festilligambe up the incline, one hand holding to the gelding's glossy mane.

The village boasted two strong gateposts of stone, but these supported no gates, nor were they flanked by

walls of any sort. Indeed, to the left of the left-hand
post grew an oak of enormous width and therefore
age. This seemed to indicate that the walls of San
Gabriele had fallen centuries before, if they had ever
been built. Damiano passed beneath the bare, gnarled
arms of the tree.

Here was life again. Stalls flanked the street far
beyond the confines of the town proper, displaying
woolens and wickerwork and brilliant dried peppers.
The first man he saw wore homespun, and the second
a robe of otter. Seven bleating ewes were driven down
the main street, dodging past a man in motley who
balanced a wine bottle on his nose.

Damiano hadn't known that he was starving for
the sight of bright-dyed bolts of cloth and piled winter
marrows, for the chatter of well-to-do peasants and the
howls of the beggars. Macchiata, too, whined with an
indefinable longing and thumped her tail against her
master's leg.

"Wait a bit, little dear," whispered the young man,
and he led the horse off the path and over the stubble
of the field. "I know the air is intoxicating, but we can't
have noble Festilligambe here eating the apples off
some fellow's cart."

The hoed field was bordered with a paling of
poplar trees. Damiano marched toward them, the horse
stepping carefully behind. Beside the gray trunks he
stopped and delved into his pack.

"Here," he said, dropping his still-folded oilcloth
to the ground. On the square he spilled a quantity of
oats. "Can I trust you to stay here and not get into
trouble until I return?"

The eyes, ears, nose, and tail of the beast replied in
unison that he could not. Damiano sighed.

"Then, as I have nothing for a tether, it's a binding
spell," he announced. "And that will probably frighten
you into hysterics. As well as tiring me unnecessarily."

The tall horse conceded. It lipped Damiano's hair.

"Good then. Trust is best. And, Macchiata—will you guard this gear until I return from the fair?"

Macchiata stared at him, stricken. Her head sank and her wormy tail crawled between her legs. "Oh, well," Damiano said. "All right, then. I'll carry it."

Piece by piece he flung over his back the saddle-bags, the wineskin, the sack of food, and the lute. Under each arm he stuffed a roll of blankets, out from one of which poked the silver head of his staff. Thus encumbered, Damiano staggered back across the field and into the town of San Gabriele.

A market is no fun for a penniless man. Damiano discovered this with surprise, for he was unused to being penniless.

There was blown glassware, both clear and in colors, some of it flawless and rounded perfect for alchemical use. Damiano was considering buying a lovely open tube, long as one's arm and thin as a soap bubble, when he realized he could not pay for it, could not transport it, and had no home in which to keep it. And there was a hat of golden marten that nearly matched the Delstrego colors. As Damiano hadn't a hat, he felt he rather deserved this one.

But worst of all were the pastries, dyed gold with saffron, blue with heliotrope, purple with amaranth, or green with parsley. There were little ones in the shapes of fish, and large ones square like castles. Some were filled with honey and some with quails. The odor of butter bubbling through wheat nearly drove Damiano to his bruised knees. Macchiata, whom he had controlled by prisoning her between his legs, whimpered with an agonized longing. He shooed her away.

"I'm sorry, little dear, but we have no money."

She licked her hairy lips. "Maybe the man will give us some anyway, because we're hungry."

Damiano snorted. "Not likely. Besides, we're not really hungry. We ate not four hours ago—cheese and bread. We just want what smells good." The dog whimpered agreement.

They passed a juggler, who had a chair teetering upon his cap of bells, and six zucchinis describing a complex orbit between the poles of his hands. Damiano regarded the man with respect, especially when he noticed the wooden bowl in front of the performer, half-filled with copper.

Damiano leaned against the white, warm wall of a stable. "We don't belong here," he whispered to the dog. "We can't eat, drink, or sleep at the inn, presuming there is one in this little place. We should just be on our way."

"Oh, no, Master," Macchiata crooned. "I'm tired, and Festelligambe is tired, and in all this crowd someone will surely drop something.

"I'll share it all with you, no matter how big or little," she concluded. Smiling ruefully, Damiano slung off his burdens and rested them against the wall.

"And Damiano's tired, too," he admitted. "Though he shouldn't be, with a long journey yet to go." He slid down the white stucco, squatting on his heels. "Still, I'd be willing to scrabble with you for the tail of one of those little wheaten fishes, even if it had dropped on the ground."

A shadow fell upon Damiano, and he found himself peering up at an urchin of indeterminate age and with the fair coloring of most of Northern Italy, topped by fox-colored hair. Damiano greeted him with a friendly flash of teeth.

The boy hesitated in response. Possibly he was deciding whether to use the familiar or the polite on this well-dressed stranger who was hunkering against the wall.

"Did that dog talk?" the boy inquired suspiciously.

Damiano nodded. "But she rarely talks to strangers."

The child was wearing a grown man's woolen shirt, which hung so long over his legs he was covered as closely as a woman. He sat down two feet from Macchiata and subjected her to scrutiny. The ugly white dog returned the favor, and her neck hairs bristled.

"'T'sokay, dog," said the boy, scowling fiercely. "I like you."

Macchiata's anger subsided into confusion. She licked her already-wet nose.

"What'r you doing here, mister? You don't live in San Gabriele, and you aren't selling or buying anything."

Damiano regarded the ragged boy more closely. "How do you know I'm not selling or buying?"

The youngster produced a true Italian shrug: one that used the eyebrows as much as the shoulders. "I been watching you. I know you don't buy anything, and you don't have anything anybody'd want to buy. So I guess you're just sitting there wishing you had two sous to scrape together."

His amusement at the boy's perception sparked both Damiano's smile and his confidence. "You are quite right, my young observer. Actually, I am of a sanguine temperament, so I was trying to think of a scheme by which I could make two sous to scrape together, or more exactly, to buy a buttered wheaten fish."

The child thumped his wiry buttocks on the ground next to Damiano. "I've been there," he said, nodding sagely. "I've been there. Why not have the dog talk? She don't have to quote Dante, or anything. Just to have her answer would bring in real silver."

Macchiata wilted visibly. She hid her nose behind her master's heel. He stroked her side.

"Macchiata is many things," he stated. "She is a ratter, an alchemist's assistant, a great traveler, and the friend of angels. You might not believe it to look at her, but she saved my life not a week ago, vanquishing three brigands who were bent on murder! But whatever she is, she is not a public performer."

The boy listened to this paean with his head cocked, as though to say whether he believed or not was his own business. "But you, mister, are a man of quality, by your clothes and also by the way you talk. Surely you have something the people want—if not a golden ring, then at least a rare skill or two."

Damiano's glance slid from the soiled small face to the road. "I have no gold rings, unfortunately. But I do have certain abilities. I can assay gold—with the proper equipment. And I can treat illness in men and animals— but again, not without medicines. I can clear the evil from bad wells and open locks that are stuck and find lost jewelry and cows"—Damiano's voice caught unexpectedly—"and cows.

"I can do many things, little friend. But I am used to having clients come to my house and request me to do them. I have never learned to . . . promote myself."

He watched the scorn on the boy's face turn to outright disbelief. "I speak the truth, philosopher. Watch—I can make myself disappear." Damiano nudged his left hand into the bedroll until his fingers touched the shoe of his staff. In a moment, he was not there.

In another moment, he was. "Stop! My friend and adviser! Don't go; I promise I won't do it again." The boy froze two steps into his flight. "You *can* disappear! You're a witch!"

Mildly, Damiano admitted to it. "Yes, I am a witch, among other things. But I'm not a street-corner sorcerer. I lived in Partestrada in a decent tower my grandfather built. There was occupation there, and it kept me comfortable. But Partestrada—or perhaps you have heard?"

The boy nodded and spat into the street. "Has changed hands. Thank Gabriele that his town is too small and too high in the hills to interest Pardo and his free company."

Damiano peered bleakly down the street, with its babble and smell. "You can never be certain of that. But as I was saying, I don't brew love-charms, and I don't engage in cursing. What effects I can produce tend to terrify people, rather than amuse them. Yet this little lady and myself have a strong desire for hot pastries. What shall I do?"

Then Damiano's eyes narrowed. "Perhaps, with effort, I could float six zucchinis in the air and pretend to be juggling them, but that smacks of..."

"What's this?" the youngster interrupted casually, knocking one knuckle against the glossy rounded back of the lute. "Can you play it?"

"The lute," said Damiano, stunned by the obvious. "Yes. I can play it. But I've never played for money. I don't know if I can."

The boy shrugged again. "The people here aren't very critical. But then, neither are they very generous. You can only try."

Damiano took the instrument onto his lap and tuned it. "Music for money," he murmured. "If you knew my teacher, philosopher..."

The little *liuto* was true-toned and clear. The boy leaned forward at the first notes. "Maybe I do. I know all the musicians who come through. And the acrobats, too. What's his name?"

"Raphael," answered Damiano shortly, for he was engaged in salting the melody with counterpoint, and he was not used to talking and playing together.

"Nope. Don't know him."

Chapter 10

The fingerboard was cold and slick beneath his fingers as his hand spidered its way through the melodies. He was not so out of practice as he had thought, and the familiar patterns came to him like old friends greeted in a strange place.

The pale winter sun seemed warm to a man who had spent the last week trudging through snow. He stretched his legs in front of him, in the hope that his boots might dry. Marketers passed by, their feet smacking through patches of mud. A matron of middle years stepped over Damiano's legs; her skirts dragged against his knees.

"Pinch that thing!" cried the redhead of San Gabriele, with the authority of a musical expert. "Let the whole town hear it!"

Damiano was no performer, or he had not thought he was, but he was well taught. He pinched the little lute, and at least a reasonable portion of the town could hear. All the old tunes—the simple, conservative airs and dances that would not have offended even dirty Marco—he played them all and he played them again.

"Louder!" cried his single listener. Damiano smiled thinly.

"This is a lute, not a bagpipe," he grumbled, but he obeyed. When he glanced up, the ragamuffin child was dancing a gavotte. No one had ever danced to his music before—not even Macchiata. His own booted toes were tapping together.

"Where's your hat?" A tall young woman loomed over him.

Red hair, a color not too rare in the more northern Italies, seemed to run in San Gabriele, for this one had hair like copper wire that hung in spiral curls down her back. Her green dress stretched tautly over her bosom, and the curve of her hips was emphasized by a belt of amber, ending in a tiny crucifix that swayed back and forth in front of Damiano's eyes. "How do you expect to make money without putting a hat out in front of you?"

Damiano stared at the crucifix, enthralled by its terribly inappropriate motions. "If I put out a hat, Signorina," he said haltingly, "will you drop a coin in it?"

She giggled as though he had said something witty. "I'm a poor woman, Signore. By your appearance, you ought to be dropping your coins into my bowl instead!"

Damiano's face flushed, and even the palms of his hands turned pink. But though his fingers stumbled, he did not lose the beat. "Fortune is fickle, beautiful lady, and yesterday's velvet purse hangs empty. Fortune is also jealous of beauty, and she uses time as her claw." He came down hard on the last downbeat of the dance and damped all the strings. His dark eyes flashed as he glanced up at the wanton. "Take care, Signorina." She stepped back, swaying, for real wit was an article she was not used to, especially on so serious a subject. Yet she lifted her chin disdainfully.

"Seminarians do not usually play the lute on street corners, black eyes."

Damiano shrugged. "I'm no more a seminarian than you are a nun, bold lady with eyes of green." Those green eyes dragged a smile from him, almost against his will.

She smirked at the wall over his head. "Then you're very little of the seminarian indeed," she said airily.

The urchin, who had stood unnoticed, following this conversation, now strode forward. "Enough! Enough, Evienne—you get in the way of paying customers. This man has a living to make, and he's not your sort of fellow at all. Go your way..." And he put one grubby hand unceremoniously against the small of her back and attempted to propel her along the street. With a scowl she slapped his hand away. "You touch me, Gaspare, and you will be floating in a well before morning!"

The youngster showed his teeth to her belligerence. "Yes? You'll stab me with your hairpin while I sleep, maybe? But that would do you no good, nor me either. And this gentleman would still not be your sort of fellow at all!"

Then he continued in more civilized tones. "Be reasonable, Evienne. Would you like me to get in between you and your work? To walk beside you when you are so beautifully displaying your wares, as though I were a jealous lover..."

"You, Gaspare? Everyone in this stinking village knows better than that!" With a toss of her head and a final wild swing of the crucifix, Evienne stalked away. Damiano watched her progress along the street and then stared with no great gratitude at the dirty face of his deliverer.

The boy made a flat, emphatic gesture of the hand. "That one's no good," he stated. "No good at all. You'll get nothing from her."

"I didn't want anything from her," Damiano answered quietly, hoping it was the truth.

Gaspare's eyes narrowed. "I mean, she won't even sleep with you; she's that mercenary. She goes from town to town on market days, because San Gabriele's too small to support a full-time whore."

Damiano's ears were prickling like sunburn. "Still, she was correct in what she said." He leaned sideways and shoved one hand into a leather pack, where he rummaged blindly. "We need a hat. Or this..." and he pulled out the wooden soup bowl that was both plate and cup for his travels. As he set it before him he stared down at his boots, for he was proud and had never before had to ask for money.

He played the old pieces through one more time, listening to young Gaspare spin and cavort before him, in the steps of the bransle and the lascivious saraband. Damiano's right hand was becoming looser minute by minute. The movement felt sure and practiced, and the sun above was yellow. Damiano swept into the French music—the music of contrasting lines.

The thump and patter of feet was stilled, but the musician didn't raise his head. He was lost in the intricacies of the many-parted music, and the rhythms were leading him as they never had before. As he played he mumbled and hissed to himself, wordless encouragement. But he was beyond the need for en-

couragement now, and if Gaspare called out to him,
Damiano did not hear.

Raphael—Raphael should hear this one day, for it
was the fruit of all his teaching. But no—placed before
his angelic teacher, Damiano knew he would stammer
and halt once more, whispering the strings as timidly
as a young girl. The difference was that here no one
knew him as Damiano, the good boy who was learning
to play the lute. Nor as Delstrego, the witch who killed
fifty men with terror. Here he was—he was whatever
he showed the people he was.

Redheaded, dirty Gaspare was kneeling in front of
him, slack jawed. "By Gabriele himself!" the boy
exclaimed. "What game were you pulling on me, asking
how you're to earn your bread? The new music!"

"Ah? You have heard contrapuntal music up here
in San Gabriele? It doesn't offend men's ears?"

Gaspare flung over the market a look of ripe scorn.
"Here? I haven't spent my whole life *here*, my friend.
But how can ears that hear nothing sweeter than the
bleating of goats be offended by what comes out of the
lute? Play on!"

Damiano raised his hand to obey, when a gleam
against the black wood of the bowl caught his eye.
"Where did these come from," he asked stupidly, nudging
the two split pennies with his forefinger. "Did you put
them in, Gaspare?"

The boy's green eye was coldly tolerant. "If I had
money, would I be dancing my hams off on the street?
That came during your last song. Leave it sit; maybe it
will breed."

The afternoon floated on rivers of tune. Intoxicated
by his own success as a lutenist, Damiano began to
sing. He had never before sung in public, or even for
his teacher, yet Macchiata had been right in saying he
had a good voice.

The bottom of the entertainer's bowl turned brick
red, lined with coppers tarnished by long residence in
sweaty, peasant hands. The glances he spared toward it

were filled with an astonished pride, as though the poor handful was the price of a kingdom. Damiano discovered that he garnered more money by his singing than by his lute playing, though singing was by far the easier of the two. He sang till he was hoarse.

His throat burned. He broke a treble string. The sun was westerly, and Damiano rubbed his face in his hands.

"Enough," he croaked.

"More than enough," sighed Gaspare, and he leaned against the warm wall, elbowing Macchiata aside. The boy's face had been washed by sweat. "The market is done for the day. Let's divide up the wealth!"

With a sly grin Damiano picked out of the bowl four ruddy coins. "This should be enough," he mumbled, and stood on legs stiff from disuse. "I'll be right back," he said, and darted away.

To the young man's immense and endless disappointment, the pastry stall on the next corner, which had filled the surrounding air with temptation, was gone. Nothing remained but postholes and the prints of the town dogs that had scoured away the last crumbs.

"The baker quits early," said Gaspare, coming up behind Damiano, "because he has to get up every morning in the middle of the night."

"You knew that?" asked Damiano wearily. "But I told you I was trying to get money for . . ."

Gaspare slapped Damiano's shoulder in comradely fashion, a gesture that required him to stand on tiptoe. "I forgot. You get carried away, dancing. But never mind that, my friend. What we have here"—he jingled a worn but serviceable leather pouch—"will buy us both dinner at any house in the town."

San Gabriele appeared tired and empty as the bright stalls were folded away and tied into bundles, and the unsold produce packed again to ride the ox wains home. Damiano led his new colleague back to the stable wall where Macchiata was guarding his gear.

"I always marvel," he commented, "at how quickly a market can disappear and become just an ordinary town again." He lowered himself onto the imprint in the dust, shaped like an upside-down heart, that showed where he had spent the afternoon. The sun crawled sideways along the side street, so low that buildings blocked it. Soon the saw-blade of the mountains would cut it through. Damiano pulled free his mantle, intending to wear it, but he noticed Gaspare shivering in his sweat. He threw the fur over the boy's bony frame.

"Here," grunted Damiano, offhand. "Save your money. I'll show you something that will surprise you." He dug into his store of food and came up with half a romano, a loaf, a piece of salt-pork, and a leathery withered trout. The cheese he divided into three pieces and the pork into two. The hard bread he used as trenchers.

"We're not poor," he admitted, waving to include the dog. "Merely penniless. And we wanted hot pastry, Macchiata and I. Well, so what? Here's to a full stomach, a full pocket, and a wonderful afternoon!" Damiano filled his mouth with rough red wine, after which he deposited the sloshing bag on Gaspare's lap, where it sat and wiggled like a puppy.

Gaspare asked no questions; he drank. And he ate Damiano's simple food with appetite. But when he was finished, or at least had slowed down, he spilled the coins in the dust of the street and divided the pile in two. He had a practiced eye for the value of liras, broken florins, francs, pfennigs, and weights of lead, and his division was eminently fair. "You owe me two," he said when he was done. "You took four coppers out of the bowl for cakes and you still have them."

Damiano blushed. "Those four coins are all I want," he insisted. "For memory's sake."

Gaspare shot him a glance of disgust and spat on the wall. "Do you really want to insult me that bad? Or are you merely an innocent from birth?

"Besides—if you leave the pile with me, I'll have to share with Evienne, unless she has had better luck. Which I doubt."

"With E-Evienne? The whore?" Damiano stuttered. "Do you mean..." and his voice trailed off, for he could think of no delicate way to phrase his question. The boy seemed hardly old enough to employ her services, and far too hungry to spend his little bit of money in that manner.

"I mean she is my sister, and the only family I have, may Gabriele pray for me!" As the boy spoke he was dropping his harvest into the leather bag.

"But you said she was worthless."

Gaspare peered at Damiano from under a ragged red brow. "She is," he stated. "She can't make a decent whore no matter how long she's at it. You saw her today, wasting time with a musician while the town is full of fat peasants with full pockets. Evienne is like me in that way—we are too civilized for our own good."

The boy obviously enjoyed Damiano's discomfiture. "I think maybe you are one of God's innocents, my friend. What's your name, eh? When you are famous, I want to be able to say I danced with you."

Damiano chuckled, opened his mouth, and then closed it again. "If I tell you my name, Gaspare, I may never be able to play the lute for you again."

Gaspare's breath hissed in. "I thought so. You play by magic!"

"No. Not magic. Just human nature. You see, I don't usually play the lute so... spiritedly. But today I forgot myself. If I tell you my name, it will remind me."

The boy burst out laughing, and the scarlet cloak slipped to the ground. Damiano felt a silly smile stretching over his face. He dropped his eyes to his knees, which were propped in front of him. "Just call me Festilligambe," he mumbled.

"Festilligambe! Is that your nickname, musician? It's hardly elegant."

Damiano shook his head. "That's my horse's nickname. And he's really a rather elegant horse; I gave him that name after a storm, when he tried to crawl into bed with me and it felt like sleeping on a pile of sticks.

"And speaking of Festilligambe—*Dominus Deus!* I left him in the field with the oxen, all this time ago. I'd better go." Damiano rose and began the task of piling his gear once more on his back. Gaspare helped him. "I'm not used to having a horse," Damiano added. "I never should have left him alone so long."

"No. You'll be lucky if he's still there," the boy agreed. "I hope you at least tied him well."

Damiano shook his head abstractedly, while he peered about him to see what he had forgotten. "No. I don't own a rope, and anyway I'm better at untying things..."

He turned then and stared full at Gaspare, as though he were trying to memorize the freckled, peaked face. "Gesu be with you," he said. "Gesu and the Virgin. I hope we meet again."

Gaspare glared, as though parting itself were an insult. "Where are you going, musician? Don't you need a dancer, maybe, and a man to pass the hat?"

Damiano blinked, startled, and almost overbalanced beneath his heavy burdens. "I'm going to the lakes of Lombardy, Gaspare," he said, "where the witch Saara dwells. I won't have time to play the lute on my journey, except around the fire at night, and there'll be no one to hear me at all."

The urchin's scowl grew more fierce. "Why? You could make a name for yourself with that lute, and it wouldn't be Festilligambe."

Damiano shrugged, and his gear rattled in sympathy. He took a step backward, away from Gaspare's disappointment. "I'm doing it to save my city," he explained in a whisper. "If I could do that by playing the lute, things would be much better, but..." He

shrugged again, noisily, and turned away from the boy
and the street corner in San Gabriele.

At his feet Macchiata spoke, breaking a silence that
had lasted all the afternoon. "He gets upset very easily," she remarked. "I thought maybe he was going to
hit you. Then, of course, I would have bitten him." She
sighed and trotted on.

"You must understand, little dear, that he is poor.
And being poor is one continuous disappointment.

"But even if he is poor, Macchiata, our Gaspare is
never mean. He is generous and fair, and a lover of the
arts, besides—which is a quality that runs in his family."

At the top of the path sloping south from the
village, Damiano stopped to drink in the sight of the
quiet, tended fields, where the colors were already
growing dim. As a man of his time, he found a greater
beauty in tilled soil than in wild grass, and he favored
orchards over forests. But then, in his travels he had
seen far more wild than tended land, and he knew
how hard it was to break the earth with a hoe.

Perhaps he would set his camp where he had left
the gelding: by the paling of live poplars to the right of
the road. The weather promised to be fair—though
Alpine weather was notoriously faithless regarding its
promises. It only remained now to see whether
Festelligambe had also proved faithless.

Damiano peered ahead as he clambered over the
roughly broken soil. He touched his staff to sharpen his
vision and could see what might be the dark outline of
the horse against the trees, silhouetted against the
setting sun. But if it was the horse, it possessed light
spots that were bouncing about in most unhorselike
fashion.

Then the witch's vision cleared (the moon was
waxing), and at the same moment Macchiata started a
growl in her belly that threatened to shake the earth.
Damiano stared, and understood, and finally broke out
laughing. He stepped steadily forward toward the pop-

lar fence. "Don't get upset, Macchiata. This is really quite funny," he said.

The black outline was indeed Festilligambe, while the white shape bouncing upon it was not part of the horse at all, but a frustrated human rider, in shirtsleeves, who had tied a crude rope bridle upon the animal and was now bounding in his seat while his heels kicked, his bony hands slapped, and in other ways he tried to encourage the horse to move.

The black gelding, however, stood with its legs braced against the earth as though it planned never to move again. Its little ears were laid back as flat as a cat's, and its liquid eyes were rimmed with white.

"Did I doubt you, noble steed?" whispered Damiano, as with one hand he held Macchiata by the scruff, lest she interfere with the comedy. He crouched to the earth and let his packs slide off his back. At that moment the man on the horse raised his head a fraction.

Damiano choked on his own breath, and his eyes widened as though he had seen a ghost (or more correctly, as though an ordinary man had seen a ghost). For in that fair and somewhat sullen set of features he recognized a man he had thought never to see again: the uncommunicative golliard, Jan Karl. And the thief had not seen him.

This was too wonderful. Quietly Damiano bent and took his staff in his hands, whispering the words of the spell that was almost his favorite, becoming invisible to prolong the wonder of the moment. Then he stepped confidently forward.

Jan Karl—or Till Eulenspiegel, as he seemed to call himself—was no danger to a wary man, let alone one with the powers of Damiano. His thin, soiled student's shirt hung on his starved shoulders as on a hanger of wood. His lank fair hair was brown with dirt and lay plastered against his face, which had been touched by that shade of gray-purple that indicated too much exposure to the cold. A rag wrapped two fingers of the thief's left hand; Damiano suspected frostbite. He remembered the golliard's frantic flight into the night, sans coat or mantle.

He remembered the bundle of letters he still carried in his pack, arrow-pierced and written in a strange tongue. And Damiano had not forgotten what Macchiata had said: this thief, at least, had not wanted to kill him. As he stood in thought beside the tableau of obdurate horse and ineffectual rider, the horse became aware of him. Festilligambe's cavernous nostrils twitched and his ears revolved like mill wheels. Macchiata, who leaned invisibly against her invisible master's calf, gave an answering whuff. With an audible snap, Damiano broke the spell.

The horse bucked in shock, and Jan Karl toppled from its bare back to the ground. A totally impossible figure loomed over the golliard, outlined black as Satan against the light of the setting sun. It growled like a dog, or somewhere a dog was growling, and the young blond's misadventures had made him very sensitive to that sound. *"Lieber Gott!* Spare me!" he wailed in a mixture of German and French, covering his face with his discolored hands. "It is all too much!" he added in bastard Italian.

Damiano peered down at his fallen enemy from under a corrugated brow. He sighed, feeling an inappropriate stab of pity for the fellow and feeling ridiculous besides. Even the less forgiving dog forgot to growl, running her tongue over her bristly lips and plopping her backside onto the broken soil. Damiano cleared his throat. "You didn't do as much," he said, in tones that were meant to sound menacing and came out more querulous, "to spare an innocent stranger who thought to be your friend."

At the sound of Damiano's voice the northerner raised up on his elbows, his purple visage paling to one of white terror. "No. You're dead! *Donner und Pfannkuchen!* Do me no harm—it wasn't I who killed you. It was that damned Frenchman, and I only met him in Chamonix..." The blond began to cry, in great, hysterical sobs.

Damiano shifted from foot to foot. "I know," he began lamely, but his words went unheard. He started again, louder.

"I know it wasn't you who killed... I mean *tried* to kill me. I'm not dead, you know," he added. "Ghosts don't generally look like this. But that's no thanks to you."

Karl's face went blank, then wary. "Not dead? Then why are you haunting me?"

Damiano snorted. "I'm not haunting you. That's my horse you're trying to steal."

With a groan and a thump, Jan Karl fell back against the earth. "*Donner und*...Blast me now. Get it over with."

Seeing the scarecrow figure lying there, limp and theatrical before him, Damiano couldn't hold back his grin. But he turned his attention to Festilligambe the honor of whose word had created this situation. "You're a good fellow, Festilligambe," he whispered into the tiny black ear. "No need to stay planted any longer. Go shake your heels in the fields a bit, and then we'll eat."

The gelding made a stiff bound into the air, as though the strings that had held him had snapped. As he descended his teeth clicked playfully into the corona of Damiano's hair, and then he was off, barreling across the empty field, sending sprays of dirt behind him.

"Eh! Watch you don't catch a leg in a hole!" Damiano shouted after him, then he turned back to his captive, whom he half expected to find gone—whom he half *hoped* to find gone.

The golliard lay as he had before, passive and shivering on the ground: the very picture of oppression. Macchiata lay next to him, her tail wagging in quiet satisfaction. "Wh...what are you going to do with me?" Karl blurted. Damiano regarded the man irritably.

"Well, since you won't run away. Or can't," he amended, sparing a glance at the dog, "I guess we'll have to do something. Let me see your hand."

Karl did not oblige. "Are you going to cut it off?"

"That may not be necessary." Damiano pulled the bandaged member from the blond's side; Karl had little strength to resist him. "At least not all of it." As he unwound the rag, the prisoner stiffened and cried out. The inner layers of cloth were blackened with dry blood.

The little finger was dead, the ring finger gone to the second knuckle. The hand itself was swollen and veined with red and black like a small map. Damiano swallowed, swept through once more by his ungovernable pity. He took a deep breath and spoke as harshly as he could. "This was going to kill you, man. Didn't you know?"

Karl's water-blue eyes widened. "But it doesn't hurt much, like it used to. With all the miserable things that have happened in the past ten days, I haven't had time to . . ."

"Eh?" Damiano interrupted, staring gently into the distance, at nothing. "It's been a hard week for you, has it? Well, things run in cycles, like the moon. And the moon is increasing. Wait here and don't move," he commanded, rising to his feet, "while I set up camp. This place is as good as any, as long as the husband-man doesn't show up brandishing a pitchfork." Damiano picked his long-legged way over the hummocks of soil to his pile of gear. He returned burdened and threw a blanket down.

"Here," he said. "Wrap yourself in this and stop shaking." When the wondering Karl had done so, Damiano plunked the wineskin on top of him. "Start drinking now, you skinny Swissman. You're going to need it later."

Picking up the leather sack with his right hand, Karl obeyed, asking no questions. After two or three good swigs he stopped to gasp air, his nose prickling

with the fumes of alcohol. "I'm Dutch," he announced.
"Not Swiss. And I'm a long way from home."

Damiano paused in the process of driving a stake
of poplar into the ground. He leaned his hammer-rock
against the butt of the stake and cocked an interested
eye at Karl. "That's true," he admitted. "I know very
little about that country, except that it is wet. But with
two rotting fingers you would never have returned to
the Low Countries. Nor would you have ever read
another letter from your dear old mother."

"My mother died when I was born," said Karl,
and he took another drink, or series of drinks.

Damiano shrugged as he pounded. "Sweetheart,
then. Whosever letters you keep in a bundle in your
pack." Seeing the dawning of slow understanding on
Karl's face, Damiano chuckled and dove into his sad-
dlebag, from which he pulled the faded, pierced bundle of letters. He tossed them onto the blond's lap.

"They've shared my dangers with me, Herr
Eulenspiegel. That's an arrow hole through the middle,
which ought also to have pierced my chest."

"This saved you?" murmured Karl, examining his
little bundle with an intensity that was already half
drunken.

"No, not exactly. It was a volume of Petrarch that
saved me, for it was bound in wood. I owe that, too, to
our convivial first meeting, for I found it in the sack of
one of your friends when I woke the next morning. It
was a bad morning, that...." Damiano finished the
stake with an extra-hard thump of the stone.

"For me too," admitted Karl, whom wine was
making more garrulous. "I lost my fingers when the
sun came up, because I lay down in the snow. They say
you should never do that, no matter how tired you
are."

Damiano nodded. "Look on the bright side, Jan.
At least we're still alive. Both of us. What about the
other two?"

Karl's brow furrowed stupidly. "You know, I never

saw them again. All I know is that I turned right at the crossroads." He swigged once more. The wineskin, though very large, was beginning to appear flabby. Damiano looked with approval. With the night's work that was in store for him, he hoped the blond would pass out.

"They might have continued up to Aosta," reflected Damiano. "But when I came there a day later, I didn't see them. And Macchiata's nose is good. . . ."

"They probably went back west, the way we'd come," suggested Karl. "To Provence. That makes most sense. This is a terrible country!"

While Damiano made a comfortable camp, Karl talked. He talked a lot. The volume of his monologue more than made up for his taciturnity on the night of their first aquaintance. He related to Damiano the story of his youth on the fishing boats at Amsterdam: he had been a poor boy but brimming with scholastic promise. He told how he had at length journeyed to Avignon, to study Church history where the pope sat. But knowledge did not come for free, nor did bread or the necessary roof. The Dutch lad had borne three years of privation and had reached no other heights than to be elected king of the pre-Lenten fete, when all went topsy-turvy for a week and the clerks ruled the roost. It was after that that he realized he had neither the right nationality nor the right friends to gain advancement in Innocent's church.

"Nor the right temperament," Damiano added silently, looking critically at the figure wrapped in the rough blanket.

Karl didn't notice his host's sharp glance, as he explained how, in great bitterness and with very little money, he had set out east to try his fortunes in old Rome itself. In the pass he had met the youth Pierre Paris, whom he had known slightly at the university, and the Breton who claimed to love Petrarch. Paris had devised the story that the three of them were retracing the poet's journey to Milan, though it was a silly tale, and the reality was that both of the others were thieves.

Damiano's hands were full of tinder. He chuckled as he sparked the evening's fire. "Both of the others?" he echoed, and turned his head to Karl.

The blond Dutchman nodded solemnly, closed his eyes and fell into a peaceful, childlike sleep.

Leaving the dog to guard both camp and patient, Damiano returned to San Gabriele, where without meeting either Gaspare or Evienne, he filled the empty wine bag at the village well. As he trudged back down the hill he could feel the chill of the deeply shadowed earth rising up through his boots, and his little campfire winked at him like the eye of a friend.

He was glad he had eaten before this necessity arose; he would not want to eat later. As he approached the light he smelled the alarming odor of burning hair. He dashed the last few yards into camp, the wine bag leaping in his arms like a live thing, only to find a picture of unbroken peace.

Macchiata lay spread-eagled over the remaining bedroll, two paws on either side, as though she were riding a log. Her dreamy gaze was fixed on her charge, Karl. The gelding quietly stood close by the fire, leaning into the warmth.

"Festilligambe," cried Damiano indignantly. "Get away from there! You're burning your tail!" He dropped the bag on the ground by Macchiata and darted around the campfire to where the big animal was now examining its disfigured tail with calm wonder.

Damiano grabbed a handful of mane and pulled the black head around. Fixing an ear in each hand, he glared at it.

"You," he pronounced, "are a most unhorselike horse." The gelding swished a tail that was reduced to half its former splendor.

"If you catch on fire, what am I to do? There isn't enough water in the entire well to put out a horse!" In response—perhaps in apology—Festilligambe raised his muzzle and lipped Damiano on the nose. It wasn't pleasant to see the yellow, boxlike teeth so near to one's face; Damiano turned away.

He had brought nothing resembling a medicinal dressing in his pack, and early winter was not the season to gather herbs. Nonetheless, Karl's fingers would have to come off, and Damiano's father had been known to resort to hot packs and lye soap when nothing else was available. The young witch filled his only pot with water and set it into the fire. Into the water went one of his two linen undershirts, torn into strips. He pulled a bundle of folded cloth out from the bottom of his pack and carefully unwrapped a little knife.

It was not terribly strong or sharp, because it was intended more for witchcraft than surgery, and its blade was silver. The handle was crystal, and was cut with all the phases of the moon, the full moon sitting at the top, like a tiny sword's pommel.

For a few moments he did no more than to kneel on the blanket by Karl, the knife resting in his palm, while his mind settled. He had never done such an operation without an effective sleeping draught for the patient, without compresses, clean linen, and a few men to hold the sufferer still should the narcotic fail. He would have to be very sure.

With his right hand—the hand that never touched the knife—he reached out and yanked a tuft of dry grasses. These he sprinkled over Karl's emaciated limbs, while he whispered a spell of binding. The gray strands clung like so many fine ropes, but as they did so his vision blurred a bit and his feet fell asleep beneath him.

Binding was a very expensive spell.

Next he consecrated both the knife and his hands to the coming task. The silver blade briefly grew too hot to touch. He twisted the knife in his fingers till it had cooled.

He lifted Karl's gangrenous hand and secured it between his knees. The sleeper didn't move. With the bright blade, no longer than a beech leaf, Damiano pierced the living skin beneath the suppuration that had been Karl's little finger. He cut around the knuckle joint.

A little spell to staunch the bleeding. Another to stir the breeze (this job didn't smell too good). Pray God this poor sinner didn't wake. The tendon and cartilage broke with small popping sounds, like sticks crackling in a fire. The blade was speckled with crimson, and thick, unhealthy blood ran down the white arm and onto Damiano's knees. The finger bone pulled free and gleaming out of its socket.

The ring finger he took off at the big joint, but after a glance at the flesh exposed, Damiano shook his head and cut again, removing the whole of that finger as well.

When he was done, he regarded the raw wound gratefully. It was simple and clean and would be easy to wrap. He had left a fold of skin hanging on both the top and bottom of the hand, to wrap over the exposed bone and flesh. Later that skin would probably fall way, to be replaced by knotted scar tissue, but for now it would close the wound.

But before he closed it Damiano held Karl's hand out from the blanket and freed the blood to flow. The oozing became a fountain that spurted with Karl's heartbeat. He heard Macchiata whine from her perch on the bedroll; the smell of human blood upset her.

After allowing the hand to bleed for half a minute, Damiano pinched the wrist tightly and reapplied the spell.

The water by now was bubbling and hissing. With the blade of the knife Damiano fished into the pot and skewered a length of linen. When he offered the cloth to the night air, a phantom of white steam coiled up from it. "That's not what ghosts look like, either," muttered the witch, and while the cloth was still hot enough to redden skin, he slapped it over Jan's bloody hand.

Then Damiano looked away from his surgery, away from the steaming rag and the three blackened stumps on the ground with the shaft of white bone protruding. He let his eyes rest on the fire for a moment, then raised them to the early stars.

The sky was a field of radiant indigo. The breeze, growing colder minute by minute, seemed to sweep directly down from that eternal, unchanging expanse. In actuality the air flowed down from the Alps, of course, but that was much the same. He let the night close his eyes.

"I would really rather not be involved in this," he whispered aloud. "He may still die.

"And there are others I would rather share my campfire with than this sullen, craven Dutchman." He longed suddenly for the presence of Raphael, so much like the night sky himself. It was on his lips to call out to the angel, to beg him not for a lesson but for a few minutes inconsequential chat by the fire. But he remembered the dying woman in Sous Pont Saint Martin. Raphael was not permitted to play a part in a mortal's trial or death, and here was poor, sly Jan Karl, his torn hand scalding under hot rags. He could wake at any moment, and it would be awkward, for he would wake screaming.

Besides, there was still the matter of his interview with the Devil. Could the archangel know what had passed between Damiano and Raphael's own, wicked brother? If so, he had not come by to ask for an explanation.

At least half the reason Damiano did not call Raphael was that he feared discovering the archangel would no longer come.

It was a weary night, for Damiano had to keep changing the hot packs. And it was a cold one, for Karl began to shiver uncontrollably and had to have both blankets. Before it got too late, Damiano rose, went into town and pounded on doors until he found a householder who would sell him more wine, at a terribly inflated price. He drank none of it himself, for he had to stay awake, but when, toward morning, Karl awoke (not screaming but weeping without pause), he forced it down the man's throat.

With sunrise, Karl became quiet. Damiano induced him to eat a piece of wine-soaked bread, and then another. He watched his patient with red and grainy eyes, thinking that it was odd to save a man's life and still not like him. "I can't stay with you, Jan," he said dully. "I'm on an errand that's very urgent to me."

Karl's face registered all the surprise his weakness allowed. "I didn't think you were going to. Why should you?"

Damiano sighed. He knew all the reasons he should remain: the wound was fresh, certain to bleed and apt to go sour, Karl was hungry and unable to work, even should any peasant take him on, and he, Damiano, had begun the job... But he set his jaw and peered over at the houses of the village, which were white and black with sunrise.

"I don't even know why you did this," added the Dutchman, as he stared fascinated at wet pinkish cloth that had taken the place of two fingers on his hand.

"It was necessary," said Damiano shortly, without looking around. "It's not the sort of thing I do for fun."

"Necessary for me, maybe," answered Karl with a sick little laugh. "But not for you. You didn't have to tend me, feed me, cover me..."

Damiano pulled up his knees, covered them with his folded arms and rested his chin on top. He was a long time answering.

"It's difficult—to learn to do a thing that not many people can do, like amputating fingers, and then to see a need for it and not to do it. You see? And then it is difficult to spend the time and effort on a man and them let him die for want of something simple.

"But I can't afford any more—time, that is. The world is full of distractions, and I must get to Lombardy

before the snows creep any lower. I'll leave you one of
those blankets and some coppers I made in San Gabriele.
Also the pot; if you neglect that wound, you'll certainly
die after all." Damiano's brow furrowed fiercely as an
idea occurred to him. An idea he distrusted. "Something more, Jan. There is a boy in San Gabriele named
Gaspare. He has red hair, and he comes about to my
shoulder. He's just a street urchin, but he has a genius
for making the best of things. He may be able to figure
out something you can do to earn your bread while you
recover and to help you on your way to Rome. He has
a sister, though, that..."

Damiano glanced over at Karl's wary eyes and
starved torso. He chuckled to himself. "Never mind
the sister. But, my dear cleric, I promise you that if you
mistreat this boy, or betray him in any way, you will
know what a curse is."

Karl was silent while Damiano rose and began to
break camp. His watery blue eyes followed Damiano
reflectively. Finally he spoke. "You're a very good man,"
he said. "Like the Samaritan, in Luke."

Damiano spun around with a face full of anger and
hurt. "Don't say such a thing. I am nothing like a good
man. I'm only...a mozzerella!"

Karl blinked in confusion. A short laugh burst out
of his throat. "A mozzarella? That's a cheese?"

"That's an Italian expression. It means..." Damiano
waved his hands in a gesture that explained nothing.
"A good man follows the commandments. I, on the
other hand, am merely softhearted. I cannot bear to eat
cows and pigs.

"—But I killed fifty men with witchcraft," he added,
and he slipped his packs over Festilligambe's elegant
back.

Karl made no answer.

Chapter 11

The road slipped east; it rolled up and down. Damiano
rode through a silence of trees. In a birch-covered
valley the sky above him was filigreed with bare branches.
Dead leaves, sodden after the autumn's rains, padded
the horse's hooves like cloth wrappings. The sun and
the trees wove a pattern of warm lace over Damiano's
head. He nodded sleepily with every step, as did
Festilligambe. Macchiata had nothing to say; she spent
the day in her nose.

The road tilted upward an hour before sunset. In
the distance Damiano could make out the crown of the
hill, with another, steeper rise behind it, black with
pine. He decided it was better to rest now and take the
climb fresh in the morning.

He brushed the dried sweat from the horse's flanks
with a boar-bristle brush that was also Macchiata's
brush and his own. The gelding's mane was tangled
and its tail a sorry sight. Before sunset Damiano gathered
wood and made a small fire, though without a pot he
had no way to cook on it. When he wrapped himself
for the night in blanket and mantle, the day's silence
was still unbroken.

Who was Saara, that he should be seeking her
across two Italies in early winter? Damiano knew very
little about her, but that little was more than most
Piedmontese knew, or most Lombards, for that matter.
He knew what his father had told him, long ago.

She had come out of the far north country, the
Fenland, in his father's youth, flying from war into

exile. Of the war, Damiano knew nothing. The exact
place of her exile he also did not know, though Guillermo
Delstrego had described it as a green hill, round as an
egg, set among the lakes of Lombardy. It was also
Delstrago who had told his son that Saara the Fenwoman
was the most powerful witch in all the Italies, perhaps
in all Europe. That was not an admission he would
have made easily.

In fact, Saara the Fenwoman (or Finn) was just
about the only other practicing witch whose name
Guillermo Delstrego let pass his lips: probably because
she dwelt too far away to be competition. He had
painted his son quite a colorful sketch of Saara, with
her braids and sing-song magic, and the birds all doing
her bidding. Being sentimental as he was, Damiano
had added his own pigments to the picture, believing
the Fenwoman to be beautiful as well as wise, and
merry and virtuous besides—or sometimes only merry.

Damiano let the gelding amble on while he sat on
its broad back and idly plucked his lute. For a week
they had traveled east: the young man in his ermine
and tangled hair, the elegant black horse, the ugly
white dog. Work and time had hardened the muscles of
the horse's back, but they had equally hardened the
rider.

Damiano had always been lean, though, and lean
and lazy or lean and tough, he looked much the same.
On Macchiata the difference was striking. She looked
every inch the fighter now, or the ratter at least, and
the bunched muscles of her thighs rippled beneath her
short hair. The fat she had lost made her triangular
head appear larger and heavier than ever. She spoke
less, following her master's lead, but she was in trim to
follow the horse all day.

Damiano's fingers spattered notes up the lute's
neck. The treble string squealed like a pig. The little
daisy-petal ears of the horse reversed, and it shook its
head.

"Eh, Festilligambe: You've become the critic?" mumbled Damiano. "Well, let me tell you, horse. You are no authority on music; you can't keep time. And if I could warm my hands up well, you would really hear something."

He raised his head and looked about him with a sigh. It was cold here, even south of the mountains. The forest of ash and oak was bare. But it was not drear to him, for he had the eyes of his father, and the moon was near the full. In the corner of his eye, beside the road, he saw a stir of the earth that meant a mouse was burrowing, and a gray gleam marked the winter nest of a rock dove. That splash of orange beneath a fallen log was neither leaves nor lichens but a fox. Damiano did not tell Macchiata.

The trees were sleeping, and their limbs creaked like the snoring of old men. Damiano imitated the sound, drumming his bass course with two fingers of his left hand, on the neck.

"If I had my way," he mused, "I'd travel like this from town to town on market days—to perdition with the higher knowledge. I'd rather make music than be wise."

Macchiata snorted, and a powder of dry leaves shot into the air. "I'd rather chase rabbits than be wise," she said.

"But you never catch them," countered her master. "Doesn't that frustrate you, little dear?"

Macchiata whuffled, sat down, and scratched the matter over. "Because I don't catch *this* rabbit," she said, "or *that* rabbit, doesn't mean I will never catch *any* rabbit."

Damiano had no answer for this. He returned to his own subject. "I really would like to find another market. Porto was a disappointment: all day playing for only a tankard of beer. And our supplies are getting lighter. I notice that every time I pick up the saddlebags. We must find Saara soon."

The dog turned to Damiano with a glance full of

anxiety. "Supplies, Master? You mean food?" Damiano nodded.

"How soon, Master? How many days is soon?"
Damiano frowned. "Just...soon," he replied.

Ludica was not holding a market, but it seemed to be a much larger town than Porto or San Gabriel. Perhaps it was larger than Partestrada. Leading Festilligambe down a cobbled street between buildings of stone, Damiano was impressed.

Ludica supported not one but two inns and a stable. Damiano left the gelding there, to enjoy for one night its fill of grain and mash. If he could not pay the keep by morning, he could surely redeem his horse with a linen undershirt.

The first inn was dim and empty. An old woman in the doorway regarded him with no great welcome. Damiano did not go in.

The second inn was called The Jolly Pilgrim. Its common room smelled like the cork of a wine bottle. The innkeeper was fat, and his black brows were the only hair on his head. He spoke staccato, with a sharp lilt, and by this Damiano knew he was in Lombardy at last. Damiano offered to play and sing in exchange for dinner and a bed, but after two minutes of bargaining he found he had promised also to cut wood for the fire and instead of a bed would get only the left side of the hearth.

Still, it was good to sit in a room, for a change, and to be warm, front and back. When the room filled up—with drinkers, travelers, and smoke—it felt even better to play the bransle and the saraband so that the men stamped their feet. Had he drunk all the wine that was bought for him, he would not have been able to see the strings, let alone pluck them, and one jolly pilgrim, a wool merchant who loved the vintage so much his cheeks had turned purple, gave Damiano a broken silver florin.

Best of all was to eat someone else's cooking—

cabbage and carrots and fresh pork in gravy, over a slice of black bread as thick as a man's wrist. And though Damiano couldn't eat the pork Macchiata was willing, and there was plenty of food for both.

The wool merchant called him Frenchie and laughed at the way Damiano slurred his words. Since the best of the new music was French, Damiano did not take offense or correct the man. Besides, it was not good sense for a Piedmontese to strut himself in Lombardy, where they who cannot swim are as proud of their lakes as the man of Turin is proud of the mountains he cannot even see.

In the morning he sought out the landlord and asked what that worthy knew of a woman named Saara.

The black eyebrows in the pink face gave the man's skepticism an eloquent frame. He stared and he sighed and he beckoned Damiano to follow him.

The yard of The Jolly Pilgrim was dusted with snow, and dry flakes like talc wavered through the air. Winter had followed Damiano into Lombardy. The bald landlord threw the hood of his tunic over his head. The steam of his breath obscured his features as he pointed up and beyond the town to where six hills stood clustered together, as if for warmth.

"See the Sisters?" asked the Lombard. His voice was sharp and harsh in Damiano's ears. "Which of them is different?"

Damiano squinted and peered, leaning on his staff. "Two of them are taller," he said. "Almost mountains. One of them is round topped and has no snow on the south side. What difference do you mean?"

The landlord stuck his hands up his sleeves. "Doesn't it seem the least bit strange to you, boy, that one hill among many, has no snow on it? And it never does. That's the hill of Saara, and she's a witch. The man is ill-advised who makes that climb."

Damiano didn't take his eyes from the high hills, where many hawks were flying circles in the gray air.

He smiled at his fortune. For here he was in Lombardy, not knowing when he had left the Piedmont, and chance or aid had dropped his desire into his lap. "I don't know if that's the result of witchcraft, benefactor. Notice that the green hill is protected from the north wind by both the taller hills. It would be the warmest, and the last to collect snow."

The fat Lombard took one step away from Damiano. He rumbled his throat and spat into the white powder. "Believe what you want, young Frenchman, but we who live here know what's what in our own backyards. Witchcraft is real under the sun or moon, no matter what you write in Latin in your books."

Damiano's eyes widened, for the man's misunderstanding of him was so complete he didn't know where to begin to correct it. But the landlord wasn't done.

"There was enother fellow like you who stopped here and asked for Saara, lutenist. He was a southerner with a sharp tongue and a sharp sword, and he disappeared into the witch's garden—that's what we call that slope of the hill—and was never seen again."

Damiano blinked and regarded that far patch of greenery with intense interest. "I have no sword," he murmured, as much to himself as to the landlord. "And, as for my tongue, I hope it is more honeyed than sharp, because I have to convince that lady to help me."

The Lombard laughed, and coughed, and spat. He left the one who he thought was a young French dandy, leaning on his prettified walking stick, his face a study in concentration, his curled black hair turning white with snow.

Damiano left the horse and the florin in the care of the stable keeper, and he and Macchiata started around the small lake that stood in between Ludica and the Sisters. It had been a while since he had done any amount of walking; his knees ached.

"I am still bruised," he said ruefully to the dog.

"Purple-and-black a week later. I wonder if that is
Satan's little joke, to remind me that I went down on
my knees before him. Though it was not my idea to do
so."

This was not the sort of conversation to interest
Macchiata. She trotted ahead along the path by the
water, her ears a-prick, her twiggy tail wagging stiffly
behind her. Damiano trudged behind, burdened with
packs, staff, and the lute, which he ought to have left
back at the inn. The snowfall was halfhearted and soon
died completely. By noon the sky was sudsy with white
clouds, and the travelers had come to the feet of the
hills.

On two of them the bare bones of rock were
exposed; these were the tall ones. Most of the rest were
weathered grassy domes, pale now with snow. The
middle hill, however, was clothed in timber, and the
south slope of it shone green. Through the gorse and
heather, a little path—no more than a goat track—led
toward it.

"This isn't difficult," Damiano mumbled, pushing
his way forward against the clinging brush. "There
must be somebody who visits here and keeps the way
passable."

Macchiata disappeared into the undergrowth; not
even her tail was visible. But Damiano could follow her
snuffling progress with his ears. "You know . . . little
. . . dear, he panted, as he fought through a waist-high
bramble. "If Saara is in truth an exile from her home,
our task may be easy. How could she not sympathize
with Partestrada?"

A black nose appeared, and then a white muzzle
hanging with burrs. "An exile is someone who was
chased out of home, Master? If this one got chased
away from her home, then how can she chase the
soldiers out of yours? I mean, she may not be fierce
enough."

Damiano stopped dead, his bags swaying at his
sides. "That's a thought, Macchiata. But we don't really

know the truth about Saara's home, only that my father said she was the most powerful witch in the Italies. And besides, here there will be two of us, she and I. And though I am not the most powerful witch in the Italies—and may not even be among the most powerful (how am I to know?)—I do know a few things."

"Of course you do, Master," attested the dog. She waggled over and placed one dirty white foot against Damiano's knee. He played with her ears while he examined the path ahead. It vanished under an arch of pines, dark as the door of a tomb. Damiano straightened and peered, then leaned on his staff and stared intently.

"There. Ahead is the gate to Saara's garden. Not welcoming, is it?

"But I smell magic," Damiano added, and strode forward.

Though it was dark within, it was also warmer, and Damiano could see well enough in the dim. The air was thick with the evergreen frankincense; like a church, it almost made one sneeze. The path wound steeply upward. Perhaps it was a goat path after all and had never been trod by man. But if it was a goat path, then there was something ahead besides pine forest, because a goat does not subsist on pine needles alone.

"It's a good thing we left Festilligambe behind," whispered Damiano. "He wouldn't do well on this road." The dog growled her own opinion.

There was light ahead, atop a rocky outcrop that reduced Damiano to climbing on hands and knees, with his staff wedged into his armpit. He winced each time the lute slapped down against his back, not for the pain of it, but for the instrument's sake. When he reached the crest, sunlight blinded him a moment. Then he saw his hands, scratched red and coated with a honey-dust of crushed sandstone. He sat up and allowed the dog to lick his hands clean.

"Look, Macchiata," he cried. "The witch's garden.
I wish it were my own!"

As a garden, it was very wild, for the grass grew
knee-high and bobbed its wheaty tails in the breeze,
and black logs and branches choked the little stream
that wandered left and right over the meadow, cutting
it into room-sized islands. Wind-carved rocks lay scattered
about, not by chance, but as though tossed by a carefully artless hand. Above rose a stand of birch, still
holding its yellow leaves, which rattled together like
flags of paper.

But as a wilderness, it was sweet and comfortable,
for the sun shone softly over grass that still held a
touch of green, and flowers dotted the meadow: late
asters and early crocuses, bronze and white. The standing stones themselves looked inviting. They were colored a deep bricklike red and pitted and hollowed all
over, so that they carried an assortment of tiny gardens
on their backs, each harboring three stalks of grass,
perhaps, or a cornflower.

Damiano felt the sun touch his lips. It made him
yawn. "We'll stop here," he said to Macchiata. "Maybe
all day. We can eat lunch on the south side of that
biggest rock."

Macchiata agreed to the proposal, and the two of
them walked through the sea of soft grass toward the
furthermost standing stone, which looked like a seat
with a huge, scallop-shell back and velvety moss over
the cushions.

At the foot of the red stone grew a thicket of
rosemary, dotted now with blue flowers and droning
with bees. "It's Dami, golden people," announced the
witch as he climbed. "Out of the way so I don't crush
you and so you don't sting me." Obediently the insects
circled wide of him.

This was a chair for a giant. Damiano could lie full
length on the cushions of moss and still have room for
his baggage and a restless dog. They ate stale bread
and cheese and a carrot Damiano had stolen from the

inn kitchen. Then he filled his wooden bowl from a
child-sized pond where a rubble of rocks had dammed
the stream. Tiny silver fish darted around his hands,
each not much bigger than a fingernail. He hoped none
had gotten into his drinking water.

A few inches from his eyes, as he knelt there, was
a patch of blooming crocuses. He broke off three blos-
soms and carried them back to the rock, where he lay
down on his stomach on the moss and peered down
the flowers' throats.

They were shining white but veined with purple at
the bottom of the petals. Within each little cup proudly
stood the stamen covered with saffron, which left a
film of gold on the young man's finger.

At this distance, too, the moss was radiant with
color: gold, green, russet, sooty black. Damiano laid the
crocuses on the moss and closed his eyes. Macchiata
lay down beside him. "I wish..." she said, and then
was silent.

"You wish what, little dear?" murmured Damiano.
There was silence. He turned to the little dog, who
licked her lips nervously.

"I...it would be fun to play with Raphael now,"
she blurted at last. "It's been a long time since you
called him."

Damiano's eyes closed again. "Yes, it has. But I
don't imagine he's drumming his fingers, waiting. He
is a blessed angel, Macchiata, and we are...creatures
of the earth. He has all eternity, while we have the
hours between lunch and dinner, as it were.

"And he cannot understand the affairs of men."
Damiano yawned again, and since his chin was resting
on the mossy stone, the effort raised his whole head.
Then he frowned.

"Actually, little dear, I don't understand the affairs
of men either. I appreciate the affairs of...bees, let's
say...much better. But I am a man, so it is up to me to
act the part."

Damiano squirmed onto his back and placed the

white cup of a crocus over each of his eyes. "I can see the sun through them," he commented. "Tinted white and pink and purple." When he took the flowers away, his lashes were dusted with gold. "These crocuses look sort of like Raphael to me: all white and gold and radiant. Though the white is his robe, of course."

Damiano yawned once more, screwed his eyes shut, and rubbed the gold all over his face. "Then again, since what we are seeing when we see Ralphael is only an image for our mortality's sake, perhaps he *is* the robe, and there is nothing under it. What man would dare lift it to see?"

"I know what Raphael looks like under the robe. I looked," said Macchiata. Damiano opened his eyes very suddenly.

"You what?"

"I looked. I stuck my head under and looked, Master. A long time ago. I was curious."

Now it was Damiano's turn to lick his lips. He tasted saffron. "And what...No, little dear. Never mind. I don't think it's for me to know." He sighed, turned his face to the sun, and composed himself for a nap.

He did miss the angel. In the three years since he had first had the temerity to speak the summoning words (that was after his father died, when many things in Damiano's life had got easier), he had never gone as long as a week without a lesson. Indeed, the lute, though important, was only a bridge by which to reach Raphael, who was Damiano's closest friend.

Second closest friend, he amended to himself, feeling a slimy nose against his palm. That made two friends in all, unless he could count Carla, whom he would never see again.

Lying there on the moss in the sun, the young witch thought of the Devil's words and did not feel in the slightest bit damned. But for the plight of his city, now so far away, he would be the happiest fellow on earth. And the sleepiest.

What instrument *did* Raphael play, by choice? The lute had been Damiano's idea, since he happened to have a lute, and the angel had never demurred. He played the lute masterfully, but it was hardly likely it was his only instrument.

Gabriele (whom Damiano had never met) played the trumpet. Of course. But there was no reason for all archangels to be alike. If they played together, it would be more reasonable to have both winds and strings. That is, if the winds could be taught not to overpower the sound of the string players. Among angels, there would surely be more consideration than among Italians.

Paintings often showed angels playing harps, but that was because harps were so common; when your imagination fails, you could always paint a musician with a harp. They were easy to paint, too, having three angles and only two curves.

But Raphael showed such a delight in shuffling between modes, and in flatting his seventh. . . . Damiano could more easily see him at a lute or chitarre. Or perhaps a large vielle—a hurdy-gurdy—with chromatic keys.

Then it occurred to Damiano that since Raphael was a spirit, he had no need for a material instrument; the trees could make his music, or the bones of the earth. So what did the archangel mean when he said, "I have my own instrument?" Next time Damiano saw him, he would ask straight out, "Raphael, what do you play?"

With this decision off his mind, Damiano fell asleep.

The bees were crawling over him: thick, droning, coating him with gold. They had a thousand voices, warm and nasal like the vielle itself. They were the voices of friends. Damiano strained to hear them, to pull out one voice and recognize it. To know a single name. "Solitary," they whispered, all together. "Solitary boy."

The weight of the bees was on him, soft and

heavy. He could feel it on his arms, his body, his lips.
The golden drone echoed in his chest. Damiano struggled upward from sleep and knew he was under a
spell.

A hand was upon him, invisible, gentle—as the
hand of a girl might cover a baby rabbit. It was at once
caressing and imprisoning. He heard Macchiata whine.
He heard a song.

> "Boy, boy, solitary boy.
> I see you in the garden,
> Alone in the garden,
> Sleeping in the sun."

It was a woman's voice, throaty and deep, rich as a
multitude of bees. "Boy," it chanted. "Solitary boy."

Damiano turned his head toward it, pushing slowly
against the invisible hand. He cracked his eyes open
and peered out from under the concealment of his
thick lashes.

Her hair was sunny brown and wound in peasant
braids. Her cheeks were blushed rose and dimpled, for
she was smiling. Her eyes were green and brown and
golden, all together, in a pattern that swam and made
his head swim. She wore a blue dress embroidered
with stars of red and yellow and Damiano found her
utterly charming.

It was not a strong spell that held him; he could
have broken it with a word. But it was the most
intimate touch he had known from any woman, so
Damiano lay still and did not speak.

> "Young one, I can see you,
> I can peel you like an onion,
> I see backward, through your days.
> I unfold you like the petals of a rose.
> Book-friend, rabbit-friend, your playmates are the
>   beasts in the stall.
> What do you study, boy, that makes you so alone?"

Her touch into his mind was like a feather under the chin. It tickled and made him smile. Then the feather withdrew in surprise.

"Dark boy, do you know who you are?
There is power in you, young one, like floods under stone."

The hazel eyes widened, and she drew back. The spell shattered, tinkling, as Damiano heaved up on one shoulder. He opened his eyes. "Don't go," he whispered. "And I'm not as young as all that."

The woman stopped where she stood, eyes wide and wary. Neither did Damiano move, and though she did not try to enter his mind once more, (he would not have obstructed her, having nothing to hide), slowly her smile grew again.

"You're a witch," she said, amusement and surprise in her words. Even when not singing, her voice had a lilt to it that was nothing like the Italian of Lombardy. "You're most certainly a witch, and you know it, too. But those black eyes are worse than witchcraft, boy. Don't turn them on me like that."

Damiano blushed to the roots of his hair. "You're making fun of me," he said. "What have I done to deserve it?" But the truth was he liked her teasing and was liking everything about the woman more and more. This was Saara. It had to be.

She had the round face of a country girl of seventeen and the knowing air of a *belle dame* of Provence and the lightness of movement of one of the wood sprites, whom even Damiano could only see out of the corner of his eye. Best of all, she was not a country girl or a great lady or a pagan sprite but one of his own kind, a human witch.

She didn't answer his question. Instead she put her hands on her hips. Damiano sat up, noticing she neither carried a staff nor seemed to need one. "Who are you, boy?" she asked. "For boy you are, to me. I

am much older than I look, I warn you. And you are in
my garden."

Suddenly Damiano remembered the southerner the
landlord at Ludica had described to him: the man with
the sharp sword and sharp tongue who had vanished
in Saara's garden. But looking at Saara herself, he was
not afraid.

"My name is Dami," he said, "Damiano. We have
traveled here from the Piedmont, my dog and I, to talk
to you."

Saara spared a glance at Macchiata, who still lay
under the spell, flattened like a white pill-bug on the
cushions of moss. With a giggle and a wave of the
hand she released the dog, who scuttled (like a white
pill-bug) out of sight behind the rock.

"I would like to talk to you too, Dami. It is rare to
find another in Lombardy who is tuned to the powers.
Rarer still to find one who is friendly. But if I allow you
to come much closer to me, you will make an enemy
you don't want to have. He might remove your curly
head from your shoulders!" She sat down cross-legged
on the green and silver grass, too far away for Damiano's
close vision.

Damiano dismissed this possibility with a shrug
and a wave, and he slid down from the rock into the
rosemary bush. Saara sang a line in a tongue that
seemed to be composed mostly of *k* sounds and long
vowels, and which was to Damiano no more than
birdsong. Instantly limber fingers of rosemary whipped
out and hugged his knees and calves, bruising themselves with the strength of their grip and filling the air
with herby sweetness.

"All right," said Damiano, and he sat down
obediently in the thorny patch. Casually, with one
hand, he reached up behind him and found his staff,
which he laid carefully across his lap.

Saara sat straight as an abbess, her feet crossed
over her knees. She pointed at the ebony stick. "Those,"
she said. "I have seen you southern witches use them.

You lock yourselves into them, like men who trade their legs for crutches. Why? Any leg at all is better than the most beautiful crutch."

Damiano frowned uncertainly. "The staff is a focus, lady—like a lens. Do you know what a lens is? It's like a drop of water, which makes sunlight into a bright point. The staff is the focus through which my craft touches the world. It makes my spells more...the same, from day to day. I have used this staff for years; all my powers are tuned to it, and without it I'd have nothing."

"That's dangerous, boy. It makes you too vulnerable, needing an outside object like that. My...lens...or drop of bright sunlight, is my song. My song cannot be taken from me."

Damiano lifted his eyebrows. "Music? Lovely lady. What a pretty thought. I play music too, but not for magic. To do that seems, somehow, to sully the tune."

Saara's little pink nostrils flared, and woody rosemary crawled over Damiano's hands. "Sully the tune? No! For both magic and music are sacred!"

"Sacred?" Damiano sighed. "Music, yes, but witchcraft...I don't know, lady. I have seen too much done with witchcraft that had nothing to do with God's will. I release my own powers into the staff because running free through me they can...make me drunk. Then who knows what deed I might do."

He raised his eyes to the pretty woman in her bright, childish dress. "Because I am, after all, a man, lady. And men at times are slaves to their passions."

Saara made as though to laugh at him but changed her mind. "You must learn to know the powers," she said seriously. "The good from the wicked. The pure from the twisted. When you are possessed by a spirit of wisdom, you can do nothing bad."

Damiano shook his head, dissatisfied.

"Perhaps for you, lady, that is true, but for me...I don't trust so much. If I allow a spirit to command my actions and then kill a child or burn down a house, who will it be who comes before the throne of the Almighty for judgment: the nameless spirit or Damiano?"

He shuffled amid the fragrant, prickling branches, trying to win some comfort. "Besides, even if the spirit is pure, I am not. At this moment, my lady Saara, I look at you and am filled with a sweet longing that is not pure at all." Immediately he lowered his eyes to the grass, overcome by his own gallantry.

The witch Saara put one braid-end to her mouth and giggled like a little girl. "We have different ideas of purity, Dami-yano. But I tell you, as long as you keep your power as a thing apart from yourself, you will not come to your full strength."

He shrugged, as though to say 'so what'? but his smile apologized for the gesture even as he made it. "It is your power that has led me all this way in the snow, Saara. I need your help."

She let the braid drop. Her greenish eyes went wary. "You mean you didn't climb here just to speak words of hopeless love to me?" Her words were lighter than her guarded expression.

Before answering, Damiano paused, running his fingers lightly over the jewels of his staff. "Beautiful lady, I think I could speak words of love to you—and more than speak—forever. If they are hopeless, then I am desolate, but since I have only just met you this hour, I may recover.

"But I have lived in Partestrada all my life, and she is in great trouble. It is for that reason I have disturbed your peace: because I am told you are the most powerful witch in the Italies." He glanced up to see whether his words had offended Saara. She looked merely concerned.

"Who told you that I was the most powerful witch in the Italies, boy? No one in the Italies knows me." But rather than waiting for his answer, she continued, "Great trouble, Dami. That would mean—plague?"

Both his eyebrows shot up. "Mother of God! No! Not that! Not again. I meant war. And tyranny."

"Ah." The syllable expressed dying interest. She turned her head away from Damiano and toward the fluttering, yellow birch leaves. "War. Well, there's nothing I can do about that."

"No?" For one moment he faced the possibility that his search had been useless, that there was no hope for Partestrada or for any small, industrious, unarmed peoples. Perhaps neither logic nor magic could hold the gates, for plague and Pardo were Fate and God's will. Just for a moment he stared at this possibility, and then he turned firmly away from it.

At a single word from Damiano, the tendrils of rosemary sprang away and hung as coils in the air around him. "I don't believe you. You say there's nothing you can do, but I read in your face that it's just not worth the bother." He stood, and Saara stood. The air spat tiny sparks that smelled like hot metal. "Well it *is* worth one person's bother, and much more, and in the service of my city I have been beaten and frozen, gone hungry and sleepless and done deeds...that I shouldn't have done," he concluded less forcefully. "In fact, I've done what no man should do. I've tried to strike a bargain with the Father of Lies, to deliver my city from bloodshed and poverty. Even he refused me. You are my last hope, Saara. I cannot believe the greatest witch in all Europe doesn't know of a way to free a town from the power of one Roman brigand.

"I'll do whatever need be done, lady. I'll fight Pardo's men alone on foot, if need be. I'll swell the Evançon to wash them from the streets. I'll go to any amount of work, and through any peril.

"I only need you to tell me how." The faith in his eyes was as unreasonable as a child's, and his jaw clenched again and again.

Saara tried to break the link that locked her green, slightly tilted eyes to Damiano's. She failed, for the power that held her was as old as sorcery and far stronger. "I'm not the greatest witch in Europe, Dami-yano. In my home we are all witches, and there are some much stronger than I, and wilder. That is why . . .

"But, boy, you are free of that place, and of General Pardo. The world is yours—although not this hill, I must remind you. General Pardo cannot follow you everywhere."

Damiano squinted painfully and shook his head. "He has my city, lady. My home. There is a great difference between a traveler and an exile. Ask Dante. Ask Petrarch."

Saara cocked her head at the unfamiliar names, and then she laughed. "I need no one else's opinion. A city is a collection of stone walls. My people need no cities; they follow the reindeer and are free."

"Reindeer?"

Saara grinned at his puzzlement. "Shaggy deer with great antlers and big feet that can stand on the snow. We ride them and milk them and also eat them, though not the same ones we ride."

Looking at the impish set of Saara's smile, Damiano was not sure he was supposed to believe her. He decided, sighing deeply, that he should let the matter pass.

"We Piedmontese—all Italians—do need cities. We invest our hearts into them. A city is like a mother, lovely lady. She gives us our food and our friends and our amusements. She sets an indelible stamp upon us. Yet a city—she can't defend herself. Who will take care of her if not her children, eh?"

The Fenwoman's elfin face softened with something like pity, yet she shook her head. "That is a pretty thing to say, Dami. But a city is not a person. Nor has it life like a tree. It's a thing like the staff—it's your choice to put care into it or to be free. I would sooner help you be free."

Hesitantly, Damiano stepped forward, trying to smile. When he was close enough to see her well, he was also close enough to touch. He put out his left hand and stroked her arm and shoulder. So roughened by the strings were his fingertips they scraped against the thin felt of her embroidered dress.

"Saara. My lady. If it is your wish that I don't live in my city anymore, so be it. I will live in a black forest. Or in a boat on the ocean—I don't care, so long as it is by your will. But first I must help Partestrada, don't you see?"

She watched his hand carefully but did not withdraw. He continued "I am told . . . by whom it doesn't matter, that a city can only prosper with blood and war, and that I could save Partestrada at the expense of her own future glory. I came to you to find another way."

Damiano spoke in a whisper, and as he spoke his fingers traced a small wheedling circle on her shoulder. So intent was Saara on this motion that she seemed not to be listening. But she answered "I know nothing about glory, unless you mean the lights in the winter sky. I won't go to war with you, Dami-yano."

"Then show me how to succeed without war," he whispered, and as she raised an ironical eye to his insistence, he kissed her softly on the side of her mouth.

Saara caught her breath and closed her eyes and stepped back from him. "This is no good," she said weakly. "Neither what you say nor what you do. Dami-yano, I have a man who would kill you for that."

She rubbed her face with both hands. Damiano's smile, as he watched her, was slow and sad. "Maybe," he admitted. "And maybe it was worth it, Saara."

"No maybes about it," she said sternly, then realizing what she had said, she added, "—about his killing you, I mean. He is just like you, too: lean and dark and unpredictable. His name is Ruggiero, and he comes from Rome."

"From Rome!" cried Damiano, stung. "Then he can be nothing like me at all. I am Piedmontese."

Her mutable eyes danced. "No difference that I can see—save that you are much younger and do not wear a sword.

"Take warning by that, Dami-yano and go back to Ludica. There is a world of charming girls out there. You need not a mother or a city or . . . a wicked old woman like me." With those words Saara vanished, and a pale gray dove flashed upwards into the heavens.

Damiano followed the flight with his eyes, till the sun blinded him. He had never seen anyone turn into a bird before; such magic was impossible to one who worked through a staff.

There was a snuffle and grunt by his feet. He glanced down to see Macchiata, obscured by a dancing, round afterimage of the sun. The dog looked earnestly into his face.

"You licked her—kissed her, I mean," said Macchiata.

"Yes," responded her master. "I . . . like her."

Still the dog stared. "I've never seen you kiss anyone before, Master. Not anyone but me."

Damiano's lips twitched, but he controlled the smile. "That's true, little dear, but does that mean that I can't kiss anyone else?"

Macchiata thought about it. "You never kissed Carla Denezzi," she commented sagely.

Damiano's reply was short. "No. But I should have." He turned back to the rock, where the bees still droned and the moss lay like a cushion in petit point: green, gold, russet, black.

"I should have." He picked up the lute by the neck and began to finger it, indecisively.

Macchiata heaved herself up beside him. "But she doesn't like you, Master. This one. She told you to go away."

The treble trilled wanly. "That's because she doesn't want me to get in a fight with her . . . her Roman friend. One must like a person somewhat to want him not to get his head lopped off. Of course, there is really no danger of that. Saara underestimates me. She thinks I'm younger than I am." He came down on the bass course so forcefully that the strings buzzed against the bridge.

"She will come around," Damiano stated. "We'll camp on her hillside until she does." Macchiata's ears flattened with doubt.

"But you said, Master . . . that we would soon be out of food. Remember?"

"We don't need to eat," said Damiano, and he set his jaw. The dog stared for a long time without a word.

The camp he set up at the edge of the birch wood that evening was small, since he hadn't been able to carry much by foot from Ludica, and neat, since he felt in a way that the meadow was the lady Saara's parlor. And although he hadn't exactly been welcomed by that lady, he hoped to make himself a pleasant guest.

He and the dog ate bread and raisins while nightingales ornamented the wind in the leaves and a single late sparrow went "peep, peep, peep." After dinner Macchiata lay before the fire and sighed.

Damiano was in a better mood. "You know, little dear, what is the best thing about Saara?" he asked as he peered down the neck of the *liuto*, checking it for wood warp. He didn't wait for an answer. "It's that she's wise as a great lady and yet free as a child."

"Those are two things," Macchiata commented, but her master was not listening.

"She was barefoot; did you notice, Macchiata? Her little white feet seemed scarce to bend the grass."

The dog emitted a slow groan that ended in a grunt. "I noticed that she had a very heavy hand, when she pushed me down on the rock."

Damiano shot her a glance in surprise. "Heavy? No, that was not heavy, Macchiata. Didn't I feel it myself? For a heavy hand, you must remember my father. Now *he* had a heavy hand."

The lute was sound, but its finish had undeniably suffered in the climb. Hoping the bass course was true, Damiano tuned the rest of the strings by it. (Among his gifts was not that of absolute pitch, which Raphael said was more of an ordeal than a blessing to the musician possessing it.)

"Yet, Saara the Fenwoman is greater than my father was. I'm sure I could learn much from her, and the learning would be more pleasant."

Macchiata raised her head. "But you don't want to be a witch, Master. You want to play the lute and go from place to place. You said so."

Damiano cocked an eyebrow in irritation, and at that moment a mid string snapped. The small explosion echoed through the little gold wood and the birds all went quiet together.

He stared down dumbly for a moment, then began to pull off the remnants of the string. "Both ways of life," he stated, "Have their advantages. And disadvantages.

"It may be I'm tuning too high," he concluded, and started the tuning again.

"But Saara has the best of both worlds, for her music is her magic. And vice versa. Her way, I think, is more suited to a woman than a man, for we are by our nature more forceful and less gentle. If my feelings ruled my craft . . . well, we'd have a lot more storms in the sky, Macchiata."

This time the tuning was completed without incident, though the empty space on the fingerboard was as bad as a missing tooth. "It must be that the lady's pure heart is her strength. That and her green eyes. Green and golden eyes. And smooth, dimpled skin . . ."

"Master," broke in Macchiata. Her own eyes, earnest and brown, were concerned. "Master, do human men ever have to go to the stable?"

He peered across the fire at her, blinking, his chain of thought—if it was thought—broken. "What, Macchiata? Do human men ever what?"

"Ever have to stay in the stable. For two weeks. Alone."

Damiano's glance slid away, and his complexion

went many shades darker. He cleared his throat. "No, Macchiata," he said with authority. "No, never."

In the dark, in the rustling quiet of the birch trees, under the round white moon, Damiano began to play. His music was French, but it was not the new music at all. He played songs that were two hundred years old: the chansons of Bernart de Ventadour, whose love of his patron's lady was so unwavering that he was banished for it, and who then chose to love Eleanor of Aquitaine.

And Damiano sang to the lute in old Provençal, a language he could barely understand. The mode was Ionian, but the tune was very sad.

> "Amors, e que'us es vejaire?
> Trobatz mais fol mas can me?"
> (Love, what is your opinion?
> Can you ever find a greater fool than I?)

He heard in his own voice greater depth and feeling than he had imagined it to possess, for there is that about any foreign language: speaking it one becomes a different person, capable of new and astonishing things. His voice carried him away, till there were tears in his eyes with pity for the song and for himself.

> ". . . Farai o,c c'aissi's cove;
> Mas vos non estai ges be
> Quem fassatz tostems mal traire."

Little wings fluttered in the tree nearest the fire: neither the wings of the lark nor the sparrow. Damiano did not look up as Saara swooped to the earth beside Macchiata and sat there, feet folded under her blue felt skirt. But he sang the last part of the verse again, in Italian.

> "I'll do what I must.
> But it does not become you
> To keep me suffering this woe."

Saara whispered "Ah," and Macchiata slunk away from the fire. The greatest witch in the Italies twisted her brown braid around and around one pink finger. "Very pretty, Dami-yano. Your music is like you: warm and dark and lonely. Only very young men are lonely in that way."

There was silence while Damiano regarded her from across the campfire. Though her face was a blur at that distance, under the full moon he saw things with his witch's eyes and was abashed.

"I've come to tell you something, Dami—I'll call you that; it's easier. I've come to tell you why I won't help you fight a war."

"I don't want..." he began, but she cut him off with a sharp gesture.

"In my home, which is Lappland in the far north, we were all sorcerers among the Haavala tribe: all Lapps are sorcerers—witches. We have power over the herds and the wild beasts and, most important of all, the weather. We keep the weather just bad enough to keep other peoples out."

"Weather? You mean raising the wind and calling clouds or dispersing them? I can do that a little."

She smiled. "I mean making a downpour in a drought, or a garden without winter."

Damiano shrugged humbly and shook his head. "I cannot even imagine that much strength."

Saara chuckled. "To control the elements, Dami, you must be willing to become one with them. That you refuse to do.

"But I want to tell you about me, and why I'm here.

"I was young, Dami. As young as you. I had a husband—Jekkinan—and two little girls with black hair, like their father's.

"Jekkinan was the head of our tribe. He was a strong man, and could cage a wolf with a song of three words. He was also proud and haughty, though he tempered his words with me.

"In the autumn was the gathering of the herds, when the men go out alone. There was a fight over the division, and a man was killed. I am told Jekkinan killed him, though I cannot believe . . .

"Whether or no, he came home and said nothing to me about a fight, but the next day I went out alone, and when I came home, Jekkinan was dead, and the— and the chil—children. Dead on the floor, pierced by spears. The open wounds were mouths that spoke the killer's name."

An involuntary cry escaped Damiano. "Ah! Lady, I'm so sorry." He leaned forward till his face was almost in the fire.

Saara glanced upward with dry, locked eyes. "That isn't why I won't help you, Dami-yano. The same night that I found my children dead I came to the house of the man who killed them.

"And I killed him with a song—him and his wife. His children were grown, or I might have killed them too. Then the tribe came together and decided—for shame—not to be a tribe anymore, and the herd was divided and they went apart, taking the names and the manners and the stitchwork of other tribes. I am the only one left wearing the two stars of the Haavala.

"That is why I won't help you, Dami. I have done what hate made me to do. For all my life."

Damiano stepped through the fire and sat beside her. "We are more alike than you know, Saara," he whispered. His sun-darkened hand rested on her own.

"Oh, I do know, Dami-yano," she replied, her hand motionless but unyielding beneath his. "When I felt you in the breezes of the meadow, I knew you, both by your delight in my garden and by the pain that brought you to it. You drew me to you like a lodestone draws a nail, and even now I cannot help but . . ."

With these words she edged away from him and turned her face to the dark. Damiano did not release her hand.

"If you know me, lady, you know that I don't want vengeance, but peace for my people."

Saara's rose pink lips tightened. "Let them find other towns to live in, as my people found other tribes."

He sighed. "It's not the same, lady. A man without property—with only a wife and hungry children—he's not especially welcome anywhere. Exiles are so many beggars.

"A city is like a garden. Everything grows together, and the roses shade the violets. A man belongs in his own city. Can't you help me, Saara? If you have the power to cage a wolf, can't you cage a brigand, or at least scare him away?"

"Can't *you?*" she replied. "Men who have no power are easily cowed by it."

Damiano smiled ruefully and scratched his head. His hand disappeared amid the tangle of black curls. "I can't think how," he admitted. "The only ways I know to frighten an army are ways Pardo suggested to me himself, and so I doubt they'd work on him.

"But with rain and lightning, lady! I'll speak the spell myself, so if it is risky or demands heavy payment, it will come back on me..."

Saara shook her head emphatically. "You can't, black eyes. Not bound to this staff as you are, and even if you let it go, you would have to learn again like a child.

"I would have to do this thing for you, and I won't." Her face was set. "In the morning you go back to Ludica."

Damiano flinched. He squeezed her hand placatingly. "Please. I'd like to stay here a few days, in case you change your mind."

Saara glared at Damiano. She pulled on one of her braids in frustration. "I told you you can't, boy. Ruggerio will go into a rage, once he knows you're here."

Damiano picked up a pebble and threw it into the fire. His own quick fire was wakened. "Well then, he must be very easily enraged, Saara. For if the truth be known, I myself am as much a virgin as a day-old chick. If I tried to do you violence, lady, you would probably have to show me how!" And with his admission he turned away from her, rested one hand on his knee and his head on his other fist and stared unseeing across the meadow.

Saara smothered her laughter with both hands. "Oh, my dear, my sweet boy. I know. I knew that from the beginning. But Ruggerio—will either not believe or not care. He is proud and quick to anger. Like Jekkinan, I guess. And it's his boast that he keeps men out of the garden."

"Proud and angry and not even a witch. What do you want with him, Saara?" growled Damiano, still with his back to the fire.

He missed the lift of her shoulders and her dimpled smile. "He's very faithful," Saara offered.

"So's Macchiata—my dog," he grunted in turn. He turned again to see the lady scratching her bare toes thoughtfully.

"Understand, Dami. When I came to this country I was very unhappy. Filled with grief and regret. When the southerners discovered who I was—a foreigner and a—a witch—they would not speak to me. The children ran away.

"A man came to me, then: a southman, but a man of our kind—the first witch I ever saw who bound himself to a stick. (How that puzzled me!) He told me he had felt my presence in the wind of his own chimney, far off, and could not stay away.

"He was young, like you, and dark. I thought I loved him. I *did* love him; he was like Jekkinan, with both his power and his storms. One night he . . . he did something very bad; he crept into my mind. He moved to steal my strength from me, and so I discovered that he had never loved me at all but had desired my power.

"It was horrible to find I had been so wrong—to

find I had lived as wife with a man and it had all been planned as a trick! He had the skill of lying with the heart itself—never had I heard of such a thing.

"But he had exposed himself too soon. I fought back, and I was the stronger. He went fleeing down the hill, and I've never seen or heard of him again.

"But I remember; I remember how I saw through a man, or thought I did, and was a fool. And I will not trust another like him! So I allow no one on the hill and rarely step out of my garden. And that was why I was surprised to find that people in the far Piedmont know my name.

"Ruggerio has no power," she continued, in calmer tones. "And his temper is a trouble to me, Dami. But he loves me, and because he is only simple I know he is not hiding..." She stopped in midsentence, staring at Damiano's face, where anguish and shame and a dread certainty were growing. "What is it, boy? What have I said?"

He swallowed and croaked, "The witch who betrayed you. His name. What was it?"

Her brow drew forward painfully. "I...don't repeat it. What does it matter to you, Dami-yano?"

His hands clenched each other as Damiano, uncomfortably glanced everywhere but at Saara. "It...it couldn't have been Delstrego, could it? Guillermo Delstrego? Because if it is, I really am sorry."

Saara's breath hissed out. She took Damiano's head between her hands and looked into his eyes, reading the truth she had missed before.

"I *am* sorry," he said, thick voiced. "I wouldn't..."

"No!" she cried out. "I've done it again! Again! Great Winds, will I never be free?" And Saara vanished upward into the trees.

Damiano huddled against a blast of frozen air. "Dear Jesu," he whispered, as the fire guttered out. A few minutes later he added, "Papa, you have so much to answer for."

Macchiata crawled out of the night and sat beside him.

Chapter 12

The cold faded soon, and Damiano was too depressed to restart the fire. He wrapped himself in his single blanket and hugged Macchiata close, both for warmth and comfort. Sleep came nowhere near.

Damiano almost called upon Raphael for comfort, since the angel, at least, knew he was not party to the wrongdoings of Delstrego, Senior. Yet that business of the interview with Lucifer stopped his mouth. Even if Raphael had no knowledge of what had passed, Damiano did, and he knew his face would proclaim his deed.

And what of Raphael's face? Now that Damiano had looked into the eyes of the Devil and recognized the angel, what would he see in the eyes of the Devil's brother? Not sin, certainly, but . . .

And on the other hand, how could he communicate to his spiritual friend his feelings for the lovely Saara, with such depths in her eye, and such sweet impudence in her mouth? Even the dog doubted the purity of his intent. Silently Damiano cursed the purity of his intent.

No, he did not want to see Raphael right now. He turned back to the comforter of whom he was sure.

"How can I be to blame, little dear? She looked into my soul so far as to see me as a child, in the days before you were born, playing with rabbits. If I was like my father, surely she would have seen it then."

Macchiata laid her long nose on the blanket by her master's head. Her tongue flicked out in consolatory gesture, touching the tip of Damiano's nose. Licking faces was a thing Macchiata was not usually allowed to do, but tonight her master didn't chide her for it. "I think I know what it is with Saara, Master," said the dog.

"Unph!" He rose up on one elbow. His dark hair snared the stars in its tangles. "What is it, Macchiata?"

The dog rolled over, presenting her unlovely belly to his scratching fingers. "It's like that with a cat. Something—anything—gets a cat upset and then there's no sense in her. No use to talk; you just have to go away and lick your nose."

"Lick your nose?"

"The scratches. Saara is upset at your father, so she claws you instead."

Damiano smiled at the image of Saara as a cat. With her little face and tilted eyes, she'd make a good cat. His sigh melded with a laugh and came out his throat and nose as a horse's whinny.

Doubtless Saara could become a cat in an instant, if she wanted to. A big cat. Damiano regarded the susurrous meadow grass with new caution. But no. Had the lady wanted to destroy him, she could have done it before, in the midst of his surprise and shame.

"Even a cat calms down, eventually, Macchiata," he murmured, reclining again. "Calms down and curls by the fire, so one can pet her. In the morning I'll find Saara again and tell her she can look into my head all she wants, till she is sure I am true. Perhaps if I put down my staff, she'll believe me."

Macchiata whined a protest and wiggled free from the blankets. "No, Master! Remember: you did that before and got hit on the head!"

Damiano grabbed at one of her feet. She evaded his hand. "Those were ordinary men, Macchiata. They were afraid of me."

"So is Saara," the dog reminded him.

Morning came, with strings of mist curling up from the waters. Damiano's blanket was damp; so was he. Breakfast was cold water and the last of the bread.

Macchiata ate a dead frog and then wandered off in search of more.

Damiano had the lute in his hands, wondering where under heaven he'd be able to find a replacement for the broken string, when he became aware of a man in the pine wood. It was neither vision nor sound that informed him, but the instinct he had inherited from his father.

It was a slight pressure, like the light touch of a finger on the face, an irritation hardly noticed. Indeed, in the streets of Partestrada, Damiano suppressed this sense, as a distraction and hindrance. But here in solitude with the moon at its full, Damiano could feel the stranger's size and shape, and even, to some measure, his intent.

He put off his mantle and laid it on the rock seat. He smoothed his clothes and ran his fingers through his hair. Since he had no sword to don, he slung his lute across his back instead. Then, with unconscious dignity, he proceeded to the edge of the meadow, where the pines cast a barrier of shadow. When the man stepped out Damiano bowed to him in a manner neither proud nor servile, and he wished him good day.

The stranger was tall, and where Damiano was slim, this fellow was lean like a starved hound. His face was long and his eyes glinted black in the early sun. His nose was so high-bridged his face would have appeared arrogant asleep. As he stood there, peering down at Damiano, the expression upon that face was an insult.

Silence stretched long. The stranger shifted his weight onto his left hip with mincing grace. His left thumb was thrust negligently between the hilt and the scabbard of a sword that was neither new nor ornamental. The worn nap on his velvet tunic proclaimed the fact that this gentleman wore the sword at least as often as he wore the tunic.

His eyes went from Damiano's dirty boots to his

rude, mountain trousers and thence to his woolen shirt, where the white linen peeped out at neck and wristline. The black glance wrote a silent satire on each article it lighted upon, and when it reached Damiano's face, its narrative was so amusing the man broke out in laughter.

"The wolf has a very small puppy," he announced, speaking to an invisible audience. "Perhaps this is only a bitch-whelp, after all."

Damiano leaned upon his staff, allowing the flush to pass from his face. "By all signs you are Ruggerio," he said. "I don't want to trade insults with you, Signor. But I do want to talk to you."

Ruggerio stepped forward in an airy toe-dance about which there was nothing feminine. He circled around Damiano to get the sun out of his eyes.

And into Damiano's. "But only one of us has anything to say, whelp. Take you from my lady's hill."

Damiano sighed deeply and scratched his head. "You have a sword, Signor, and I do not. That is a strong argument in your favor. But much as I would like to avoid trouble with you, I cannot leave without seeing the lady Saara again."

Ruggerio paused, a black shape against the sun. "I see, fellow. And that in itself is an argument almost as strong as a sword, for my lady is more beautiful than the new rose, and her speech is like water to a man in the desert. If I prevent men from Saara, it is because otherwise her garden would become a litter of broken hearts.

"But, little wolf, with you the matter is different. It is not I but Saara herself who has ordered you gone from here. Isn't that enough, fellow? You have seen my lady's face; how can you not now bend to her wish?" Damiano heard the practiced, smooth draw of the sword from its scabbard.

He stepped back behind his staff, as though it could conceal him. "I would indeed bend to her wish,

Signor. Every wish but this one. If she told you who I am, she must have also told you why I am here."

The sword reflected light like water. The long grass stood away from the base of Damiano's staff as though blown by wind. "Like your dog of a father, fellow, you covet my lady's powers," said Ruggerio.

"I don't want her powers, Signore, but her help. I need her to save my city from destruction," replied the witch, and he raised his staff off the ground. As the Franciscan in his homespun robes may raise the cross before some Muslim caliph, so Damiano raised his black staff before Ruggerio. And Ruggerio laughed.

"You have a pretty name for ambition, churl. I'll admit that.

"But enough, now. Go." The sword made an abortive feint toward Damiano's midsection. "Or I'll prick you with tiny holes, like bedbug bites, that will get bigger and bigger as I lose my temper. You see?" The steel flickered in motion and was deflected by Damiano's staff. A sweet tinging like that of a bell cut the air. Ruggerio circled his wrist, and the sword lunged again.

Sparks flew as steel hit silver, and again the strike went wild. Ruggerio grunted in his throat.

Damiano's eyes (never very useful to him) went soft and vague as he turned his inner attention to Ruggerio. He swayed to the right out of the path of the swordsman's attack.

"I'm not about to let you stick me with that pin, Signor Ruggerio," Damiano said aggrievedly. "Not even a prick like a bedbug bite."

It was not agility alone that preserved the young witch, for with each sword thrust his staff called out to his opponent's blade and took the force of the blow upon its own wood and metal. Three more times Damiano evaded the taunting feints, till the tall southerner stepped back with a hiss of breath.

"You will drive me to kill you, fellow," Ruggerio spat.

Cautiously Damiano stepped sideways, until he

could discern the features of his enemy's face. "Is that what the lady said, Signore? That you were to kill me if I did not run away?"

The Roman snorted. "She didn't stipulate. Being a delicate creature, my lady leaves such necessities to me. I am very willing to..."

Ruggerio's sentence ended in a scream of rage, which turned to one of pain as ivory dog-fangs clashed against the bone of his ankle. He kicked, and Macchiata flew through the air above the meadow grass. Seeing the tip of the sword touch against the ground, Damiano stepped down upon it, but Ruggerio withdrew his weapon, slicing halfway through the wood and leather of Damiano's boot heel. "Leave us, Macchiata," called Damiano. "I can handle him; you'll only get yourself killed."

Ruggerio's cry was wordless. The edged blade flashed in a scintillating arc toward Damiano's head.

"Mother of God, help me!" whispered the witch, as he threw his staff into the path of destruction. The blade sparked and recoiled, while the wood itself sang like the reed of a cathedral organ. "Don't do that, Signore," Damiano warned.

Ruggerio switched his sword to his left and stuck a numbed right hand into his belt. "Ah? So it's the stick you need, puppy. I forgot my lady said something to that effect. Then I'll cut it out of your hands or cut your hands off with it; that's the fitting punishment for a thief."

The knowledge that Saara had given away his weakness hit Damiano like a slap. For an instant he heard the forest ring in its own silence and felt a weakness in his chest. Ruggerio swung again, scraping his blade along the surface of the staff. Damiano spun the ebony length just fast enough to escape with his hands. The knuckles of his left hand oozed blood.

But it was Ruggerio who cursed aloud at the pain that shot up his wrist and arm. "Let the staff be,

Ruggerio," shouted Damiano, drawing back a step. "Striking it is deadly."

The tall swordsman stood motionless a moment, eyes intent, face expressionless. He swayed lightly, as though to music. "Is it, fellow? To me or to you, I wonder? Where will you be, if I cut off that pretty silver head with the yellow stones? Will your own head roll in the dust? Let's see." And Ruggerio's blade whirled above his own head.

Damiano yanked sideways on the staff, and the sword flew clean. He started to step away. "No, Signore. You will only get..." And in that instant his torn heel caught in the grass and Damiano went down, falling flat on the body of the lute. He heard the snap of wood, Ruggerio stood above him, and the blade was falling.

"Mother of..." Damiano whispered, expecting to end the phrase in heaven or in hell. But the blade came down with terrible force not on flesh but on the silver head of the staff, where five topaz made a ring, almost directly on top of the single, small ruby.

The sword itself made a noise like a broken string that echoed through earth and air. Ruggerio dropped the weapon, shuddered, and put both hands to his heart. On his greyhound features was a look of embarrassed surprise. He dropped beside Damiano, who still lay with one foot trapped in the long grass. The witch saw the man's spirit, like light, like water, like wings, shake itself free of the body and be gone.

The wind made mumbling sounds in the grass. In the birch wood a single sparrow repeated "peep peep peep." Damiano knelt before the body of the swordsman. He began to shake his head, though he himself didn't know why he was doing so. He closed the man's eyes and arranged the sprawled limbs, then he leaned back on his heels and folded his hands on his lap. He began a Paternoster, for want of anything else to do.

The wind grew louder, its wailing growing moment by moment until the wind became a white bird,

which became Saara the Fenwoman. She took the body
of her lover in her arms and cried out in a strange and
bitter tongue. Her face was white and unbelieving. Her
eyes stared, and she, too, shook her head at the sight
of death.

Damiano shuffled back and rose to his feet. His
jaw seemed to be locked; there was nothing he could
say. He staggered, dragging one wooden heel held only
by a strip of leather. Macchiata whined and thrust her
head between his knees.

Saara looked up slowly. Her face was ashen and
blank. Her eyes were dry. It was a long time before she
saw Damiano standing there before her.

The single sparrow went "peep peep peep." The
wind sorted through the grass. Damiano noticed his
left hand was red with blood. Blood from his knuckles
had slicked the black staff, but the wound itself had no
feeling.

Then Saara opened her mouth and began to keen.

Cold struck Damiano like so many blows to the
face. His nose stung, and the roots of his teeth. Frozen
air scraped at his lungs as he raised his hand to his
face. In another instant the wind had knocked him
from his feet, and he rolled on grass that snapped like
ice beneath his weight. He closed his eyes to the cold
and cried out.

His ears felt Saara's song as a deadly pain. Damiano
screamed as his right eardrum burst. He clambered to
his feet and ran toward the pine forest, horribly dizzy,
stumbling as he went.

Saara's song reached before him, and the gentle air
froze, leaving each green needle clothed in ice. There
was a crackling like a fire, as branches too suddenly
stressed broke and fell to the ground. Snow came out
of nowhere and stole Damiano's breath. He fell again
and gobbets of snow and frozen stream water pelted
him from behind, beating him, seeking to bury him
alive. From nearby Macchiata howled "Master!" He
freed his face of the drift. He called to her.

Then the rough black tree trunk at his right hand cracked like a twig underfoot, and forty feet of pine loomed over Damiano and came crashing down.

He couldn't move, trapped under the weight of snow. But by instinct he twisted, and he raised his staff to the falling monster as he had done against Ruggerio's sword.

"No!" he shouted, with his foolish little protection waving above him.

The air crackled with a smell of burning metal. Damiano's hair stood away from his head, and the black wind whistled through his ebony staff.

The tree stopped falling.

Its mammoth bulk lay suspended in the air for three seconds, then it caught fire. Rude orange flames lit the shadow, and the sound of burning was like an enormous, damned choir. Damiano lay half-buried and helpless as the heat of flame warred with winter, and feathery ash fell upon his face. It began to rain in the covert.

And then the tree was gone.

He rose slowly, unhindered, and stared down at his bloody hand. He mouthed the words *"Dominus Deus!* Did I do that?" Wondering, he shook his head again.

Yet, even now, Damiano wasn't weary. Destroying the tree had been easily done. It was as though he had all the fires of hell to draw upon. The very idea of that made him shiver.

He peered all around himself at the blasted wilderness that had been a garden only minutes before. The red rocks glistened beneath jackets of ice, and the flowers in their tiny rock-bound plots lay frost-white and broken. The bed of the wandering stream gaped empty, while snow bent the grass double. Nowhere was there body or bird that could be Saara.

And it was quiet. Even the sparrow had ceased its din, either frozen or frightened away. Damiano stepped into the meadow again.

There was the body of Ruggerio the Roman, lying upon grass untouched by frost. And there, very near to it, was the little lute, broken like an egg. Damiano sighed and came closer.

As Damiano stepped his toe thudded into a lump in the snow. He caught his balance with difficulty and glanced down.

The snow was white and the lump was white, but there was a red spot like a bloodstain upon it. Damiano went down upon one knee and touched not blood but ruddy short fur and the hard, cold ugly bulk that had been Macchiata.

"Macchiata?" he said stupidly, and he turned the dog over. "Little dear?"

The body was stiff as wood, with three legs folded under and one held out, little toes spread like the fingers of a warding hand. The lips were pulled in a perpetual smile of terror, and the eyes—the eyes were dull chestnuts, no more.

The obvious truth hit Damiano slowly. He took the frozen dog on his lap, hugging her to him. Then he grunted, dumbly, and for the third time he shook his head. His staff clattered to the ground, and Damiano wept like a child.

Saara came toward her enemy, stepping through the snow barefoot. Her face was colorless; her eyes round. Beneath the gay felt dress her small shoulders were hunched stiff, as though she expected blows.

One hand she raised, finger pointing, then she dropped it. She stood motionless and unseen before Damiano's grief.

"Ah, Macchiata," he crooned to no one but himself, and he stroked the white head. It was like petting a piece of wood; even her little petal-like ear was stiff. "Little dear. So small a thing to be dead. Why does it have to be?"

And his unthinking question awoke in him the memory of Macchiata's own words as she mourned the murdered infant in Sous Pont Saint Martin: "It's so little. Can't it be alive?"

"No, Macchiata. It can't," he had said. And with that memory his grief grew harder.

He looked up and saw Saara standing barefoot in the snow, hands at her sides. The simple, girlish figure wavered in his vision as though he were looking through water. He rose. The staff was again in his hand.

"He was my man," she said. "He loved me. He thought I was beautiful. I'm not young, Dami. I'm old. Where will I find another like him?"

Damiano did not reply. Perhaps he did not even hear her. He heard the sound of fire in his ears, and he knew the flames were near, to be drawn through his staff like air through a flute. He tilted his head to hear what the fire was saying.

Saara looked at his face and turned to flee.

The white bird rose, but fire seared the sky like the lick of a whip. She dropped and dove, and a beast like a shaggy deer sprang away. It carried backswept antlers, and its hooves were wide like the pads of a camel.

It was true, Damiano thought distantly. She was not lying; there is such a deer.

A tongue of flame raced toward the pine wood; where it touched the snow, the air went white with steam. It reached the edge of the meadow before the leaping animal and flashed sideways, turning the reindeer, prisoning both it and its captor with a wall of deadly heat. Grass sizzled. The fire burned wood, earth, snow. It needed nothing but itself to burn.

I have only begun, thought Damiano without emotion. Hell is vast; I could char all this hill. All of Lombardy.

Saara turned at bay, and as she cast off her animal form, she was hidden by the thickening mists. It didn't matter. Damiano could feel her presence on his closed eyelids. He advanced toward her.

Suddenly the air dazzled and snapped with thunder. Above both witches the heavens convulsed, and a drenching rain smote down.

The ring of flame guttered, and for a moment Damiano saw Saara plainly: a small and slender figure kneeling on the flattened grass, streams of rain running along her long braids and down her breast. Her hands were raised to the sky. She was singing.

She was as fair as a dryad, as a child. Her beauty hurt him, and with his pain he built the fire higher. Saara screamed at the touch of boiling steam. Damiano felt nothing.

The clouds lifted, but there was no woman on the grass, merely a flock of doves, watching him. He closed his eyes and stepped toward Saara.

A white bear rose above his head, black mouthed, ten feet tall. It swung a paw at him that was thicker than Damiano's waist. He dodged and thrust a staff of fire at the creature's eyes. It turned and faded.

Lightning smashed down upon him, and the mad staff drank it, singing as though with joy. He threw the bolt at the woman before him, and she fell.

Damiano leaned over her. Water ran from the snakelike curls on his head to spatter in her face. He put his boot upon her stomach; the broken heel snagged and tore the red and yellow stars. The silver head of his staff he pressed against her throat. "No more singing," he said.

Then he raised his head. The ring of fire, unattended, had flickered out, but Saara's rain continued, cold, dull, and gray. Damiano ground his teeth and stared without seeing.

In another moment he would kill her. Or walk away. He desired . . . what he wanted he did not know. He flexed his damaged knuckles on the staff.

The staff knew what *it* desired. It told him, speaking the same language as the fire had used. It desired increase—power. It vibrated in his hand.

Saara cried shrilly and gasped for air. Damiano

glanced down in surprise, all hate forgotten between one moment and the next. He lifted his foot.

And then he was struck by a blow of greater power than that of the lightning. It came through the wood of the staff itself and ascended his arm, striking into his heart and his head.

It was cold rain and distance and falling. It was sunlight and unrecognized tunes and a wealth of meaningless words. Damiano floated in stunned silence. He would have flung the staff away, had he known how. But he was not now master. The staff had been created by Damiano's father, and in this moment, it reverted to type. It was strong, and it was thirsty. It dragged the young man into its own magic.

But it was the only weapon he had or knew how to use, so he fought the chaos with that length of black wood, until it was subdued to it.

Time and time and time passed away.

Saara was still screaming. Rain pelted him in the face. Damiano climbed swaying to his feet. He stopped the rain.

She stared up at him in horrified wonder. "You have it all," she whispered, and huddled in a ball on the mired grass. "What your father wanted."

He looked down at the woman's full hair, gray at the temples, and her eyes, which were seamed by sun and hard weather. On the backs of her clenched hands the tendons stood out clearly, and veins made a faint, blue lacework. Her face was burned by steam.

But nothing he saw was a surprise to him now, for he knew Saara very well—in her body, in her song, and in her power, which had become his.

"You are still beautiful, *pikku* Saara," he said, not knowing he spoke the far Northern language. "And you are not very old."

Saara turned her head to him, and what she saw hurt her eyes. She started to shiver.

Damiano limped away from her. In the middle of the waste that had been a garden he stopped and tapped his staff upon the soil. Grass roots ripped, and stones. A black hole gaped before him. Within it he placed the corpse of a dog. He made again the small journey to the dead man's side, and he picked up, not Ruggerio's body, but the pieces of the broken lute, which went into the grave beside Macchiata. In another moment the earth shut its mouth.

Leaving the grave unmarked, Damiano turned away from the meadow, where a winter wind blew across the sullied earth. He did not look back at Saara.

Chapter 13

When he was well into the privacy of the pines, Damiano sat down on a log. He stuck a bit of moss into his painful ear, to keep out the cold, and with this his dizzyness grew less. With a bread knife he pried off the heel from his intact boot, making his steps level.

His new powers whispered in his right ear, like a friend standing too near for comfort. That broken ear could hear nothing save the memory of chants sung long ago, in a language repetitive and strange, yet to Damiano understandable.

Fly, the words repeated. Find the sky. Leave vestment and body behind. He clung doggedly to his clomping staff.

"It isn't what I wanted, lady," Damiano said aloud, his voice echoing oddly through his left ear only. "I am not my father."

Suddenly it occurred to him that even he did not believe himself. He stopped in his tracks, chewing his lower lip. He began to review his actions, step by step, since leaving home, both through the eyes of his memory and through this strange new vision that had become his. He sat down.

Before Damiano moved again, the endless evergreen twilight had deepened. An owl stretched its downy wings in the crotch of a split fir, and cold spread down from the high meadow into the wood.

Only the silver on his staff was visible as Damiano hauled himself again to his feet, using a sapling for support. He cleared his throat and glanced about him, marking each mouse-stir and badger's yawn: the living rustle of the forest.

This time the invocation should be easier. He had merely to follow his own fire to its source, and he would locate the spirit he sought. Closing his eyes Damiano descended within himself until he touched, far down and glimmering, the trace of the fire.

This he followed, through blackness and void, and it grew stronger and brighter as he approached its source. At the shore of a molten ocean he stopped, daunted not by heat but by terror.

I was born for this, he thought, and with that understanding he might have wept, except that he had used up all his tears. He did not kneel, but stood with his knees locked, braced by his staff. "Satan!" he called. "I am here."

There was no response. Damiano opened his eyes.

He was in the black forest, in full night. His journey had gone nowhere. Puzzlement knit his brow. "If those are the fires of hell," he mumbled to himself, "then this Lombard hillside must be hell itself. And I've been many places worse."

Frowning, he dismissed the matter and began his conjurement in the traditional manner, with staff and palindrome. At the word Satanas, he again felt the pull that would wrench him from the damp pine needles to the Devil's palm. Every weary bone in Damiano rebelled at the thought of that wild flight.

"No," he stated, and rooted himself to the earth. The spell tightened like a rope around him, but it

neither shook him nor did it tear. The jeweled head of
his staff sparked, then glimmered like an oil lamp, and
Damiano found himself staring at the fine ruddy features and elegant poise of Satan, who shook the dead
needles from his shoes and bowed.

The Devil was just his size.

"So you are no longer the sympathetic little dove
who had words with me a week ago," he said to
Damiano.

The witch shrugged. "You don't have wings," he
remarked, pointing. "I didn't notice before, when you
were so big. You don't have wings anymore."

The red face twitched with scorn. "I am what size
it pleases me to be. And as for wings, young mortal, I
don't need them to fly."

Damiano blinked and scratched his chin. "Perhaps,
Signore, but I don't need my eyebrows either, and yet I
don't pluck them out."

Scarlet deepened to crimson, but the Devil's urbani-
ty remained otherwise intact. "Did you bring me here
to throw insults at me, Delstrego? If so, I warn you,
you are not yet that powerful..."

"No, Signore." Damiano ran one hand through his
hair in a businesslike manner. "I... asked you here
because I want to take the bargain you offered me last
week."

Satan's smile was slow and grudging. Under the
flickering staff-light it looked a bit... satanic. "But you
were sure there was a better way, little witch."

Damiano nodded, lips pursed. "Yes. I'm still sure
of it. But not for me. Everything I have done has led
to blood."

Very quietly the Devil said, "You are one of mine."
Damiano stared down at his boots and nodded.

"The bargain," he repeated.

Satan sank indolently down upon a chair that
hadn't been there before: a chair that looked very much
like the one Damiano had seen burnt in the guard

shack at the crossroads below Aosta. He fixed Damiano with a knowing eye.

"Why that?" he began diffidently. "Now that you know the truth, I can give you freedom itself."

"The bargain. I will trade the future of my city, and my own, for peace."

"Renounce the shackles of the Beginning, and you can have whatever you want."

Damiano snorted and sat also, not on a magical chair, but on the ground. "Why would I renounce my Maker, Signore. He has done nothing ill."

Satan's eyes widened in shock. "He has covered the earth with pain and despair, Damiano. His cruelties are so enormous that even his ministers curse him in private. You have seen his work well these past few weeks. Open your poor, nearsighted eyes."

Damiano took a deep breath, and still regarding Satan, he scratched his forehead on the wood of the staff. "I have seen cruel and angry men and men who are mistaken. I have seen my own misbegotten nature. And I have seen a lot of bad weather.

"But the world He made, Signor Satan, does not despair. It is beautiful. No, I admit that I am wicked, and that my destiny is hell. But that does not mean I must love hell, or all that is wicked, and I do not.

"I love the green earth, Signore, and the Creator who made it. I also love your gentle brother Raphael, and the city of Partestrada in the Piedmont. What of the bargain you offered?"

The Devil's eyes flickered. "Don't be a fool, Dami. You can do better than that."

"That's what I thought, once. The bargain."

Satan folded his florid and shapely hands in his lap. Damiano noticed beneath his chair a settled pall of smoke, and the tang of burning cut the incense of the pines.

"The situation has changed," announced Satan. "You yourself have changed it, youth, by your . . . adventures. It will have to be approached differently."

"Explain," replied Damiano, drumming his fingers on his staff.

"You have become larger, Damiano. Much larger. And you are a disturbing influence, with your ultra-modern ideas and your quaint morality. Men such as yourself exist only to make trouble." The Devil grinned tightly.

"And you will make trouble—for your village, for the Piedmont, for the Green Count himself, in years to come—for you will inevitably come to disagree with Amadeus, whatever the man does.

"If you want what you wanted last week for your village—pardon me, your city—peace and stagnation, you will have to pay a higher price."

Damiano's black eyebrows came together in a V between his eyes. "You said the city would fade and be forgotten. And I myself. Have you found something worse to offer, Satanas?"

Satan's smile was pained. "I? Damiano, I'm trying to help you construct the future. You have created the possible choices, not I.

"And this one...isn't good. In order for Partestrada to squat in comfort for the next half-century (before decaying into the soil), it is necessary that you be out of the picture."

Damiano shrugged and watched the smoke crawl like so many snakes over the forest floor. "So I can't go home?"

The Devil sat immobile. "That's not enough, as it was not enough to exile Dante from Florence. You must die," Satan said calmly.

Damiano's eyes shot to the red, expressionless face. "Die?"

"Yes. Die. And soon. So you see, Dami, it's not much of a bargain after all, is it?"

The young man's mouth opened. His black eyes stared unseeing. "How soon?" he whispered, repeating Macchiata's words once again. "How soon is soon?"

A slow smile pulled at the perfect lips as Satan

watched the mortal man shiver. "Soon. I can't say,
exactly. Perhaps a year or two. Perhaps tonight. It is
certain, if you strike this fool's bargain, that you will
not live to become wise." And he observed Damiano's
misery with trained appreciation.

But his enjoyment was short. Damiano raised his
head, met the Devil's gaze, and nodded.

"Done," he said.

Satan scowled, and his huge anger cracked through
the carnelian mask. "What game do you think you're
playing? You can gain nothing by theatrics, boy! The
Beginning has cast you off already, and mankind will
never know!"

Damiano placed both hands on top of his head and
rubbed his face against his knees. "Eh? Yes, but I will
know, Signor Satan, and that is something."

The Devil stood up and flung the spindly chair into
nothingness. He spat on the forest floor in front of
Damiano, leaving a spot of smoking ash. "You will
know, boy? When you are in my hand you will know
what I permit you to know, no more. You will remember only the idiocy of your actions, forever!"

Damiano rose slowly. "Then I know it now, and
that will have to be enough. Come, Signor Satan. It
was your bargain to begin with; hold to it. Shall I sign
in blood?"

Ruddy nostrils twitched, and Satan glared at the
man with barely disguised rage. "Unnecessary, Damiano.
I will have blood enough at the end.

"So be it, fool. I give you your bargain." The Devil
sighed, and his pale eyes narrowed. "Go back the way
you came. What you see on the road will make your
path obvious.

"As for what you are to do, do what seems best to
you. Employ what tools you are given."

Pulling on composure like a cloak, Satan bowed
and was gone.

The young man drew his hands into his mantle
and leaned against the rough trunk of a tree. "I'm

cold," he said aloud, with no expression in his voice. "And very tired."

But the full moon and his unfamiliar and exotic powers pulled upon him. The staff in which they were caged was warm in his hand. He scrambled down the steep incline toward the lake.

A patch of moonlight stopped Damiano. He focused on the knobbed head of his staff; something was different.

Indeed. The silver had gone black—black as soot. And the jewels at the top were six small chips of jet. What was more, his clothing had turned an equally inky color; ermine shone like sable.

"So he has put his stamp on me, for all to see," whispered Damiano, speaking aloud because he was not used to being alone. Horror chilled the blood in his fingers. His shoulders drew up to his ears.

"Mother of God, keep me from hurting anyone else!"

He reached Ludica in the gray-violet light of dawn. The streets were empty, and Damiano went directly to the stable. Festelligambe whickered at his smell.

From a pile of hay and blankets came a phlegmy snoring. Damiano nudged it with his staff. "I have come for my horse," he said.

The stableboy crawled out of his nest and stood upright before the shadowed figure. Then, with a cry of terror, he fell to his knees, hiding his face, praying and babbling together.

The witch stood puzzled, then his back slumped wearily as he turned toward the horses. "It seems he has most certainly put his mark on me," he said.

The ride west from Ludica was quiet, very quiet save for the tumult in Damiano's injured ear, where foreign speech, foreign desire, and homeless memory mixed together in a murmurous yearning. But either the eardrum was healing rapidly or he was getting used to the voices, for they no longer bothered him.

During Damiano's few days in Lombardy, November had given way to December. Damiano reflected that his birthday had passed unnoticed. He was now twenty-two years old. Twice that age would be younger than he felt himself to be.

But he would not live to be forty-four, he reminded himself. He would not live to be twenty-five. It was quite possible he would not live past the night. With consuming fire at the end of it all, it didn't make a pleasant subject for thought.

Snow was falling and had been all morning. Damiano was sincerely tired of it, as well as tired of the wind, the frozen ruts, and the bare trees. His only comfort was that he was also too tired to question both what he had done and what he was about to do.

He huddled in his furs and began to sing a sad ballad of Walther von der Vogelweide. It sounded odd in his own head, as though the singer were actually someone standing near him on the left, but the familiar tune comforted him.

Was he still able to pray? he wondered. Well why not? He'd said his little Paternoster by the swordsman's body, and the only difference then had been that he had not known he was damned at the time.

"Sweet Creator," he began, in Latin as was proper for all prayers, "of this green world . . . I thank you for it, though it is not to be mine for very long. And though I am wicked in nature, I hope you will not take it amiss if I ask you to take care of certain people. . . ."

Damiano broke off suddenly, blinked, and stared at the road ahead of him. As he saw the delicate glory of white wings rising upward in twin interrogative curls his face stretched into a welcoming, gently relieved smile.

But the expression was stillborn. With the sight of Raphael, Damiano's plodding numbness broke in pieces, and he remembered. Shame froze his heart and heated his face, which went dusky. His hands twisted into the horse's mane. His eyes slid down to the road. "Seraph," he said thickly. "I didn't mean to call you. It was only a prayer."

"I know." The archangel Raphael did not try to smile. He gazed intently at Damiano on his horse, and the wind riffled his yellow hair.

The angel raised one ivory hand, and Festelligambe loped forward, lipping the air and nickering. The heavy, swart head pressed against Raphael's bosom.

"I know, Damiano," Raphael said again, scratching the beast forcefully behind the right ear. "But I wanted to see you." And the angel's gaze was simple and open, yet so searching that Damiano felt himself go red from head to foot.

That's why Satan looks red, he thought to himself. Bold as he is, his spiritual body is ashamed of itself. As I am ashamed. And now I understand why he hates his brother.

Damiano's jaw clenched. "You do see me, Raphael," he snapped, more sharply than he had intended, and he stared over Raphael's shoulder, where black trees gave way to fields of dead grass, crusted in snow. "And now that you have seen me, what is there to do but go away again?"

The young man waited. Out of the corner of his eye he could see the easy slow drift of a wing, like the twitch of a cat's tail. He dared not look at Raphael's face, to see why the angel stood there, not speaking, for Damiano feared that either the beauty of that face or the compassion written upon it would knock him to the ground.

"Go back to heaven, Raphael. My lute is smashed. My dog, too."

"I am sorry for you, Damiano." It was said coolly, as a statement of fact. "But you must not grieve for Macchiata."

Damiano's answer was flat. "I have not been. I haven't had the time. Or perhaps the feeling.

"It's my life that is smashed, Raphael. I have no more use for a teacher." Then his need to know how the angel was reacting outweighed both fear and shame, and Damiano's eyes turned to Raphael.

Slowly the angel smiled. "I love you, Dami," he said.

Damiano's head sank forward onto the gelding's neck. His face hid in the long mane, rough and black as his own hair. He shuddered until the horse's black back twitched beneath him. "Oh, no," he cried softly. *"Dominus Deus!* No. Don't say that. Not to me."

Raphael stepped to Damiano's side. "Why, Damiano? What is this distance? Do you no longer love me? You said that you did, not a month ago, and you said I was not to doubt it. I *will* not doubt it.

"—I can be very stubborn."

The witch flinched at the gentle touch on his knee. He screwed shut his eyes and ground his teeth together. "Of course I love you, Raphael. And that is turning me on a spit!

"Go away now. Begone! Fly! You can do it fast enough when you want to." And Damiano made blind, ineffectual bird-shooing gestures.

The touch of the hand grew heavier for a moment. "I go," said Raphael. "But we will meet again, Damiano. I am sure of it. At least once more. And then we will talk this over."

Suddenly the horse snorted and turned his head left and right. He stamped an iron-shod foot in disappointment, and his breath blew a cloud of steam. His whinny rang among the iron-gray trees. Damiano opened his eyes, knowing the angel was gone.

Chapter 14

The weather continued inclement, with the sky a dark nimbus and the earth cold and wet. Damiano made slow progress westward, waiting for a sign.

He encountered a girl with a shoulder yoke and two baskets of hens. After one look at him she fled screaming, abandoning her squawking wares. Damiano righted the baskets and continued on his way, wondering what it was she had seen in him. When he placed one hand on each side of his nose, he felt the same face beneath them.

That same day a man on horseback approached from a side road. His antipathy was as pronounced as the peasant girl's had been, and what was worse, his champing horse seemed to share the terror.

"This is good," mumbled Damiano sullenly. "No one here to bend my ear with unwanted company and bad jokes. I can have some peace for a bit." And he sighed.

He had been riding for almost a week along the empty road when his witch sense felt the presence of people ahead, thick and hot like the smoke of a wood fire. He took a deep breath, closed his eyes, and listened with his mismatched ears.

There were many men ahead—more men than women. Soldiers, in fact, if his powers were any judge. The part of him that had been Saara grew very wary, feeling this.

But at least there was no sound of fighting. Damiano urged the gelding forward.

Half the walls of San Gabriele had gone to make rubble for the barricades. Behind these makeshifts, the black leather and brass of the army of General Pardo filled the town. Because the men were Romans, mostly, they cursed the wind and the constant cold. Because they were soldiers, they glanced dourly over the barricades and the ploughed fields to another camp, where blue tents flapped in the wind and the flag of Savoy was pitched, and spoke of other things.

Ogier, illegitimate son of Aymon of Savoy, sat in his quivering tent and also cursed the wind. He wanted to mop up this little pope's man—this upstart—and go back to Chambéry.

But Amadeus had given him only three hundred troops for the task, while Pardo had at least five. True, Ogier had been able to gather together a few score of the peasants uprooted by Pardo's passage, men with a grudge who would fight for almost nothing, but these were not soldiers, merely angry queenless bees.

He rose from his leather-seated campstool, stretched to his full six feet in height, and scratched the scalp beneath his yellow hair. As soon as he started to release the tent flap, the wind caught it and snapped it out of his hands.

Spread before him was the three-day-old camp of his little regiment. The loose earth was dotted with man-sized shallow holes, which some of the men had dug as a protection from the wind. These made a depressing sight, resembling graves as they did. The air smelled of smoke, human feces (the men were not used to the water in this place), and burnt mutton. No one was doing much; till Ogier gave the order to attack, there was nothing to do.

But his men were not fools or chattel. He could not send them blindly into a bloodbath, hoping in the process to somehow dispatch the Roman. They would not obey such an order. Nor would Ogier have given it, for he was a civilized man; he respected his soldiers, and he knew that giving orders that will not be obeyed only serves to break an officer's authority.

He wondered, not for the first time, whether his half-brother had assigned him this task in order to shame him. Certainly that would be unlike the Green Count, whose obsession with honor and chivalry had caused him to storm off under the banner of Jean le Bon, fighting Edward in Brittainy merely because he had sworn to do so.

The gesture had made Savoy appear weak in the eyes of jackals like Pardo, and sending a force of three hundred men after the Roman had merely reinforced that impression.

Which was false. Savoy was not weak; it was merely led by a ruler whose moralities were passé. Ogier scratched the yellow stubble on his cheek.

No, Amadeus had not sent him after the brigand to shame him. The count was not subtle enough for such maneuvering, and besides, Ogier had to admit that he himself was not strong enough to be a threat to Amadeus. Still, by plan or no, this encounter could shame him.

He needed a stratagem to get past the relative weakness of his regiment. But what was strategy without cities or rivers to work around, and when two small forces can see one another clearly? Twice he had sent mounted patrols into the surrounding hills, attempting to circle San Gabriele, and each time enemy trumpets sang out the Savoyard position. Men on hillsides could not hide very well.

He fished for the rope closure of the tent flap, secured it again, and sat down heavily on the camp-stool. He absently fingered the tip of his long lace collar. It found its way into his mouth, where he bit down upon the already draggled fabric.

He had been gone from his estates six weeks now. He wondered if his wife had yet taken a lover.

At the hour of sunset, as Ogier took supper in his tent, alone and thinking, he heard a single scream, and then the hubbub of raised voices. He cursed himself for delaying too long, and he cursed Pardo for a treacherous Roman bastard. Snatching his sword from the tent floor, he leaped through the open tent flap and landed, rolling, on the stamped earth outside.

There was no battle, he decided in one swift glimpse. The men sat by their cook fires, necks craned to the east road. Or they stood, their hands at their sides or their fingers pointing at a thing that approached through the fading light of day.

Ogier, too, stood motionless and staring as the creature approached, riding a horse of white bones.

The rider was black, save for a bone-white face, and it wore the shape of a man. Two eyes like spear wounds, black and ragged, peered over the blue-clad assemblage. Ogier froze with the sudden belief that those deadly eyes were looking at him.

The worst of it was that the apparition was burning— burning like a doll of pitch, like a witch's toy made for a curse. Its murky red-orange light lit the trees from underneath and shone through the gaping eye sockets of the horse's skull. It advanced.

"Let us shoot it, Commander," urged Martin, his second. "Before it does us harm. Look, it steals men's courage by its very presence!"

The second's teeth were actually chattering as he spoke. This observation broke Ogier's paralysis. "Not . . . yet, Martin," he replied. "It is hideous enough, surely, but it's done us no damage. And what if our weapons can't touch it? Then we will be sorry. Wait," he concluded, adding, "and pray to Saint Michel the archangel, whose duty it is to rein in the hosts of Satan." And Ogier strode forward into the apparition's path.

With one will, the men drew back from this encounter. The burning figure stopped before Ogier; its mount's grisly head turned left and right.

At close range it was the same, or worse. "At least there is no stink of burning flesh," said Ogier aloud, in order to be saying something.

The dead face peered down. "Mutton is what I smell," it said in tones unexpectedly mild, and with a strong Italian accent to its French. Its voice gratified Ogier, who had always suspected the Devil was Italian.

It slid down from its seat of bare ribs, and for a moment the Savoyard's vision wavered, and he thought he saw an ordinary fellow (though rather small) standing next to an ordinary horse. But that glimpse was gone in a wink, and Ogier could not be sure he had ever seen it.

"You are the commander of these men?" the apparition inquired casually.

"Ogier de Savoy," he found himself saying, and he executed a precise, ceremonious bow. Somewhere in the crowd of soldiers one man cried out and clapped his hands. Ogier smiled tightly to himself, thinking this interchange would do his reputation no harm, assuming he lived through it.

When the apparition returned the bow, flames hissed like a flung torch. "Well met, Marquis. I know well the House of Savoy."

Ogier raised one eyebrow and tilted his head. He was not a marquis, but it did not seem necessary to correct the thing. "So? I hadn't thought my family had lived so ill. But no matter, Monsieur Fiend, I stand here at your service. For what have you come so far?"

The creature sighed and patted his skeletal horse. "I would like to talk to you in private, Marquis. It is to both our benefit."

Ogier's other eyebrow joined the first. "The only private place in the camp is my tent," he said. "And I greatly fear you'll burn it down."

The cadaverous head jerked around. "Burn...? Marquis, I promise wholeheartedly I will not burn your tent down. Why did you think... Am I glowing red in your eyes, or something like that?"

A smile twitched over Ogier's long face. "Something like that," he admitted, and he led the apparition through the hushed camp to where his blue tent flapped and fluttered in the wind.

"Leave the horse alone," said the creature unnecessarily, but as it stepped away from the structure of bone, that monstrous steed wavered, and in its place stood a black gelding of good breeding, wearing no trappings of any kind. "Stay," the apparition commanded, as though the horse were a dog.

Ogier and the fiend disappeared into the tent of

blue silk, which shone then like a lantern in the gathering dark.

"You have men from Partestrada in your army, my lord Marquis," Damiano noted. As there was only one seat in the tent (the folding leather campstool), he settled himself upon the dirt.

Ogier also sat, his face expressionless, his eyes watchful. "I have men from all over the Piedmont in my retinue, good Devil, but only the ones I brought over Mont Cenis are soldiers."

The witch nodded appreciatively. To Ogier the effect was like that of paper shivering in the blast of a flame. The Savoyard sat bolt upright and suppressed a shudder.

After a meditative pause, Damiano spoke again. "Am I correct in assuming you are pursuing the condottiere Pardo and have him cornered in San Gabriele?"

Ogier sucked his cheek before answering. "Aside from the fact there are no corners left in the village you speak of, the situation is as you say. May I inquire, Monsieur Demon, how it is you involve yourself in this matter?"

Ogier found himself confronted by two earnestly gaping eye sockets, filled with night. "I, too, am hunting General Pardo. I think you and I can save each other both time and bloodshed.

"In fact, my lord Marquis, I was promised I would find a tool to my purpose, and I believe your army is the very thing."

Promised? Ogier's mind raced, and the hair on the back of his fair neck stood on end. He repeated to himself "Jesus, Marie, et Joseph," three times. "I regret, Monsieur, that I am not empowered by the count to make treaties, neither with man nor with man's Enemy. I do not wish to offend a being of your evident grandeur, but..."

Two arms rose, leprous white and burning, burning...Damiano slicked his hair back from his face. "I

do not ask you to make a bargain with the Devil,
Marquis. Nor with me, if there's any difference there.

"I am merely explaining to you that I need your
men, or at least a goodly portion of them. I am going
into the village tonight, and once I have captured the
general, I will need troops to keep his own men from
causing trouble."

Ogier started, snorted, and then thought better of
it. "You are going to kill General Pardo, spirit? Tonight?" As if by chance, the blond shuffled his left foot
forward until it almost touched the flickering figure: *no
heat*.

Damiano frowned. "If need be. I had hoped to
deliver him to you, though that would be hypocrisy on
my part, eh? Since you would, in turn, slay him."

There was a moment's silence, broken by Ogier.
"Why do you seek the Roman's life? What could he
have done..."

"I was born in Partestrada, Marquis," answered
Damiano.

Ogier leaned forward on the stool, his revulsion
tempered by sudden interest. The lace of his limp collar
hung in the air before his coat of sky blue. "So you
were mortal once, Monsieur Demon?"

Damiano blinked in surprise. Feeling a chill, he
drew his soot-colored mantle closer. "Yes, Marquis. But
it was a very short life and painful at the end.

"Enough. It's dark already, and there's no reason
to delay. Assemble your men now, and the battle will
be done by midnight." He rose to his feet, using his
black staff for support.

Ogier remained seated, staring at the ground. After some moments he shook his head. "I am sorry,
Monseigneur Demon, but I may not do that. You see,
although I am a soldier, I am still a Christian."

"Then I will," said Damiano easily. "But they would
be happier led by you, I think." As he turned away, the
witch heard the now familiar sound of a blade pulling
free. He swiveled and pointed his staff.

With a cry Ogier dropped the weapon and cradled one badly singed hand in the other.

Damiano bent and stepped through the tent door.

The night was windy but clear. None of the Savoyard soldiery seemed to have moved during their commander's interview with the Devil. Some shadowed figures were standing, weapons in hand, while others squatted by the meager cooking fires. All faced toward the hellishly radiant tent, and when the burning corpse appeared again, they backed slowly away.

Damiano felt the fear and hostility in the air he breathed. He glanced up at the uncaring stars, as if borrowing their indifference. He raised his staff just as an arrow shot out of the night toward him. Its bright yellow length splintered against the tarnished silver midband, and the goose-feathers sizzled and stank.

"None of that," said the witch quietly, staring past three fires into the crowd, directly at the archer who had loosed the arrow. "The next man who tries to harm me will flame like that arrow.

"And he will die for nothing, because I cannot be hurt as easily as that."

Damiano glanced around him, and his nostrils flared. The skin of his face sorted the men around him. He strode forward at last, and men squirmed out of his path like the Red Sea parting.

He stopped before a cluster of fires a little apart from the others. "Belloc," he said. "Aloisio. I am glad to see you still alive and healthy.

"Tell me, old friend and benefactor. Where is Paolo Denezzi? Is he not among you?"

The square blacksmith gasped. "God's wounds! It's young Delstrego!" Then a form stepped between them.

"I'm here, monster," growled the bass voice Damiano knew and disliked so well. Though his full beard hid most of the expression on Denezzi's face, the small, ursine eyes held more challenge than fear. Damiano met his gaze and said nothing.

"My sister," Denezzi announced, "is locked in the convent at Bard. She is of no use to anyone, that way, but at least she's safe from you."

Damiano nodded. "Good. To be locked away is by far the best kind of life." Then he turned his attention to the men huddled by the fire.

"I am going to take Pardo tonight, men of Partestrada. I thought you might like to ride behind me."

"Behind you?" repeated Denezzi, in tones evenly divided between hate and scorn. "We will take Pardo, all right, Devil's spawn, but not behind you."

Damiano shrugged. "As you like." He turned away. Over his shoulder he called, "We will all be going to San Gabriele soon, however."

He returned to the middle of the camp, in front of the gay tent, which night had reduced to a lumpish shape like a couchant cow. Ogier stood there, weaponless, saying nothing, his face taut and sharp. Damiano ignored the man, for he was preparing himself for his work.

He gazed left and right into the distance, examining his canvas. The half-moon beat down on the low hills as though its light and nothing else had flattened them. The grassland before San Gabriele and the half-forested hills behind the village lay open and empty of man. The sky was clear and translucent, not yet black. The Savoyard camp was a small blot of shadows on the soil. The ruined village was another.

Wind blew Damiano's mantle back from his shoulders, and its silver chain pressed against his throat. With his right hand he pulled against the chain. His left hand held his staff—held it so tight he felt it pulse and knew that pulse for his own.

"You are perhaps planning to slip through Pardo's sentries in secret, Monseigneur Demon?" Ogier's dry words broke the witch's concentration. "Or should I call you Monseigneur Lost Soul? Either way, your peculiar . . . ornamentation will make it difficult."

Damiano was aware the men were slipping away into the darkness. He could feel the terrified feet stumbling over the barren fields like ants on his skin. He took the staff in both hands. "Why so, my lord Marquis. What is it I look like, anyway?"

Ogier smiled with an odd satisfaction. "You are aflame," he said.

The dead white face split in a laugh. "Appropriate, Marquis," it whispered, "for you are about to see quite a lot of flames." As he spoke a serpent of fire hissed and spat from the swart head of the staff. It wriggled after the fleeing men, who screamed at the orange light. Some fell to the earth, while others huddled where they stood, praying and cursing together.

But the gaudy snake passed them, burning nothing but the ground and the night air. Damiano slid his hands to the foot of his staff and swung it over his head.

The serpent of fire became a ring, a wall, a prison for the Savoyard soldiery. When the witch set the foot of his staff back upon the earth, the ring of fire remained, taller than a man and booming thunder. Ogier put his hands to his ears. The cries of men faded and were lost in the wail of the fire.

"But as you see, Marquis, I am not planning a secret approach." Damiano shouted above the noise. "Such would be a mistake, I think. My weapon is terror.

"Using terror, I will save men's lives," he added.

With an effort, Ogier dropped his hands to his belt. "Save men's lives?" he repeated. "You are the tool of the Father of Lies himself. May Saint Michel the archangel fling you to the bottom of the deepest hell if you destroy my good and true men!"

Damiano stopped, a word on his tongue concerning another archangel, but he turned his face to the sky again, and the word went unsaid. "Weave me a storm," he whispered to the foreign powers trapped within his staff.

The stick throbbed and went warm in his hands, warmer than it had been belching flame. A wind whistled somewhere far away, from the north.

Dusky clouds snarled and tumbled over the distant Alps, moving with impossible speed. Out of the west, where the land was flat, blew skeins of mare's tail. The gleaming hills emitted white fog like breath. Minutes passed while Damiano watched this tumult in the sky.

Fire shrieked a protest, and two cloud-soaked winds smashed together above the circlet of fire that held the Savoyard forces. The sky was ripped by lightning, again, again, and again, and thunder drove men to their knees.

A spatter of rain caught Damiano across the face. "Enough," he muttered absently. "We don't need to put out the fire." He fingered the staff. "Wind, little instrument. Not wet."

The wind raged, and the circle of fire bent like the black shadows of the trees. East it went, then south. The silk tent took sparks and blazed suddenly. The men crawled to the middle of the circle, hugging the bare earth. All the air smelled of pitch and metal.

Like a flute, the black staff sang, and Damiano fingered it gingerly. It was not meant to channel such power, let alone to imprison it. The silver bands burnt his hands when he touched them.

He took a deep breath of the clamorous air and let it sigh out again. "This will do," he announced. "Now we ride."

"Ride what?" shouted Ogier, terrified and angry. "The horses are all on the other side of that . . . that . . ."

Damiano glanced around and noted the truth of the statement. "Eh? Well, I ride. Everyone else walks. After all, the village is very close." And he whistled for his horse.

The black gelding cantered over, eyes rolling and ears flat. In another instant it had become the grinning mount of Death.

"Forward!" he cried to the despairing company.

"Follow me, soldiers of Savoy, men of the Piedmont. Follow me, and you need not fear the fire, for it will be your friend." He added in a lower tone, "And with that as your friend, I doubt you will find many enemies to fight."

As he nudged the horse forward a hulking man's figure appeared in the way, blocking him. "Give me a horse, Delstrego," rumbled Paolo Denezzi, "and I'll ride beside you. Not behind."

Damiano peered down. With the staff whining in his hand, he had not much mind to spare for this. But as he glanced up past Denezzi at the ring of fire, a dark gap in the brilliance appeared, and a confused chestnut mare trotted through, dragging her tether rope. The beast was blind to the fire and heard nothing except Damiano's undeniable call. "There's your mount, Paolo," the witch snapped. "Don't ask for a saddle to go with it."

Awkwardly Denezzi hefted his bulk onto the chestnut's back, and the two men started forward.

The fire parted before them and ran, twin trellises, toward the hill and the village. Behind them it herded the Savoyard soldiers like sheep.

The air was seared with the unending lightning. All sight was confusion. Damiano's left ear was stunned with the bellow of the elements, and in his right ear was a passionate, seductive keening. He had the staff in his hands, it whispered and moaned. He could suck all the power from it and be free. He could fly over the village, alone, bodiless. He could pluck Pardo from hiding and carry the Roman high, up past the storm to the lucent air where the stars sang. The heavens themselves, then, would kill the fleshly man. Or he could drop him.

Or better, far better, sang the voices in his right ear, he could simply forget this onerous task and fly away.

He raised the black wand before him. After tonight, he said to the voices, you will be free. After tonight.

A white-hot bolt smacked down ahead of them, at the top of the hill of San Gabriele. It spun over the earth and hit the dusty oak by the broken village gate. The old tree flamed.

San Gabriele itself was coming apart: dark fragments rolling and scuttling down the hill in all directions. "Pardo's men are deserting," commented Damiano quietly.

Denezzi glanced at Damiano. The man's heavy face might have been made of wood. "Where?" he asked. "I can see nothing but blackness and the fire."

"And you call me Owl-Eyes," was the witch's answer.

They were at the base of the hill. There the repellent corpse-thing stopped and descended from the horse of bones.

The wall of flame split again, and a black gelding trotted through, followed by the pretty chestnut.

Damiano and Denezzi climbed the rutted market road to San Gabriele. Ogier followed, with his empty scabbard, and then the Savoyard troops, all slave to the constricting fire.

Pardo was not one of those who fled; Damiano was sure of that, as he had been sure of the general's presence since first riding out of the woods and beholding San Gabriele. Pardo was unforgettable, like a blister on one's palate. But the general was not in the open, at the barricades of rubble by the gateposts. At that moment, to be exact, there was no one manning the barricades. Damiano smiled and passed under the blasted oak. Almost three hundred men followed him, their faces gleaming with the heat.

Then the fire trellis parted, and two raging streams of orange raced each other over the heaps of rubble Pardo's men had built. They met behind the ruined village with a smack like canvas against water. San Gabriele was enclosed, as were both the panicked

Romans and their terrified conquerors. Now there was only finding the general himself.

But Damiano glanced around uneasily. Pardo was not the only person in town whose feel he could recognize. Other presences licked his skin, tiny as the tongues of mice. He felt, obscurely, that these presences were not things he should ignore.

"Wait here," he called over his shoulder, but seeing Ogier's expression of open, though impotent, insolence, he stopped in his tracks.

The Savoyard troops were huddled in sullen unity just inside the gates. The displaced men of the Piedmont made another group. Ogier's blue gaze was hard steel directed toward the witch. And Denezzi—well, Denezzi stood by Damiano's left hand, hating him.

These were not horses or dogs, or even human friends, who would stay at a word. These men had wills and plans of their own. If the Savoyards engaged with Pardo while Damiano was following his own curious nose, there would be unnecessary death. And it was to avoid that that Damiano had devised this bizarre attack.

With a gesture he drew a fiery chord through the circle of fire, separating the forces of Savoy from those of Pardo. Two rams in a pasture, he thought with some amusement as he turned away.

He strode down a street made unrecognizable by the ruin and by the multiplicity of dancing lights and shadows. Halfway along its length, on the right-hand side, stood a shed of dry stone, its stucco facade crumbled. This edifice seemingly had been too solid for the soldiers to destroy. Perhaps it was old Roman work. Damiano's smile flickered wider. He stopped at the door of brass and wood.

"Gaspare," he called. "You are in there, aren't you? And . . . is that your sister? Or no . . . that's my old friend Till Eulenspiegel, no?"

There was a buzzing of speech, and then the heavy

door rattled. Damiano flattened himself against the wall.

"Don't come out! Don't look at me. Just talk through the door."

But a pale, freckled face, topped by greasy red hair, peered around the doorjamb. "Festilligambe!" shouted the boy. "Why not? You're alone on the street. Is the village burning? How could that be? There's no wood or thatch left in it. What a time for you to return, you old . . .

"Eh, Jan, did I ever tell you about this one? He can make lute strings cry for Mama. . . ." Gaspare reached out and took Damiano's wrist in his scrawny, strong grip. He pulled him in.

Within the stone shed, the air smelled of old wood and wine. Light filtered between the naked stones, and Damiano's eyes discovered rows of barrels. One of these had been rolled into the middle of the shed and turned on end, and on it lay a huge sheep cheese, broken and gouged at random all over its surface.

Jan Karl slouched next to this makeshift table, seated on the rounded surface of another barrel. His bandaged hand rested on the greenish, mold-cased surface of the cheese wheel in proprietary fashion. Beside him, very close, sat the beautiful Evienne in her dress of green.

Damiano took a slow breath and felt his shoulders relax. "What do you see when you look at me?" he demanded of the company.

Methodically, Karl reached out and clawed a morsel out of the cheese. Methodically, he chewed it. Evienne giggled. "What should we see?" asked Gaspare. "It's pretty dim in here. You look tired, I think. That's understandable, considering the political situation."

Damiano closed his eyes in simple thanks. "I am under a curse," he tried to explain, as he sank down onto the barrel across from the redheaded woman. "Or perhaps it's not a curse but a premonition. People tell me I appear to be burning alive. They run. They cover their faces." He sighed and leaned on his staff.

"It's been very useful to me."

Jan Karl swallowed. His narrow blue eyes regarded Damiano doubtfully. "Maybe you are the butt of a joke, Delstrego. You don't look different to me."

"Nor to me," added Evienne. She looked like she might have added more to that but for the restraining presence of the Dutchman next to her.

Damiano shook his head. He realized there was too much to explain, and he could only devote a part of his attention to the amiable scene before him while his fire imprisoned both the village and the Savoyard forces.

"Where's your lute? And your dog?" asked Gaspare, standing near the open door. He didn't wait for answers. "Have some cheese and put your mouth to the bunghole of the barrel under it. You spill a lot that way, but we've got a lot.

"I really do think the village is burning."

"Broken," replied Damiano distantly. "And dead. No, thank you. I don't feel like cheese, tonight. Nor wine."

Gaspare stepped over and looked his friend in the face. "I'm sorry, Festilligambe, if your dog died. I liked her. I like dogs. And your lute, well..." The boy shrugged. "These are terrible times to live in."

Both Jan Karl and Evienne grunted in unison. "Midwinter, and they tear all the buildings down," continued the boy. "Then they make campfires of the thatch and furniture. Was that sensible, I ask you? Everyone with anywhere to go gets out.

"Me, I stay to watch over Evienne, but it's no good for her, either. Lots of business, yes..."

"If you can call it that," introjected the prostitute, glaring vengefully at the wheel of cheese.

"But they don't pay," added her brother. "And Jan Karl here... Where's he going to go with a hand like that, too tender to touch anything yet and not a sou to his name? Where is San Gabriele when we need him?"

Damiano shook his head to all these questions.
"Well, my friend. It's over, now, for Pardo. The army of
Savoy is in the town." He rose to his feet.

"As a matter of fact, I must get back to them,
now," he said, and turned to the door.

"The Green Count?" Gaspare gasped, and he danced
from one foot to the other. "You are with the Savoyard
army?"

"They are with me," corrected the witch. "And
they don't like it much." He stepped out.

"Gesu and all the saints guard you," Damiano
added, quietly, and with a certain formality. The door
creaked shut.

The flames flapped and roared, and he passed
through them. The Savoyard company turned to him
as one man. "I know where Pardo is hiding," he
announced briefly, and the fire that bisected the village
stuttered and died.

Ogier snapped a word, and the men, for the first
time that night, made ranks. Damiano led the way
along the central street of the village.

He found Paolo Denezzi at his side. The man's
bearish aspect was much reduced, for the hair of his
face and head was singed to the root and his naked
skin gleamed a taut and ugly pink.

"You attempted my barrier," remarked Damiano.
"That was a mistake. The fire is not an illusion."
Denezzi made only an animal noise.

Damiano turned to the commander. "My lord Marquis," he began. "Do I still look as I did before?
Burning?"

Ogier concealed his amusement behind a mock
civility. "You must forgive me, Monsieur Demon, if you
have been engaged in *la toilette*, and I did not notice. To
me you appear much the same."

Damiano merely nodded, and they passed through
the smoke and wind to the center of San Gabriele,
where a few stone buildings stood undamaged.

"He's here," said the witch. He stood with his eyes closed before a squat square tower. His head moved right, then left, as though he were rubbing his face into a pillow. "He's in the cellar, with a few men. Follow me, please."

Before Ogier, or troublesome Paolo Denezzi, could object, Damiano raised his staff before him and leaped onto the outside staircase. He bounded up.

At the door to the interior he was met by a sentry with a sword. The man cried out and dropped the glowing weapon. Damiano passed in.

It was like home, this place: the well-built tower of a family with means. The floor of the entranceway was tiled in red and blue, and the walls were soot free, washed fresh white. None of these carved oaken chairs or velvet divans had been burned for campfires, and woolen tapestries added their warmth to the rooms.

Damiano passed down the long stairs; no man dared to face him. Behind him was a cry and the sound of massed footsteps. Damiano ground his teeth against the knowledge that someone had slain the weaponless sentry.

The cellar had not been meant to be lived in. It was a warren of boxes and barrels and furniture stored on end. Though he could see reasonably well in this darkness, certainly better than any ordinary man, Damiano sent light into his staff.

General Pardo, neatly built, clothed in black leather, lounged amid the clutter on a chair upholstered in cloth of gold. His sword lay on his lap. Before him stood three swordsmen wearing his colors, each with sword and round shield. These men wore hauberks of link-mail. Pardo did not. All four faced the apparition without flinching, and the three guardsmen advanced upon Damiano.

At the moment Damiano saw Pardo his attention snapped away from the fire, and all around the village it fluttered and died.

"No, Carlo," called Pardo in moderate tones.

"Roberto, Gilberto, no. I fear your techniques will be . . . worthless here."

Pardo stood and bowed. "I take it, Signore, that the Devil has allied himself with the cause of Savoy?"

Damiano was struck by the literal accuracy of that statement. "Yes," he admitted. "You may say that."

Pardo looked about him and rested the tip of his sword blade upon the earth. "Well then. By all rights I ought to have made an alliance with the Almighty against that possibility, but . . . unfortunately . . . I neglected my strategies there."

"Your men have all run away." Damiano stared at Pardo. The lithe dark figure was fascinating in that it was only that of a man.

"Run away?" echoed Pardo, raising his head with a glimmer of hope. "They were not all burnt to death, then, or swept into hell alive?"

"There is only one man dead, that I know of," said Damiano, and Pardo's eyes narrowed.

"Do I know that voice?" he asked aloud. "Yes! Are you not the young patriot from the town below—the one who claimed he could not use witchcraft for the purposes of war?"

"I am," Damiano admitted, and he heard men on the stair behind him. He did not turn to greet Ogier and his men. Paolo Denezzi advanced to the witch's side, growling like a beast at Pardo.

"I am, General, but you yourself convinced me otherwise."

"What about the price, witch, that you said was too high for a man to pay?" Pardo's eyes shifted from face to face. Recognizing Ogier, he bowed insouciantly.

"Ogier de Savoy, I believe. I think we met at Avignon last spring, at the salon of our Holy Father."

Damiano could not see whether Ogier acknowledged the salute. "The price?" he said. "Look at me, General, and you will see the price."

With a theatrical sigh, Pardo let his sword drop to the dry dust floor. "It is too bad, then. You could just as well have damned yourself for me as against me. I admit I was a bit precipitous at your first refusal, but..."

"You could not rape Partestrada and expect me to join with you, General."

Pardo shrugged. "Why not?"

Damiano took a deep breath and adjusted the flaming stick in his hand. As he glanced behind him he saw only a wall of hate, directed at the Roman general and directed at him. "Because a man's city is like his mother."

With a snort and a sigh of weariness, Pardo sat back down on the glittering cushion. "That again." He looked up at Damiano with his dark eyes steady and fearless.

"It is idiocy that has damned you, Delstrego, and ideas wildly mistaken. A city is not a woman, and its affections are purely...commercial."

There was a titter from behind Damiano, probably from one of the Piedmontese, since the Savoyard soldiers generally spoke French. "It is true," admitted Damiano, thoughtfully, "that Partestrada never really loved me, but she was a kind enough mother for all that, and it is for her sake I have worked toward your fall."

Pardo glanced meaningfully from the apparition to the blue coat of Savoy. "And this one," he said. "Will he be any better?"

Ogier put his hand on the pommel of the plain infantry sword he was now wearing. He smiled dryly. "That should be of no interest to you, pope's man," he said.

"I have it on authority that he will be," said Damiano. "He or his brother, or his brother's son. For the next fifty years at least." Ogier's eyes widened.

"Kill him!" bellowed Denezzi in Damiano's ear. The witch jumped at the sound, for he had begun to think of the big man as a mere brute. "You've talked enough. Kill the southerner already and be done!"

There was a murmur of support for this idea and Denezzi stalked forward. Pardo, in his chair, froze, his fingers clutching the carving of the arms.

Damiano felt a sudden sweat break out on his face. This was not what should happen, though he was not at all sure what the alternatives were. But not Denezzi— it should not be the brute Denezzi.

The witch waited for Ogier to say something, to call the man back. But the Savoyard stood there, his blond hair gleaming in the torchlight, and he said nothing.

There was a sound of clashing swords as the three Roman guardsmen sprang out of hiding and made for their chief. Paolo Denezzi paused, uncertainly, his head lifted toward the sound.

Pardo struck so fast only Damiano saw him move, and he could only blink and watch as Denezzi was tripped and grabbed from behind. Then Pardo had the big man bent backward and a dainty dagger prodding at Denezzi's short, trunklike neck.

The three guards making for their master's side were met by a dozen swords of Savoy.

Denezzi shouted in rage, and he kicked, helpless as a bull locked in the shackles. Damiano raised his staff.

"I can kill him very quickly, Signor Delstrego," shouted Pardo in warning. "See the position of the knife? It's at the big vein; I can feel the pulse up through the blade. Though you strike me into a toad or sear me to ash, this one'll be dead with me. He's your townsman, isn't he? Perhaps you would have reason to miss him."

And it seemed to Damiano that he had stepped out of the path of time, and this cellar in San Gabriele was as flat as the tapestry on a wall: a picture of men locked in combat and men lying dead and men watching. In the wild torchlight the picture wavered, like a tapestry in the wind.

And he, in the center of the composition, had all the time in the world to make a decision.

Reason to miss Denezzi? How ironic. Of all the people in the world Damiano could do without, Paolo Denezzi . . . He looked again at the big man with singed chin and eyes rolling like an angry bull's. But for Denezzi, he might have had Carla.

Better he didn't, seeing what he now knew about himself. But Denezzi was everything the young witch disliked: boorish, bullying, crude, self-important . . . He had made life difficult for Damiano in every way he could, for years beyond remembering.

And Pardo was dangerous; Damiano had not suspected how dangerous until that lightning grab for Denezzi's throat. With his men alive, though scattered, Pardo was deadly. He had to be eliminated, for the sake of peace in the Piedmont.

As all these reasons lined up in Damiano's mind he knew absolutely he could not allow Denezzi to die. He let the heel of his staff thump in the dirt. Pardo smiled.

But other parties had made decisions as well. *"Coupe sa tête!"* drawled Ogier in a bored voice. A hundred men surged forth.

Denezzi bellowed like a bull, like a cow in the shambles, as Pardo's little knife opened his throat. His frantic, unavailing kicks scratched the dirt. Martin, Ogier's second, scrambled past Damiano and raised his blade over Pardo's head.

"No!" cried Damiano with almost no voice, and then again, "No!" His staff slipped in his sweating palm, and at that moment Denezzi's dying spasms kicked the object out of the witch's grasp.

Pardo's head bounced and rolled on the ground unheeded, for almost every eye in the company was locked in fascination on the slim, motionless figure with tangled black curls and black eyes that peered back at theirs, uncertainly.

Ogier leaped forward and kicked the staff out of

Damiano's reach. It rolled over the hard floor like the stick of wood it was, and it disappeared into the shadows.

"Take him," said the Savoyard commander, and a dozen soldiers bore Damiano to the ground. It was a deed quickly done, for Damiano hadn't the slightest idea how a man ought to fight.

Ogier paused and examined the field. He rubbed the fair stubble on his jaw. "An excellent engagement," he remarked to Martin. "I don't think we lost a man, except this poor lout here. And we will give thanks for it by sending this creature back to his rightful home.

"Tomorrow, though. Not during the darkness it has made hideous. If the oak at the village gates is still standing, hang a rope from it."

Chapter 15

Half the night passed over the village of San Gabriele, while dead fires and crawling fog wove a net of tangles in the air. The last of Pardo's soldiers slunk out of the cellars in which they were hiding and vanished over the stubbly fields. Before the week was out many of these would be recruited by the polyglot Savoyard army, but tonight memories were too green, so they departed quietly.

Most of the natives of San Gabriele were gone as well, save for those who, having nothing, had lost nothing. These roamed like dogs around the broken houses, avoiding Ogier's soldiers and sorting hopefully through the rubble of the streets.

Damiano lay in the cold on the wine-soaked floor of the very stone shed where he had found Gaspare, Jan, and Evienne. His wrists were bound behind him.

Where his three disreputable friends had fled to, and whether they were still free, still alive at all, he had no way of knowing, for without his staff Damiano was like a man struck blind and deaf. Nor had he much time to care, for the stars heaved slowly to the west, pulling the sun behind them, and with the first light he would die.

They had thrown his mantle over him, lest he freeze during the night and cheat them of their revenge. Soldiers outside guarded the corners of the shed; their slow passage blocked the moonlight that seeped in between the stones. Their presence and the dry, choking fear that filled his throat kept Damiano from weeping.

Instead he shook uncontrollably, until his shivers caused the fur mantle to slip off, and between the pain of his wrenched shoulders and swollen hands, he could not crawl back under it.

The earthen floor smelled strongly of wine and mice, and as he twisted to free his nose of the caking dust, the wad of moss in his ear fell out and cold lanced in. No voices, just cold.

Why would the marquis do this to him? Couldn't the man see that Damiano had given him better than any commander could hope for? Victory with no loss, all in an evening. And if a man was damned, then that was his misfortune, and nowhere was it written that he should be murdered on top of it. To kill a damned man must be a crime worse than to kill a saint, for a damned man had no good except that found in this life—forever.

Damiano's eyes stung in self-pity, which he forced back, lest he lose control and begin to howl. He had only a few hours, and then, according to Satan's promise, he would remember nothing good, nothing of beauty, nothing he had loved.

Yet he didn't regret his bargain with the Devil, for it was not his bargain that was sending him to hell. The bargain was only to die, and all men must die sooner or later. "Later!" cried a voice within him—not a voice

of power, but a small, insistent voice like that of
Macchiata, like that of Dami the boy. Later would be
better. Much better!

What had he answered Satan, when the Enemy
had told him he would not remember, nothing except
what Satan desired? "I know it now," he had said.
"That will have to be enough."

So. He was still alive, these few hours. He would
remember: what was good and beautiful, what he . . .

Damiano swallowed the pungent odor of mice. He
curled his knees to his chest and closed his eyes. Then
he heard another small voice, not in his head, but from
outside.

"*Hein!* Festilligambe," it hissed. "Or Delstrego—
whatever you call yourself. Are you awake?"

Damiano's eyes sprang open. "Gaspare!" he hissed.
"What are you doing there?" There was a vague dark
blotch behind the fieldstones. It shifted and the boy
replied.

"One of the soldiers went to take a leak. Only a
moment. What can I do? To . . . Wait . . ." Starlight
appeared where the blotch had been.

Damiano waited as still as a man carved of stone,
his eyes wide in the darkness. Then the shape of the
sentry passed by again and despair crept back. There
was a lock of iron on the door anyway, and Ogier de
Savoy had the key.

Gaspare was a good fellow. That was something to
remember, as long as it did not make him weep. It *was*
making him weep. Ah well, he could do that quietly.

"Hsst!" came the voice again, from the front wall
this time. Damiano lurched over, and when his weight
fell on his pinioned arms, he whimpered in pain. "I'm
here now. Evienne is . . . distracting the guards. What
can we do for you?"

He swallowed twice before he could reply. "Nothing, Gaspare. You can't help me, except that you have,
a bit, by . . . Run off, now, for if they catch you, they'll
hang you too."

Gaspare's inaudible reply was probably a curse. Then he hissed, "Become invisible, Festilligambe. I'll say I saw you run down the street, and they'll open the shed to see."

Damiano had to smile at the plan. "I can't," he replied. "They took my staff. I can't become invisible. I can't do anything.

"Go away, Gaspare. This is something that was decided before. I can't escape it, and I'm not Christ, that a couple of thieves should hang beside me. Go away."

He had to repeat it three more times before the shadow faded off.

What day was it, anyway, or *would* it be with the first morning's light? One ought to know what day of the week one was dying on. He figured in his head, counting the days since the full moon. It was coming Sunday, the twelfth of December.

O Christ! It was a terrible thing to die cold.

Suddenly Damiano's weary, strained body stopped shivering. His mind was flooded with the pictures of a spring he would never see, and he smelled not mouse droppings but the breathing earth and the scent of lilacs. He grunted and sagged down against the floor, regardless of the pain.

To see the spring again, and to lie in the grass. To be investigated by silly lambs, newborn, all knees and nose, with their placid mothers bleating. To see silk dresses on the street again, when the girls' faces and necks were pink with the sharp morning air, and they were determined to wear their dresses anyway, for the calendar said spring. To go out into the fields and search for blooming herbs, arrowroot, angelica. Spending all the day and having little to show for it, because the fields were bouncing with new rabbits, like the children's little leather-sewn balls.

To endure the last fasting week of Lent, while every oven in town was baking for Easter, and then the great gold and white mass on Easter Sunday morning,

and all the townsfolk singing together in their terrible,
wonderful, untutored Latin "Alleluia, Alleluia, He is
risen, He is not here."

Last year, on the day before Easter, he had spent
all day in the hills and come home with two armfuls of
flowers and a burnt nose. The best of these: the pink
early rose and the lily of the marsh, he had put in vases
and left them for Carla to find, stealing onto her
balcony at night while Macchiata had kept watch. (He
had never told Carla.) The rest of them—the yellow lily
and bright mustard, and the tiny nodding snowdrops
on their stems—he had put into a bag and had dumped
the lot on Raphael, like a shower bath. Though Damiano
couldn't remember the expression on the angel's face,
he remembered one fluffy brush of gold mustard dan-
gling at the end of a fluttering wing, and the white robe
gilded with pollen.

The act had been neither very respectful, nor very
manly, but no matter. Raphael had taken it well. And
now...now Damiano sank into memory. His mouth
softened.

To die in the spring would be easier, for one would
die drunk.

The winter was beautiful, too, or had been beautiful when he was warm, climbing up the road to Aosta.
And of course, the gleaming high Alps were lovely,
despite what Macchiata had said.

Macchiata had been beautiful, too, the most beautiful thing of all, in some ways. But her he could not
bear to think about.

"*Dominus Deus*," he whispered, his lips brushing
the dirt, "you made a pretty world." It was not meant
to be a prayer.

Cold air on his injured ear was making him dizzy
again, for he could not feel the ground, and the room
was swimming with lights of pearl, lights of sunstruck
clouds. Damiano's head was gently lifted. He looked
up into the eyes of Raphael.

Great wings curled in, hiding the walls of stone.

The archangel took Damiano onto his lap, and the young man felt no cold at all.

"That's right," whispered Damiano. "You said we should meet once more."

Raphael did not smile. He stroked the young man's hair back from his face. "I said *at least* once more, Dami. And I said we would talk."

Damiano raised his head for a moment and let his eyes rest on the figure of quiet beauty. Then he let it fall back. "Once is all I have time for, Seraph. And there's not a lot to say. They're going to hang me at dawn.

Raphael looked down at his friend like a man staring into a well. He said nothing.

"Did you know that already?" asked Damiano, looking back.

The angel nodded and touched Damiano's face lightly with the backs of his fingers. "That's why I'm here, my friend."

"This will be it, for you and I—for our friendship—my dear teacher. For I am damned and am going to hell, where I doubt very much you will come visiting."

Both wings exploded outwards, slapping the little shed walls. "Damned, Damiano? Damned? What are you saying?" For a few moments the angel was speechless. "Where did you get this idea? I never heard you speak such... such..."

Damiano had not believed the perfect face could assume such a blank, startled, almost silly expression. Nor had he imagined that the celestial wings could rutch so like a sparrow's.

"... such miserable folly!" Raphael concluded with effort.

Through his crushing misery Damiano almost laughed, but his face sobered with the effort of explanation.

"It was Satan himself who first told me..." he began.

The complex play of feeling on Raphael's face was replaced by simple anger. "He? He is the Father..."

"...of Lies. I know. I've heard that many times, especially recently, Raphael. But forget that. Not all he says is a lie, and I have my own evidence in the matter. I have touched the unquenchable fire, Seraph. I have traced it back to its source, and I know now that its source is within me."

One wing went up, and the other went down, and Raphael's head tilted in balance to the wings. "Dami. If you are trying to tell me you have fire in you, save your breath, for I've known it long since.

"You are as warm as a hearth, young one, and like a hearth fire, open and giving. Till this moment, I would have said as ... as confident as a hearth fire, too, for I have seen you go through pain and horror, and glow the brighter for them. Do you think it is out of a sense of duty that I love you, Dami? Or that it is your witchcraft that has compelled me to teach you music these three years?

"I have no duty toward mankind. None. I was created not for duty but to make music. Nor can the actions of mortals force me into time's stringent bondage.

"But you are such a silly one, Damiano Delstrego. Your hands are too big for you. Also your eyes. And your opinions. You try so hard, in a world whose pain I cannot bear to comprehend. And within you, you know what is best and love it despite all error. That's why I cannot understand how you could be so cozened as to believe...

"Ah, Dami, Dami!" And Raphael held the young man to him and rocked from side to side. "Do you know what it is to be damned? It has nothing to do with fire. To be damned is only not to love."

"Not to love God, you mean, Raphael," murmured Damiano, who lay with eyes closed, feeling his pain ebb away. "I've heard something like that from Father Antonio."

Raphael paused, and his fair brow frowned in concentration. "All created things," he said at last, "are the mirror of their creator. Can one love anything, with whole heart, and not love its source?

"Maybe a man can—men are a mystery to me—but I cannot. And, Damiano, look at me.

"You are a sudden flash of light, child. A tune rising from nowhere. I am not flesh, and I cannot understand you, but I love you, and I know you are not damned!"

Damiano blinked up at the angel. Raphael's face blurred in his vision, and he blinked harder. "Is that so?" he asked. "Is that *really* so? Then I'm very glad to hear it," he added, "because I didn't want to go to hell."

Then he wept without shame against the spotless white robe.

Minutes passed, and then Damiano lifted his head. "You know what, Raphael?" he asked. "I'm sorry to say this, after all you have done for me, but . . . but . . . I find I still don't want to die, either. Isn't that petty of me, after all I've done to get myself in trouble?"

And then the angel pursed his beautiful lips and rocked Damiano back and forth. "We all get into trouble sometimes," he whispered, "doing what we shouldn't. Sometimes we *should* do what we shouldn't. Don't worry about it, Dami."

This statement was difficult. It was also dubious morality. But Damiano was past trying to make good sense out of Raphael, or good morality, either. Perhaps angels were not expected to be moral, but just to be angels. Were they even Christians, these pure spirits?

No matter. It was better just to listen and to trust Raphael. And it was wonderful, being rocked by him. It was music and it was rest. It was falling, falling weightlessly like snow, his face against the spotless white garment, falling through a room filled with the lights of pearl.

Pain was forgotten, and fear. And if tomorrow—today almost, for it was near dawn—if tomorrow the rope worked properly, and he did not strangle, then perhaps death would be no more than this.

He was not damned.

Damiano almost slept, curled on the angel's lap, his hands bound behind him. He would have slept, except for the irritating, familiar poke against his hands and the awkward voice calling "Master, Master, Master," incessantly and too early in the morning.

Damiano opened his eyes. "Macchiata," he whispered, and the heavy triangular head thrust before his face, and she licked his wet eyes. She was as solid as life, and almost as ugly as she had ever been.

"Oh, poor Master, poor Master," she crooned. "All tied up. It's terrible to be tied up. I remember."

Damiano slid to the floor and sat upright. "Little dear," he said. "It's so good to see you. I...I...don't know what to say, except maybe we can be together again tomorrow."

But she left him and struggled onto Raphael's lap. "We're together right now," she said, and then turned her attention to the angel. "I got it," she announced. "I dragged it all the way up and down the stairs of the big house and nobody saw me. But I can't get it through the door. Help me; I can't get Master's stick through the door."

Raphael petted her from ear to tail with easy familiarity. Damiano had to smile.

"Don't ask him that," Damiano chided the dog. "Raphael can't arrange a man's life. Or death. He can't interfere, being not of this world, Macchiata. I've told you that a dozen times."

But the little white ghost with a single red spot ignored him. She trotted to the door on her bandy legs, then back to Raphael. "Open the door," she insisted. "I can't do it, and it's late. Open it."

The angel looked over at Damiano, until the young man hung his head. "Stop, Macchiata," he whispered. "He can't do it."

Then Raphael, still sitting, leaned over and opened

the door of the shed. Starlight flooded in, and the iron padlock, still intact, swung back and forth against the wood.

Macchiata scuttled out and then in again, dragging the ornate length of ebony wood. She maneuvered it, with much thudding and thumping, till it touched the fingers of Damiano's bound hands.

He cried out as power flooded into him. "Raphael! What have you done? You have . . . have interfered!"

Raphael's smile was contained and inward-turning. "Yes, I have, Dami," he said, and he laced fair fingers over one white samite knee. "It feels very interesting," the angel added. "I wonder . . ."

Damiano could wait no longer. He spoke three words.

The massive door was flung back against the shed wall with such force the stones shook, and the one iron hinge burst in fragments. All through the ruins of San Gabriele rang the echoes of similar doors swinging open and parchment windows ripping open. The sword belts of the sentries writhed unbuckled and fell.

The laces of jerkins and tunics sprang free of their eyelets, and Damiano's bonds escaped him like frightened snakes, and at the gateless gateposts of the village, a noose of rope, prepared for the morning, spiraled free of the tree and lay limp as a worm on the trodden road.

Damiano crawled to his feet. With one numb, purple hand he scooped up the small ghost of a dog. He embraced Raphael and kissed him enthusiastically on both cheeks. Then he stepped out into the street, where night and morning were touching and the east was gray.

The sentries saw him emerge, splended in his tunic of gold and his robe of scarlet, lined with stainless ermine. He was young and unwearied and fearless. He grinned at them as he passed, thumping his tall staff in time. And if they saw the archangel, or even the spectral dog, they gave no sign of it but stood frozen, holding their clothes up with both hands.

Before the square tower Damiano stopped and called out until a blue form appeared on the balcony. "Marquis?

"There is no need to hang me after all. I'm not damned; it was all a big misunderstanding."

Ogier made no answer, so after a moment Damiano added, "I'm Monsieur Demon—remember? But maybe I'm not so hideous after all, in the morning light."

"I see you," said Ogier, and the marquis looked left and right along the streets. "You look much more comely this morning. Am I to understand that none of my men are willing to take arms against you? Yes, well, I quite understand their reservations." For five seconds the marquis stared fixedly at Damiano, and Damiano beamed up at him.

"What are you going to do, Monsieur who is not a demon?" he asked finally. "Seeing we cannot prevent you, that is."

Damiano shrugged loosely. "I'm going to leave, of course.

"But I thank you for your assistance last night. It saved much bloodshed."

"Overjoyed to have been of service," responded Ogier, with chilly, ironical politeness.

There was a drum of hooves, and the black gelding racketed into the village, passing between the gateposts and spurning the fallen rope. Damiano turned to the horse, which snorted delicately and bit its master's curly hair.

He pulled himself up. Raphael stood before him on the road, wings outspread and glorious. The little dog sat beside him, scratching impossible fleas. "Seraph," he said, leaning left around the black gelding's neck, "I have one more debt to pay, and it's one that should not wait."

"I know," answered the angel quite calmly. "We'll come along, if we may." The little dog chimed in, "Of

course we'll come with you, Master. We haven't been
here any time at all!"

He left San Gabriele with his scarlet cloak flying
like a banner in the early light. Bright wings soared in
the air above the galloping horse, for any to see who
had eyes to see, and a small dog ran at his left hand,
trotting easily over the ground and never falling behind.

Chapter 16

It was a ride like all rides through the Piedmont during
this bleak season of the Nativity. Mud spattered the
horse's cannons, and ice crusted its shaggy face, till it
scraped its muzzle with its hooves like a dog. But the
mud was rich, and the ice was glorious, and the snow
that whipped Damiano's cheeks and caught in his
hair—that was so much eiderdown. He rode singing,
sometimes sweetly, sometimes voice-cracked and hoarse,
sometimes in strange harmony to tunes whose burden
no one heard but him.

And he laughed at nothing, wiggling on the patient gelding's back. At night Damiano nursed great
bonfires and squatted by them, talking like a crazy
man. Talking, talking, talking to the air.

Beside a cairn of rocks crouched Saara the
Fenwoman, wrapped against the cold in a rough wool-
en blanket. Still she was cold, always cold. Being cold
didn't interest her.

She brought a few rocks every day, and though
sometimes wolves or dogs came and dug a few of them
away, Ruggerio's grave was becoming more secure.

One dull brown braid flapped in the wind. She
tucked it back into her blanket. She should go down to

Ludica, she knew. This high hill was no place for her, alone and in the winter. The steam-burns on her arms and under her chin pulled in the cold and ached. She would go down to Ludica; when hardly mattered.

She could sweep floors. A woman could always sweep floors.

The wind sang over the flat, marshy field. It had done so day after day, singing a bleak, mindless, winter song. Though her ear was trained to the sounds of wind and water, she was rapidly learning not to hear this song of despair.

But now she had no choice but to hear, for the tone of the wind was changing. She cocked her small head to one side, and her tilted green eyes narrowed.

This was a south wind, and a very familiar one. As any weaver can recognize her cloth, even when it is cut out of shape and sewn, so Saara recognized her own soft south wind, woven to cover her garden.

She stood, and she saw Damiano step out from the pines, swinging his black staff and striding toward her. His raiment shone under the winter sun, and his hair was black and free as a horse's mane. His eyes were filled with the beauty of youth and with purpose, and in his face shone power.

Saara turned from him, anger warring with shame. She thought to run into the birch wood where all the leaves rattled. But anger won and she stayed, standing between the witch and the grave of the man he had slain.

Damiano looked down at the stones. "Lady, please let me by," he said.

"Why?" she asked in turn, and her voice shook like paper, like a dead birch leaf. "What more harm would you do to him?"

His nostrils flared. "None. He is beyond harm, and I intend none." Then his face softened. "Please, Saara. Let me by and you shall see why I'm here."

His pleading was more painful to her than his presence, and she stiffened under it. "See what? Can you bring Ruggerio to life again, after weeks in the earth?"

"No," replied Damiano, and with his staff he forced her aside. "All I can do is this." And holding the staff by its heel, he raised it high over his head.

"Leave the grave be!" she shouted in rage, but the staff whistled through the air and smashed down.

There was a snap and a screech of wood and metal. The staff cracked. It split up the middle and broke into two pieces.

There was no flash of light, nor booming of thunder. The air did not smell burned. Yet Saara staggered as all that was her own came back to her, and more, and more. She shook her head against memories she had never known before: books unread, unfamiliar flowers and faces.

A girl's face, with yellow hair. The face of an air spirit, awesome and mild. The face of a dog.

Then she saw the face of Guillermo Delstrego through other eyes.

Daily lessons in the great stone workroom with the wood fire hissing. Daily dinners, crude but filling, cooked on the same enormous hearth. Whippings—both the deserved and the undeserved. A gift of apples. The gift of a staff.

And finally the screams from above, and, oh, pray for my father, he is dead, my father is dead. Saara cried in anger but could not resist, violated to the depths by the pity she was compelled to feel for Guillermo Delstrego.

After minutes or hours she sighed, putting the images away.

The young man—the boy—stood unmoving, staring stupidly down at the piled stones and the shards of wood and silver. The heel of the staff dangled limply from his hands. His mouth was open. Finally he dropped the stick and rubbed his face in both hands. He cleared his throat.

"It's what he wanted, Saara. Ruggerio, I mean. He

had a chance to kill me, but he chose instead to try to break the staff. Well, no one but I myself could do that, while I am alive." He turned to her, squinting as though the light was too bright.

"My lady Saara, you are so beautiful! A beautiful witch and a beautiful woman. It's not just the witch power. When I came up the meadow, you were beautiful then, too, but you didn't give me a chance to mention it."

Saara took a deep breath, sorting the chaos within her. "I don't want all this," she said to him. "Only what was mine. Take back what is yours."

He shrugged and dropped his eyes. "I can't. Besides, I don't want it anymore. Your song, my lady, was never meant to be bound in wood—it wasn't happy with me—and as for mine, well I give it freely, so it won't make any fuss. Please accept it; it's like a homeless dog. It can't survive alone."

Saara stepped forward, letting the blanket slip from her shoulders. Her embroidered dress shone gaily under a sun that was growing warmer. Rags fell, leaving her feet pink and bare. She touched Damiano.

"This is too much to understand," she said, and he nodded.

"I find it so myself. But, lady, I trust you with power more than I trust myself. I told you so once before.

Besides—what is all power but fire? And I have had too much of fire, lately." He stepped away, then glanced again at her, one hand scratching the side of his head.

"Please forgive me," he said, "for all I've done to you. It was never the way I wanted it." And he walked away.

"Wait," Saara called. She opened her mouth to sing his feet still, but shame stopped her. Instead she ran after Damiano, her bare feet splashing over the wet ground. "Where are you going, like this?" she demanded. "You're helpless as a baby." He turned to her in surprise.

"I'm going west," he said. "I thought to Provence, or as far as I get. And, my lady, don't worry. I'm no more helpless than any other man."

"Go home instead, if you can," she countered. "Or if that general will not let you, then stay in Ludica.

"You'll learn what it is to be alone, now, Dami. Cold and alone. Believe me: a witch without power . . ."

He scratched his tangled head again, and he grinned at her. "Don't worry, I said. I know what cold is like already. I've had a lot of practice.

"And alone? Saara, *pikku* Saara! Our closest friends are sometimes those we cannot see."

He leaped one coil of the broad, choked stream that cut the meadow into islands. Landing, he slipped and fell on one knee, then stood again, laughing at himself. He met the Fenwoman's gaze, he squinting with the distance between them. "What a body this is; nothing seems to work right." Then his grin softened. "Look at me, Saara. I'm happy. Haven't you eyes to see?"

Then he turned on his heel and darted across the meadow. Saara watched him until, slapping a low branch with his hand, he faded into the dark trees. When he had vanished, she lifted her head to the high, singing brilliance that went with Damiano, shining above the pine wood.

She had the eyes to see.

OUT OF THIS WORLD!

That's the only way to describe Bantam's great series of science fiction classics. These space-age thrillers are filled with terror, fancy and adventure and written by America's most renowned writers of science fiction. Welcome to outer space and have a good trip!

FANTASY AND SCIENCE FICTION FAVORITES

Bantam brings you the recognized classics as well as the current favorites in fantasy and science fiction. Here you will find the most recent titles by the most respected authors the genre.

SPECIAL
MONEY SAVING
OFFER

Now you can have an up-to-date listing of Bantam's hundreds of titles plus take advantage of our unique and exciting bonus book offer. A special offer which gives you the opportunity to purchase a Bantam book for only 50¢. Here's how!

By ordering any five books at the regular price per order, you can also choose any other single book listed (up to a $4.95 value) for just 50¢. Some restrictions do apply, but for further details why not send for Bantam's listing of titles today!

Just send us your name and address plus 50¢ to defray the postage and handling costs.